THE BIG WINDOWS

THE BIG WINDOWS
is part of the
Classic Irish Fiction Series
edited by Peter Fallon
and published by
The O'Brien Press Dublin

Also by Peadar O'Donnell

Peadar O'Donnell

THE BIG WINDOWS

A Novel

The O'Brien Press Dublin

PUBLISHED 1983 BY THE O'BRIEN PRESS
20 VICTORIA ROAD DUBLIN 6 IRELAND

REPRINTED 1986

ORIGINALLY PUBLISHED BY JONATHAN CAPE 1955

British Library Cataloguing in Publication Data

O'Donnell, Peadar

The Big Windows. — (classic Irish fiction, ISSN 0332-1347:4)

I. Title   II. Series

823'. 914 [F]   PR6029.D543

ISBN 0-86278-090-X

PUBLISHED WITH THE ASSISTANCE OF
THE ARTS COUNCIL (AN CHOMHAIRLE EALAÍON)
BOOK DESIGN: MICHAEL O'BRIEN
TYPESETTING: REDSETTER LTD.
PRINTED IN THE REPUBLIC OF IRELAND

for Lile

1

ON towards mid-morning the people of the island began gathering by the gables and open doorways within easy reach of Miley Dugan's house. Miley's daughter, Brigid, was to leave the island that day for her new home on the mainland. The neighbours had no need to go in on the floor to her as yet, for they took their leave of her the night before, one or other crying a little, just as she cried a little, and it was right that Brigid and her mother should have this hour alone together. The neighbours would have time enough to move in when smoke arose over the grey flags on the mainland to make it known that Brigid's man, Tom Manus Sharkey, had arrived there with his cart. It would be their task then to raise a cheery noise and gather the whole Dugan family into it, so that any sadness in them would get no chance to show itself, and, above all, so that Brigid herself might enter the boat in a right way; for the island, attentive to all things that touched on its people, had a saying that the girl who went forth in tears got good reason for tears before life was finished with her. 'So, bear in mind now, cheer let you, and shout.'

They knew well what to do, but the thing was to be in good heart doing it, and they would be glad of easier minds that morning than they found in themselves. Brigid had their good-will beyond any girl that ever went out from among them, and they would be anxious she should be carried into her father's boat on a strong tide of gay voices, without a trace of let-on or put-on in any one of them. The thing was, how to free their minds of any last doubts about her. They could wish, indeed, for a clearer view of what kind of life awaited her in this man's home, in a townland in the heart of the hills away back in the bend of the sky, where she would be beyond the island laneways of traffic to mass on Sundays, to fairs, wakes and funerals. She would be more among strangers from now on than if she headed for one of the lake cities of Canada or America.

By all appearance she had done well enough for herself in marrying this man. The word they got in Carrick village of his way of life was favourable; like their own idea of the man himself. He was from the townland of lime carts, Glenmore, and he drove a long-shafted, red-wheeled cart over the roads of the parishes selling lime. He had a name for good sense, and thrift, and money. They saw themselves that he was lighthearted, in a quiet, watchful way; and open-handed too. He lived with his mother, so Brigid was not going in on a crowded floor. They met his mother. She was in the church for the wedding, and she caught their eye going down the aisle before they knew who she was; a tall, spare woman, big-framed, with a light stoop and a way of crooking her arm across her breast. They heard what she said to Brigid when they met, good firm words that you would like and they were said in a good firm way: 'Thank God for you, oh, thank God for you.'

Brigid's mother hurt her knee in a fall among the rocks, gathering dilsk for Brigid to take with her fresh, and it was a bad hurt and it helped this man in their eyes that he should put back the day for Brigid's journey home until her mother would be on her feet again. But then there came a whisper, a bad whisper, that it was not out of good nature he did it, but to give himself time to overcome some sourness and confusion among his relations over his marriage; that was the whisper, 'sourness and confusion among his people'. Island women on the mainland took the word off the wind, and they spoke it carefully to neighbours, warning everybody that no breath of it must come to Brigid's people, since now there was nothing they could do. Anyway it might be a whisper that should never have been let loose, for it was entirely against the sense of things. Brigid chose this man herself out of all the men that had an eye on her, and she had no need in the world to say 'run' to the first man who said 'come', and she took him in the serious, warm way that was her gait of going. Brigid was a good-looking girl in the tall, light-bodied mould of her people. She had their black, black hair and the palish face, and the blue eyes of the island. Her home was no place of hardship — far from it — and it had no wish to lose her; far from it again. And this man of hers, he was her match, thirty-one years against her twenty-four, a big-boned, strong man in whose hands any girl's living would be safe; to be sure he was gawky and clumsy in a boat but then he was a mountainy man. Brigid and this man would make a go of life, so they would. 'So leave it at that: Bear in mind now, cheer let you.'

'Cheer let you, but is any of you noticing the morning itself?' And right enough the morning was between two minds, too. It was mostly a bright morning with a light, white wind, but every now and then a wisp of cloud sneaked up the clean sky and pounced on the sun, and draped itself over it, and the day darkened and black blasts, with a whistle in them that could be snow, raced up the bay. So far, the sun freed itself in time to put a stop to the gathering shower, but let it fail once and there was no telling how this day would turn out; the wind might even back round. If the mountainy man had sense he would hurry. And then suddenly there it was, the warning smoke over the grey flags. 'Cheer let you, and shout.' They closed in on Miley Dugan's, with their melodeons and tin whistles, their fiddles and their antics, and their mildly bawdy talk, and they surged round Brigid and warned her to show signs of her feeding soon, and to make place for other island girls near her, and Brigid held her own with them and the procession and the confusion crossed the green to the creek, and Brigid stepped lightly into the boat. She put her back to the mast and her shawl slipped from her shoulders and she laughed back into the great uproar of their send-off. Her brother Ned, who was a youth, flung the main-sheet back to his brother, Hugh, who was man-grown, and he entered the sprit in the peak of the sail and he hoisted the heel into the bicket and Miley, her father, raised the gib; they all worked quickly for this was no time for dallying. Nobody at all raised an eye to the sky, just then, and nobody heard the trip of the hailstone shower galloping up the bay. The hail struck and it cut like a blast of sand, and the day darkened and the hail trampled every sound but its own drumming into the earth. The boat shied away, wildly, and the shower engulfed it and the darkness, and the storm.

Brigid ducked at the first blast of the hail. Ned snatched up her shawl and draped it over her head, and he caught the oil coat his father thrust at him and knotted the sleeves across her breast. He swept a taft with his cap and guided her to a seat and he stood over her to make a shelter of his body. The hail rattled on the sail and the timbers and it whipped the sea to a boil of bubbles that burst into a white stubble. They all crouched and waited and the boat leaped and strained.

As suddenly as it opened the shower ended. It was a strange thing to see. A flash of sun crossed the boat and the burden of the hail in the lap of the wind above it fell straight down, without force or passion. The shower itself was cut in two, one half making noisy tracks back into the wind, the other in white-heeled panic flying ·up the mountain. The boat prattled and rattled against the short waves of the cross tide. Brigid stirred within the cocoon of frosted snow in the ripples and folds of her clothing. Ned helped her to her feet and he brushed the snow from her shawl with his red hands. 'Will you look at you, Ned?' Brigid scolded picking up his cap, 'will you look at you, in your gansey and no cap.' She brushed the snow from his hair with her hand, and beat it from his shoulders with his cap, and she scolded her father and Hugh for going aboard without coats on such a day, and she made them rid themselves of the snow. 'Beats all,' Miley said, 'beats all ever I saw, that shower.' And there was silence among them and they were alone together. Brigid sighed. 'Look-at, here,' Ned blurted, anger in his voice, 'I still say she should not take that net with her. I tell you that net will look out of place. People will laugh.' He poked the neatly tied herring net with his foot. 'If you will listen to me, Brigid, you will leave this after you.'

'Let her bring nothing with her she thinks she will be better without,' Miley agreed. He bit a chew of tobacco. 'Ah, that fellow,' Hugh scorned, 'he has to make a row over something. Better for him check did we forget anything. Isn't every island woman that ever went to live on the mainland, for ever cadging nets to save her from herding hens in the harvest time. Have we fourteen things?' 'There you go,' Ned protested, 'there you go, fourteen things, after telling me there were only thirteen, that the carrigean moss and the fish are in the same bag. I'm telling you I will ask Tom does he think the net will be out of place.' He began to check the items of Brigid's gear, counting out loud naming parcels, and he went astray in his count and blamed Hugh, and he began again and he was still at it when they rounded the creek by the grey flags that opened the Caslagh, and caught sight of Tom's cart. Tom rose from among the rocks, his hand high in greeting.

When Ned put it to Tom to say whether the net was to go on he nodded decisively. The net would be the greatest wonder that was ever brought to the glen. It would be his idea to say nothing at all about it, but to sneak it in and hide it until the sowing of the oats, and then put it up at night and let the glen get the full wonder of it in the morning. His mother would make a to-do over it and his Aunt Peggy, but that would be nothing to the shout others would set up. 'Did you hear that?' Ned whispered to Hugh when he got a chance, 'did you hear him saying it would be his idea to sneak the net into the glen and hide it? Is not that my talk?' Hugh struck at him with his elbow and growled at him to shut his mouth. Three men gathering seaweed left their work and came up to give a hand with the loading and unloading. 'That is the mainland man for ever,' Ned grunted, 'a great nose for a free drink.' This time it was his father growled at him.

Tom hoisted the net into the cart, and he boosted Brigid in over the wheel to see would it serve as it lay as a seat for her. He drew a bottle of whiskey from the haybag and he handed it to Miley, and it passed round among them all and they drank, and Tom, laughing, stepped to the cart to make a show of handing the bottle to Brigid, and the horse took it for a signal to be on his way — it was a cold day and he was restive — and he started forward. The rattle of wheels on the flags startled him and he bolted. Tom flung the bottle on the grass, snatched the reins, ran a step, bounded on to the shaft, climbed in over the high side-rails. He did not get the horse under control until he was out on the main road. Ned, half way up the side of a turf stack, was the only one in sight. Tom and Brigid waved to him, and Ned half raised his arm and held it there. 'Poor Ned,' Brigid sighed, 'Ned will miss me.' Tom gave the horse his head. 'Maybe it was best that way, Brigid, maybe that way was best. . . .'

The road was newly metalled and the iron-shod wheels made noise on it, and the dogs were roused and they dashed up barking. People stirred, too, for they knew what was afoot and they wanted a look at the mountainy man and the island woman and they jostled inside their doorways, where the light just caught them. The dogs kept up their barking, forming a pack on either side of the cart. Tom drove steadily looking ahead, without a glance at a door or a flick of a whip at a dog. When the dogs gave up, after a short stretch of empty road, he took out his pipe. They could talk now. Ever and always that stretch of townland had bad-tempered dogs. It was a bad-tempered townland. People from that townland took more oaths in court than the rest of the parish put together. That was one thing about his glen, no neighbour ever set the law on another. That was how it was in the island too. He knew other townlands with dogs like that, and they had bad names, too, for contention among neighbours. He cut tobacco into his palm. 'Cranky neighbours, cranky dogs.' He teased his tobacco. 'Ho, ho, here is a right bad pill.' He laid his pipe and tobacco on Brigid's lap as a policeman came round the bend of the road walking quickly. 'A right bad pill, this.' The policeman raised his hand and Tom drew up. The policeman took out his notebook and stooped to read the name, painted roughly on the shaft. He found fault with it. 'A shameful piece of work, that barely brings you within the law. A shameful piece of work.' He gestured them on their way.

'You heard what he said, barely within the law. He has that word well off. That man is never done searching what he can throw up at glen people. The like of him will get worse now when the Boers are making a show of them. They know our glen favours the Boers.' He picked up his pipe and tobacco. 'The police have a down on us anyway, since Parnell; our glen was the most place stood by Parnell. Then there was a thing Black Donal did.' He pushed back his cap and chuckled. 'Black Donal is Aunt Peggy's man, a quiet man every way except in his mind. His ear is for ever cocked for what goes on in the world. You would never know that until he gets himself a pup. Every new dog is a new name and every new name has to do with things far off. His dog now is Kruger. Not like us. From as far back as I have memory our dog was "Cois". So Black Donal named one dog, "Buckshot". I mind him fine, a big red dog. One fair day Black Donal drove sheep to the market and Buckshot was with him. Black Donal sold his sheep and he had a drink, and two drinks, and then he bethought himself of his dog; but no dog. Out through the fair with him, searching, and in the end he got up on a cart and in the throng of the fair he roars out, "BUCKSHOT, BUCKSHOT." The fair thought, like the police thought, that it was a rage of politics was in Black Donal. The whole fair got up in a roar, some booing Buckshot, some cheering Parnell and the police blew their whistles and there was murder. Black Donal was dragged to the barracks beating round him. The police would never believe in the truth of it all. They said it was politics. . . .'

They entered Carrick village. Its one long street was empty except for three carts outside Garvey's shop. Tom pulled up there, too, for Brigid had a mind to buy some groceries. An island woman, married in the village, was on the look-out for them and nothing would do her but they must go with her and have a meal. It made for more delay, that as they rode out of Carrick village by the church, they went inside together to say a prayer and they crossed the graveyard to Brigid's people's graves and when they came out on the road they saw that night would catch them before they got home. Brigid had not travelled this road before, and when they got to the top of the brae it was a surprise to her to see a great countryside of cottage-laden townlands. The sun had a good moment just then, and the slanting rays beat on the gables and the bits of white road across the shoulders of the hills, the strips of river and the shiny faces of rocks, and on the bleached fields, and they all tossed light from one to the other so that the whole floor of the evening was in a flutter, and Brigid wondered at it all. It was strange to her, too, that so many people could live in townlands so far from the sea.

Tom told her they made a poor enough living. They had no worth-while grazing for sheep; not like his glen. Then again they had no lime; not like his glen. Lime and sheep were a great backing to land. All the townlands in all the parishes round had two classes of people, families that could not buy their passage to America but must carn it in Scotland, and families that could shoot past Scotland and pay their way straight into America. Many a man who went to Scotland to carn his passage money never got beyond Scotland at all, and that was a great trial to his people. Glenmore men always went straight to Boston from their own homes. If you were born in Glenmore you were either there or in Boston; or in the graveyard; except for an odd man like the Sapper. . . .

The road curved with the mountains which grew in bulk as the dusk fell, and ripples of shadow spread outwards from them. Brigid glanced uneasily at the peaks that seemed to stir and move forward and she shut her eyes and prayed and she drew her shawl over her face and wiped away a tear. Tom flicked the reins and the horse lengthened his stride, and he pranced as he turned in on a narrow road that headed straight for the hills, and Brigid, glancing up, cried out and grabbed the reins, 'Mother of God, Tom, we're not going in under their feet?' He pulled up sharply. She let go her hold on the reins. 'Don't mind me, don't mind me. It's just that I got used to us going by them, and then all at once I looked up and we were making straight for them.' He slid on to the net and put an arm round her. 'I'll put my back against them so they won't fall on you,' he laughed, and she embraced him back. 'Oh, thank God,' she murmured, 'all day it was like there was some strangeness between us.' The horse jogged along on his own.

2

THE road across the moor into the glen passed over the limestone muscle which cradled the townland above the bog, and ended on the floor of a used-up quarry at the foot of the inner brae. Tom thought it best that Brigid should take a foot-path through the field with his mother, who would likely head for the old quarry as soon as the dog barked, for the cart-way was rough. They sat side by side and he pointed out the light of their home, and Black Donal's light, and he named other lights, and Brigid was silent, attentive only to the great bulk of the mountains. A woman rid her throat and Tom knew his mother, Mary Manus, was at hand so he helped Brigid down and he led her to the slap, and Mary Manus was there. She raised her two hands and Brigid gave hers and Mary Manus said 'Thank God, oh thank God' and Brigid bowed as to a blessing. The chains jingled as Tom led the horse away. His mother cried out sharply but Tom did not hear her, and she was upset, and Brigid told her that Tom thought it best they should go over the casan together, and she said she was glad to stretch her legs and look around her and get a right sense of being close to the mountains. They walked out on a level patch of frosted grass that shimmered faintly, so that it was grey, like a patch of sea against the dark night of land. And out of the night suddenly there came voices in a low muttering as of the sea itself; a gust of angry, smothered voices that startled her. Mary held her hand and she kept pace with her. A spatter of words came in out of the muttering, and the words were clear-spoken and sharp as the hailstones of the morning, and Brigid stood frightened and defenceless before them, and she moaned. 'Hurry, let us,' Mary said, 'hurry let us.' She raised her voice, 'Such children. Such children.' The muttering was nearer now and there were faces, as well as the bulk of bodies, darting to and fro, and the words were more shameless. Brigid grabbed at Mary and asked her what, under God, was this but Mary only raised her voice a little more and cried out 'Children's work' and Brigid noticed that Mary's voice, too, held itself strangely in check. She let herself be hurried onward. Clods fell on the hard ground and a clod struck her. Mary pushed her in the door ahead of her, and shut the door behind them.

Brigid stood on the floor facing Mary. She brushed a crumb of earth from her cheek. Mary came forward slowly, her right arm bent across her breast. She was as tall as Brigid, even with her slight stoop. 'Yon is what is, children's work.' Brigid frowned. 'It was the night did it. The night makes children of people.' She took the shawl from Brigid's shoulders and draped it over the back of the chair. 'Don't let yourself be upset. This night of all nights don't let yourself be upset.' Brigid walked slowly to the fire and rested a hand on the mantelpiece, 'What do you make of me that you think I can make light of what was said out there? All that was done and said, I am to brush away and say "children's work"?'

'But it is like I said, Brigid, it was the darkness.' Brigid turned wearily and found herself a seat. Mary came close to her. 'Will you listen to me, girl?' Brigid raised her head slowly. 'Listen to me and be said by me, for what I say is true; I would wish the like not to happen. What is done is done. Now you will have to give yourself time. You will have to give the glen time. You will have to put this night out of your mind, else for ever, in the days to come, it will be an upset to you. If it was a thing that had a root other than in the darkness, would they keep their voices down so Tom would not hear?'

'And do they think Tom won't hear?'

'If you are said by me he will not hear. This is what I

would ask of you, Brigid, to bear this in mind: what was done out there was like a shower. Noise among women in this glen has that nature. It is a noise, it rises and it passes. But if one woman carries that noise in among the men and makes men angry, men's anger has many hiding places in their minds and it is like a burn, in the way it leaves a tenderness after it. The anger of Tom is a terrible thing.' Brigid poked back her hair. 'I want to do the right thing, Mary. I would do the right thing if I could only see it, but there was all that talk.' She rose slowly. 'There is one thing I am forgetting, maybe. Am I welcome on this floor?' Mary's eyes met hers steadily. 'I thanked God for you before I ever laid an eye on you, from what I heard of you. I thanked God for you when I saw you, and I thank Him more than ever this night.' And then, the impulsive ways of the sea in her, Brigid smiled at Tom's mother. 'I'll give myself time.'

The dog scratched at the door and Mary opened it. Tom carried in Brigid's trunk, and they both scolded him for taking such a weight in his arms and they helped him manœuvre it through the room door. There was a glowing fire in the bedroom. Tom was full of talk. With the threat of snow for all to see why did not the men of the glen go to the mountain and shepherd in the ewes? It was daft of the men of the glen to let this day pass. He would have to be on his feet early in the morning. He would rap up Dan Rua and Wee Conail and he would give them a bit of his mind, so he would. Mary had things to tell, too, and she told them while she served the supper, and when the three of them were at their ease together by the fire Mary asked Brigid about her family, and Brigid named them one by one, and she told of the one the sea took, and when they went on their knees Mary added the name of Brigid's brother to the trimmings of the family Rosary, and Brigid laid her head on her arms and wept quietly.

There was nobody by the fire when Brigid came from the bedroom the next morning. The two doors were shut. There was only the small four-paned window to let in light. A thin breath of steam rose from the spout of the kettle, hung high over a crumbling fire. Brigid drew one of the doors open and stepped outside. The mountains were taller now, and farther away. The peaks were notched and scarred, like sea-scourged crags. The floor and sides of the glen were a crazy quilt of small fields, basted together with every-way stone fences. There were no full-length, up-and-down mearn fences, like on the island. The houses were set here and there, facing this way and that without pattern. At the end of the glen to her left there was a lake — the Loch — and a stream came out of it (the Sruthain), and in the middle of the glen the Sruthain made a pond, the Big Hole. The Sruthain went on from there in a shiny, thin glint until a ridge hid it. Up by the Loch there was one house alone, away from the others, its soot-marked gable towards them. She sauntered along the side of the house, and a woman driving a cow raised her head. She was big with child, her face strangely small and in-drawn, so that her eyes seemed too large for it. For a moment they stared, and then the woman raised her elbows and, prodding the air with them, walked away, and a young woman by a haggard noticing her, rid her throat angrily and her elbows went up too and she walked quickly. Mary came up breathless. 'Did I not say to you, Brigid, to take a rest in the morning? I had to go over to Peggy. Peggy is nailed to the bed with pains in her back. I had to milk for her.'

'Looks like the daylight makes no difference to them, Mary. Look at them, with their elbows out, putting you in mind of nothing so much as hatching sea-gulls, trailing their wings in anger. Looks like it was not the darkness.'

'Ah, there let them, Brigid. Can't you say "there let them"?' She took out her snuff box. Brigid looked out towards the mountains. 'One good thing the mountains are not as close as I thought last night.'

'You'll get a great liking for the mountains, Brigid. When people from this glen go to Boston that is the one thing they miss.'

'They hide the best part of the sky. I will not know how to judge the weather, the way they hide so much of the best part of the sky.'

'But it's the mountains, not the sky tells the weather. That is where you read what the day has in mind.' Mary took in the line of hills in the sweep of her arm. 'Whatever the day has in mind the mountain knows of, and tells you.'

'The way to tell the weather is from the butt of the sky.' Mary looked above the mountains as if she was noticing the sky for the first time. She shook her head. She led the way inside. Half way up the floor Brigid turned back to the doorstep. 'I am going to have trouble with myself, getting used to the mountains. I thought it was only last night, in the dark, but it is in the day too.' She leaned against the door-jamb. 'A body can see there is great space in the glen, but when you go inside it is like the mountains followed on your heels.'

'Lower your voice.' Mary spoke urgently. She beckoned Brigid to her. 'There will be always some child with an ear cocked for any word by you he can pick up, and do not satisfy them to let any word out, until you are more yourself.' She linked down the kettle. 'The word that sounds strange sounds foolish. They would laugh at you making a wonder of mountains. I would not give them that satisfaction.'

Brigid shrugged. 'That first woman I saw, that was Nelly?' Mary nodded. 'And Nelly is Tom's full cousin?' There was a flash of anger in her voice.

'Ah, poor Nelly.' Mary spoke lightly as she wet the tea. 'Now will you pour your own tea, Brigid, while I milk.'

'I will milk,' Brigid said sharply. 'It will do me good to milk. You sit there and leave it to me to milk.' She poked her fingers into her hair.

Mary blessed herself. 'God protect us, girl, talk sense. How can you say such a thing?'

'I will milk,' Brigid persisted. Mary was stern now. Brigid faced her sternly. 'Look, Mary, I'm here, and I'm half out of my senses, because of things I see that I don't know the

22

why of. It will be good for me to milk.'

'But under God, Brigid, will you listen to me: do you understand anything about the nature of cows? Do you think you can walk in on this floor, and take off your shawl, and go straight into the byre and sit down under cows that never had the smell of you, nor a word from you, and put your strange hand to their teats and get their milk?'

'I tell you, Mary, I am going to milk. The cows may as well get to know I am here.' She bit her lip. 'You will have to let me have my way in this.' There was a moment's silence between them. Mary slumped back on her creepy in the corner. 'You are not doing like you said, you are not giving yourself time. But let it be as you say, only you will have to take care. You will have to put on my neck shawl. You'll not cough, nor as much as rid your throat, and you will promise me if you scare the grey cow — you will start with the grey cow — if you scare the grey cow you will rise from under her at once.' Brigid took Mary's neck shawl and draped it over her shoulders and she made no promise. 'This is the kind of cow the grey cow is,' Mary pleaded, 'she is a nervous cow, a good cow but a nervous cow; maybe a spoiled cow, for there never was a hand under her but mine. I reared her. She wouldn't let me out of her sight for two days before her first calf. If you frighten her she will go into a tremble. The milk will scatter back through her body, and she may never be the same cow again.'

Brigid picked up the milk-pails and crossed the gravel path — the street — to the byre. There were two cows in the stalls and they made low, eager sounds in their throats. There was no milking stool. Brigid went on her hunkers under the grey cow. The grey cow fidgeted. Brigid dusted the teats and the udder, her fingers gentle, confident. The grey cow moved closer to her. She felt for Brigid's shoulder with her body and snuggled against her. She gave her milk freely.

Mary waited inside the kitchen door. She spoke in a whisper as if afraid the grey cow would overhear her. 'I was listening; I was listening and I could not help laughing. I stood well back from the door for fear she might get a whiff of me. You must have a grand pair of hands, Brigid. I did not think the like could happen, a stranger to sit under the grey cow. It was the shawl. And you got every last drop of her milk . . .' Mary chattered on, while she strained the milk. She handed back the pails. 'Bear in mind, now, when you sit under the black cow to keep the shawl well down on your right side, and be doubly on your guard. Push out the shawl to her if she fidgets. The black cow has her own nature. She would not take fright, but she would sulk. The milk would be there but she would not let it down. She would go into a sour and she might get cross, and maybe turn on the grey cow. The thing is, keep the shawl well down on your right side.'

Mary promised to sit in her corner this time and take her ease, and on her way to the byre Brigid heard the tinkle of the tongs. The ducks were stealing morsels of food from the hens' board, and Brigid shooed them away and they ran out of the gap, and she turned to watch them, and a woman came around the corner, and it was the young woman she noticed before, and she was smiling to herself over something, and Brigid in a happy mood was smiling too, when their eyes met. She was a comely young woman. She gave the cow an angry slap of her hand and looked away. Brigid still watched, frowning, and the other turned, and she laid her hand flat against her face and she drew the skin down from under her eyes, and flashed the red of them at Brigid. This was a thing Brigid knew, for this was Balor's eye, the Evil eye, and Brigid moaned before it, and she stumbled into the byre and she prayed under her breath and sank on her heels by the black cow. The cow danced away. She swung her tail and struck Brigid against the face and left a mark. She swung back and Brigid had to bound to her feet to save herself. She wiped her tears, settled herself on her heels, and touched the udder. The cow lashed out with her foot. The hands wandered over the udder and the cow danced, and Brigid pushed against her and she squeezed a teat and there was only a thin trickle of milk. 'All right then,' Brigid challenged, 'this is not Mary but a stranger, one that met your kind before.' The cow raised her foot again. Brigid laughed, and she spoke softly and she dug and the milk came, and the raised foot jabbed feebly. It wavered, fell slowly, and the fidgeting tail drooped and rested into place. The cow gurgled low, plaintive cries. The milk trummed into the pail and Brigid, moved by her sadness and her hurt, raised her voice in a chant of the island. Mary, stumbling on the kerb, staggered into the byre. Brigid looked up wearily. She pressed closer to the black cow and went on with her song. Mary withdrew and, when she was finished, Brigid dabbled her thumb in the milk foam and she made the sign of the cross on the cow's flank. She laid the pail aside and went in between the cows, and she threw Mary's shawl from her so that they might get the full shock of her strangeness. They sniffed her clothes. They touched her hands with their tongues and they whimpered. 'So you don't know what is going on,' Brigid crooned. 'There are you and there is myself and we do not know what is going on.' She picked up her pail. On the street outside Mary grabbed it from her, and she cried out in wonder when she saw that it held its full complement of milk. She gave it back and she passed on into the byre. Brigid washed her face to rid herself of the dirt mark of the cow's tail. She strained the milk. Mary stalked back to her corner. Brigid took the basin of strained milk in her hands, to put it aside on the bench in the spare room, and she stumbled over the cat. 'Put down that basin.' Mary's voice was friendly. Brigid put down the basin. 'Here, now, is a thing to keep in mind: to get the cat away from under your feet, you empty the froth in the strainer into that hollow in the flag in the middle of the floor. You'll see it is clean. Put a splash of milk out of the jug in with the froth, and that takes care of the cat.'

Brigid did as she was bid, and she put the basin away. There were other things on the bench in the lumber room.

The room itself was in thick gloom for the pile of thatch straw half-hid the window. Brigid noticed the wicker basket that held her delph, and then she saw that all her gear, except her trunk and the net, was here. She dragged the bundle of blankets into the kitchen and Mary rose at the sight of the first blanket, and she was taken aback that there should be so many blankets, and she said it was a wrong thing of Brigid's mother to deprive herself of so much bedclothes. No young woman beginning life had need of all this, and it was not right. She helped Brigid carry them to the bedroom, and there was some embarrassment in her. 'There has to be more things in the island houses than in this glen,' she worried. 'There has to be more place for things than in this house.'

'This is a fine big room,' Brigid said earnestly. 'We would be the better of a press. Now on the island the men make such things. Men that go to sea become useful with their hands. They like making things. Maybe Tom has such hands.'

'No, no,' Mary said quickly, 'the only such hands in this glen are Black Donal's hands. Black Donal makes all the coffins for the glen.' 'All the coffins,' Brigid murmured, and then suddenly she laughed, and she laughed and laughed, and could not check herself and she flung herself on the bed and in the end she cried. Mary left her and she shut the room door behind her. When Brigid went back to the kitchen Mary was not in her corner, nor in her bed nor in the byre. Brigid had more to do in the bedroom, so she went back there, and she was still in it when a man came in on the kitchen floor. He rid his throat and he rid it again, and Brigid discovered herself to him. He was a light-bodied, somewhat worn man in a dickey and a glaze peak cap. 'Tom is abroad on the mountain and Mary is out,' she announced. He nodded, shifting his pipe to his left hand. 'I know,' he said quietly. 'I thought to come in and bid you welcome to the glen. I have need of Tom's ladder so I thought it civil to come in and bid you welcome. I am Briany. This is my house with its gable to your door.' He held out his hand.

26

'It would be good to be made welcome.' She was suspicious. His dickey popped up from under his waistcoat and he put it back in its place and he patted it. 'Thank you for bidding me welcome.'

He went by her to the fire and picked up a coal to light his pipe. 'Like I said, I have need of the ladder.' He drew a few puffs on his pipe and found it alive. Brigid pushed forward a chair. She found one for herself. 'It is because of a hen I need the ladder; a broody hen. This time of the year the like is scarce.' He waited for a moment and Brigid nodded. 'Now Kitty — Kitty is my woman — Kitty likes to put down an early hatching of eggs, and she is always on the look-out early for a broody hen, so Peggy sent her word she had one — you know about Peggy.' Brigid nodded. 'Well, Kitty went across for the hen, and she put the eggs under her, and the hen settled on them and does not Kitty let the hen out to feed with her own hens when, lo and behold you, did not they turn on her and slash her head with their nebs.' He found his pipe dead and he relit it. Brigid waited. 'Kitty raised the besom to her own hens to scare them, but it was Peggy's hen took more fright at that. She took wing and up with her on the roof, and there she is now, snug as you like, in the heat by the chimney hatching nothing. So I have to get Tom's ladder and go up and catch her and take her down.' He rose, and Brigid rose with him. 'Kitty should know better than let a strange, angry hen in among her own hens,' she said. He paused in the door, and nodded. 'If you buy a cow and take her into this glen, it is strange, but you have to stand by her with a rod in your hand till the other cows come up to her, and sniff her, and lick her, and maybe push at her a bit with their heads, and you may have to do that for long enough before they take up with her.' He raised the ladder and balanced it on his shoulder. 'That's the kind of world it is. Kitty should have had more sense, like you say.' He trudged off, and Brigid watched him go.

Brigid was still busy in her bedroom when Mary returned. Mary was full of talk. Peggy had a wish for Brigid to go across to her that evening, but Mary was of the opinion it might be too late when Tom would come home, and that the morrow would be a better time. Peggy made a great wonder of the way the cows took to Brigid, and Peggy did not know which wonder was the greater, the grey cow to be taken in or the black cow to be bested. Brigid watched Mary pick up her knitting and she felt guilty before her friendliness. 'It was not like you think, Mary. I did not give myself away on purpose to the black cow. It was that I let myself get upset over a thing that happened.' Mary laid her knitting in her lap and when Brigid told her what was done to her, she got to her feet quickly spilling the knitting on to the floor. 'What kind of woman was she — was she a strong stump of an old woman that had her hands down stiff by her sides and out from them?' Brigid shook her head. 'Was she a light wisp of a woman, with a skip in her step, and her head in and out in her neck for ever like a duck?' Brigid raised her hand against this spill of talk, and she told what manner of woman it was who turned Balor's eye on her, and Mary raised her two hands to put a halt to Brigid's talk and she relaxed again on her creepy. 'Oh thank God, Brigid, thank God. That was Susan Dan; a lumpy poor body, Susan, but there is no evil in Susan Dan; only, shame on her, she did a wrong thing.' She picked up her knitting again. 'You took a fright out of me, Brigid. You did a wrong thing not to run back and tell me, so that I could put your mind at rest, or, if it was the thing that the person who did it was a danger, so that I would let you know what to do to overcome anything with evil in it.' 'No, no,' Brigid protested, 'it is not scared I was, but upset. I smiled at her and it was like she spat back at me. What sense is there in the like, or what cause has she, or what excuse have you for her, now that it is daylight?'

'She did a wrong thing. She'll be sorry for it. Susan is like that. She can be the friendliest woman in the world, and then she can get thick; mostly she is friendly. She has no hold on herself when she gets thick. I mind one time . . .'

Brigid walked to the door. Mary in her corner watched her. 'You had Briany in with you while I was out,' she said at the end of a stretch of silence between them.

'I had Briany in with me,' Brigid said sharply, 'and I think Briany was trying to tell me something. He was an example to some other people.' She leaned wearily against the jamb of the door.

'A friendly man Briany surely,' Mary agreed, 'and an example to the world. It is Briany's one misfortune that when he came back from Boston he did not take the whole of his mind home with him from there.' Brigid delayed in the doorway. 'Briany had to come home, for his mother got a stroke, and it was in the spring time. He said he would not be for staying, and that, when he saw his mother into her grave, he would be on his way back to Boston, and to let people see he had no mind to settle here he kept on wearing the dickey, and people looking at the dickey made no wonder of it that he put in no crop. But, instead of dying his mother began to mend, and then the glen turned round and put in a crop for him; and Briany kept on wearing his dickey. He was still here when the harvest came and, beyond taking the dickey off him now and then and leaving it on a sheaf, he never parted from it. Now it is more than twenty years since Briany came, and he is still like you see him, and there is no bother on him, for the man in this house has a great liking for him. I saw Tom leave his own haggard and go to Briany to build a stack of oats for him.' She leaned forward on her creepy. 'I would have to say this to you some time: you will have to keep an eye on Tom. Tom is far too ready to take his hand out of his own work, and go to help another. It is right to be good-neighbourly. It is wrong to be soft. A man needs to have a good greed for the world in him.'

'I'm glad Tom likes Briany.'

'Everybody has a liking for Briany. In his own way Briany is a good neighbour. Briany has a gift in his fingers. He has the cure of the rose in his fingers and there is no man brings such comfort to a woman when her face or breast is

29

all swollen and red, and in a roasting pain, as Briany. And Briany has an understanding of things. Some people say Briany could write a ballad of this glen if he put his mind to it. But it is not that but this: Tom has no right to take on Briany's burdens. It is Dan Rua's job, for Kitty is Susan's aunt, and Kitty's people are long lived, and Kitty will be here after Briany is gone, and it is one of Dan Rua's children will get that place. So it is Dan Rua's right to take on Briany's burdens. A body has to have a hard face on him for the world, and go against his own feelings by times.' She gestured Brigid to sit on her creepy. 'I mind my mother telling us often, that on the day she married my father her mother, my grandmother, took her aside when she was leaving to go to her new home, and she said this to her: "Here now is my last word to you. You have my blessing. If you are short of anything do not come to me for it, for I will not have it to give you." And my mother always said that that was the best advice any young woman could get; to gather her mind to her and settle herself. Briany had not sense to take his mind back with him from Boston, and settle himself inside the glen, and make his own of the glen.'

'A woman of the island would never say that to her daughter. How could she, and no woman knowing when the sea might take her man? Maybe land is not like the sea.' She stood by the doorway again and Mary kept furtive watch on her. Brigid stepped on to the street. 'An island is not like a glen. There is more sky over an island. The sea itself is like a turnover of the sky. There is more light on an island; inside a house and outside a house there is more light.' She went inside.

'I can see I was wrong this morning, Brigid. You are having trouble with your mind, and you went after it in the right way this morning, when you said you would milk. What you need is work. Every time your mind gets up on its elbow set some work in front of it. There is wisdom in you, Brigid. I went through a time of great upset after Manus died. I was a young woman and, everywhere, I met things to put me in mind of Manus. Everything I laid a hand on Manus was in it. Work saved me. All day long I worked, and before long I began to see Manus in everything I had to do, and when the children's strength crept up on me, to take over some of the burdens, I often said to myself that Manus and myself reared them. He was that much with me.' She raised her hand commanding silence. 'Do you hear that hen? That's the red hen. That hen will not lay her egg anywhere except on the straw in the grey cow's stall. Get your ear used to her, so that you will always give heed to her and let her in. She'll walk up and down past the door making that noise.'

Mary laid her knitting aside and went out, and Brigid heard her talking to the red hen, and laughing. On her way back from the byre Mary paused on the doorstep, and she whispered Brigid to come to her. 'Is that the woman who did yon?' Brigid nodded. 'Like I said, Susan Dan. I was afraid maybe it was Nappy, Susan's man's mother. I was more afraid it was Ann the Hill. Ann the Hill is from that house back there by the lake. I best tell you about Ann the Hill.

'Ann's mother was from the lower glen. She kept to herself. She was friendly when you came her way but silent in herself. From the first she had a habit of looking the other way across her shoulder as if she did not know you were there, and when you spoke she would let on you took a start out of her, but she would be friendly, only somehow neighbour women began to let her go by, looking over her shoulder. Children came, a houseful of them. One of the children died, without a word being said that there was sickness in the house. Within the year a second died, and then she began burying things in neighbours' gardens to shift the sickness from her own house to some other house, and the whole glen got a fear of her. She would come out at night her shawl out over her head. She would race this way and that over the casans and next you would hear that something was dug up in some garden or out of the mouth of a ridge of potatoes. She never came near me. She had some friendliness for this house. One by one her children died, until there was only Ann left and Andy, and Ann was the pick of all the children. Then Ann was missed and nobody knew for sure was she sick, but people all watched, for they knew this was the most terrible blow of all, and they were afraid, and then one night the poor woman was heard crying, and in the morning she was heard crying, and in the broad light of day she was heard crying, and nobody could get near her for if she saw you she ran and she kept the door shut. The glen waited to hear Ann was dead, and then Ann's mother did a terrible thing.' Mary paused. 'I will not say what it was, but a man died, a strong man died, and Ann was given back to her mother out of a bed of sickness, when she was so near death she should not have been asked back. And what the mother got back was a broken thing, Ann without her senses, a ghost for ever juking and hiding in sally gardens. If ever you are going by a sally garden and you hear a screech like a hare in a snare you must not take a fright for that will be Ann. A thing happened to a child when Ann looked into the cradle. . . .'

'I won't listen, Mary,' Brigid protested. 'I tell you I will not listen. I do not give in to such things. The island would laugh at such things. The island knows of Balor's eye, but it is a story and that is all the heed they put in it.'

'Don't talk like that Brigid.' There was alarm and sharpness in Mary's voice. 'Make it a rule never to dare and never to mock and never to deny. Give yourself time. Give the glen time to get a hold of you. Let you give your mind over to it.'

Brigid turned away wearily, and for a while each did her own work, and there was no talk between them. The red hen having laid her egg raised a cackle, and Mary, grumbling that she had her suspicions of Dan Rua's dog, went out to collect the egg.

3

IT was dusk when Tom got back from the mountain and he was well pleased with his day. All his ewes were now in the near folds of the hills. He met men from across the mountains and there was no word of any mischief by dogs, on one side or the other. He promised a man from mid-glen to go down and have a look at his horse. He would be back soon because, by what he heard, there would be a gathering of men into their house that evening.

Brigid looked at Mary and she said nothing, and when Tom went out Brigid asked Mary would Tom be put about, if it should be he was mistaken and no men came, for it was her belief the women would put against them, and she warned Mary that if Tom said anything to her, while she might make light of what took place she would not make little of it; she would not withhold a word from him, while not making out to be overcome by it. But Mary was at her ease. Black Donal would come, for there would be no let nor hindrance on him, and Sean Mor would come, and so would Briany even though Kitty might put against him if Susan Dan said to her to put against him, and Nelly's man, Wee Conail, would come. If the glen got time to work itself out the glen and Brigid would get on together. The thing was, everything would take time. Women who did what was done last night would sulk for a while. They would be afraid. . . .

It came to pass as Mary said, for the men came shortly after lamplight. They came in a cluster, and Sean Mor was in front. He was a great hulk of an old man, and there was still a tinge of red in his grey whisker. He halted half way up the floor, and raised his hands sideways to hold back those behind him. 'Let you step forward, island woman,' he ordered in his great booming voice, 'let you step forward, island woman.' Brigid sought guidance from Tom who was behind Sean Mor and Tom winked. She came forward slowly and she curtseyed easily. 'So this is you. And by my soul, Mary, a fine frame of a woman. Turn round let you. A fine frame of a woman, Mary; no fat on her rump. She is nature's own woman, Mary, for like I often said, no matter what it is rears its young from milk if the fat is on the rump it will not be where it should be.' He rested his two hands on his stick. 'Turn round again let you.'

'That will do you Sean Mor,' a man behind him growled. He pushed past and held out his hand. 'I'm Black Donal. You are welcome, and do you know what I am going to take and to tell you, girl, the regular fact of the matter is, you will think us daft if you go by some people.' He shook hands with her and found himself a chair. 'Mary, I'm pleased with her,' Sean Mor continued. 'She is the right strain of a woman for this glen. She is light in the bone. I'm saying all the time that this glen needs a lighter strain than is in it. People are getting too bulky. Too much bone. It is the lime, Mary, that's what I say. Tell me, island woman . . .'

'Tell him nothing, island woman.' Wee Conail came forward now, and he made Brigid welcome. He wore a slope with large ivory buttons, and his broken peak cap was set sideways. 'If it turned out you were a fat, stumpy lump Sean Mor would find something in you to praise.'

'I would not,' Sean Mor bellowed, 'I would not. Mary didn't I often say it to you, this glen needs a lighter strain of a woman?'

'Do you know what I am going to take and to tell you the regular fact of the matter is Sean Mor, you're not decent. Let the girl get her breath. Sit you all down.' But Sean Mor would not be gainsaid. 'And by what I hear, Mary, she has nature in her for things. Peggy told me about the cows.'

Mary let them settle themselves by the fire and she told the story of the milking and she found new wonder in it herself as her mind went back to it and she made a great tale of it. Brigid made light of it. 'I never heard such nonsense,' she protested, 'I like milking. I always liked milking. A strange cow is no newens to us on the island, for you never get to know a cow on the island. If you keep a cow two years on the island you will lose her. There is something in the grass.'

'Ho, ho; ho, ho, now we are learning something, Mary,' Sean Mor rejoiced. 'Now I can see this will be a great winter for discourse.' Brigid had to tell of the strange ways of cattle on her island, and it was a miracle to them all that people could make a living in the shadow of such continuous danger to their cattle. Sean Mor wanted to know what kind of living the sea gave people, where the land had such a weakness, and he asked and she told him, what they had for their breakfast, for their dinner, and the others put questions to her and she answered them, and Mary could see the doubt rising in them that such a place should permit people to live in such a way, and so she told them about the blankets, and she went to the room and she carried down an armful of blankets, and Sean Mor wondered loudest at what he saw.

'There now, is the one fear I have in me since I heard you were coming, Brigid,' Wee Conail confessed, his keen face turned to her in friendliness. 'I asked about you in the town of Carrick, and from what I heard I said to myself, "take care would this woman bring a new way of living with her".' He leaned forward and picked up the tongs. 'The way it is with this glen, island woman, half of it is here, and half of it is in Boston. There is no end to what Boston can carry. If all the people in this glen went to Boston, Boston could take them in, and nobody would notice. But suppose the people of this glen begin to want more things.' He pointed to the blankets. 'I am finding no fault with you, Brigid, but if you have to have things, beyond what people know of, other people have to be like you and the glen will not be able to give more things to all the people in it.'

'It is hard to keep up the world,' Mary agreed, 'beyond what used to be. I mind when a woman going to Carrick would carry her boots until she came in sight of the town. I mind myself out in the frost in the bare feet. I mind when a quart of oil would last half the winter, using it only Sunday nights. I mind . . .'

'That is what is wrong maybe,' Briany grumbled, 'the meanness and the scraping instead of more sheep on the mountain, with winter feeding. If people listened to The Sapper. . . .'

Mary blessed herself, scandalized that Briany of all should speak of better husbandry and Wee Conail blazed out against him. There was little use in more sheep and more wool when the glen was at the mercy of the rogues and robbers of Carrick; doubly at the mercy of their teeth and their claws from the day Parnell died. No, the glen had to live within itself, and not raise its head to what went on outside. If the glen began to give itself airs then the glen would begin to empty itself. He turned to Brigid. 'The sea is like that too is it not? If it is the sea alone has to carry people they have to content themselves with what it gives, or does the sea get a backing of any kind, like from sheep?'

'No sheep,' Brigid said promptly, 'not sheep but hens.'

'Hens!' Black Donal roared. 'I like you, girl. I was listening. There is truth in you, but do you know what I am going to take and to tell you the regular fact of the matter is, if you bring a plague of hens down on us in this glen then, we will have to get rid of you; or leave the glen to you and the hens. Mary, I ask you, was there ever words between two families in this glen but hens were at the root of it?'

There was confusion of voices around the fireside. Sean Mor rapped his stick and he got order. The island woman must tell them more. Brigid laughed at Black Donal's fear of hens. People had to know how to handle hens. She thought it likely the women of the glen did not know how to treat hens. Mary made a face at her but Brigid would not be turned aside. She found fault with Mary's henhouse, and she asked if all the henhouses were like Mary's henhouse, and the men said they were, and Brigid said that when she got time, she would show the women how to make as much use of hens in the glen as on the island. Mary took issue with her. What Black Donal said was true — hens needed herding. It was a poor thing to make ready ground, and seed it and then in the harvest to have a scourge of hens threshing your oats. You could not depend on children. Sean Mor rapped for order. He had a question. What was the number of eggs Brigid's mother sent to the shop in one week in the laying season. And Brigid took her time answering and she told them that there were weeks when her mother carried out fifteen dozen of eggs, and everybody by the fire was silent then, until Black Donal slapped his knee and bellowed his laughter. 'Do you know what I am going to tell you the regular fact of the matter is, this is the best night ever I had. Ho, ho . . . My jewel, you Brigid, to come here and you only a slip of a girl and tell them a wonder story, and make them all sit with their mouths open swallowing every word of it. Ho, ho, fifteen dozen eggs. Do you know what I'm going to take and to tell you . . .'

A new hubbub arose and Brigid looked at Tom, and he went out and came back with the net, and he laid it on the floor and they all got to their feet, and Tom stretched it across the kitchen to show them how the people of the island took care of their hens. Now Mary, really roused, raised her voice: This net was a wrong thing. Even if it could do what was said of it, it would still be a wrong thing. She would not be for it. It would not be in the ways of the glen for any one family to have a thing that could not be of use to every family in its turn. For, was it not the way of the glen that one man had a ladder and his neighbours could have their turn of it, and one had a cobbler's last and it went from house to house, and one woman had a quilting frame, and one house had a saw, and one house had the candlesticks for use when the priest came? This net would be a yoke, no neighbour could have a share in, and she wouldn't like her house to take the first step in such a thing. But Brigid fought back. Every island girl with a home on the mainland brought a net, and when her neighbour women had a wish for one she cadged it, for the island made little use of old nets because people on the island put in little crop and had not much heart in the land.

And when bedtime came and the men went out and Tom walked out with them Mary took Brigid to task. 'You did a wrong thing, Brigid. All you were doing, all night, was putting fight on the women of the glen, sending out a challenge; making little of them. Sean Mor will go through the townland now, and he will roar out your words and the women will be angry at you for finding fault with them. They will know you had in mind to make little of them. You said you would give yourself time, Brigid, and that you would give the glen time.' They went to the byre together and Brigid strained the milk and took care of the cat, and Mary spent a long time on her knees after the rosary.

4

THE next day was Sunday. Brigid was the first afoot that morning. Mary peeped from behind the bed-curtain. She watched Brigid pour water into a tin basin, and dashed it on her face, and she shook her head in disapproval. When Brigid stooped to build a fire she spoke. 'This is how to open your day, Brigid: Let your first race always be into your byre to your cows; always have your cows first in mind in the morning. Let you race back and put down your fire, and put on your kettle. A kettle is long-some to boil on the first fire, so out with you to let out your hens, and let you feed your hens before you let out the ducks, and if you have a duck among your ducks that you have a suspicion of, see is she still carrying her egg, and if she is let you hold her back. Milk your cow, and if there is a calf feed the calf, and then make your breakfast. Get on top of your work in the morning and you will have the upper hand of your work all day.' Brigid knelt to say her prayers. Mary dressed quickly, praying loudly, and Brigid had to cut short her prayers and take her share of the milking. 'This is how I prayed always,' Mary explained: 'As soon as I opened my eyes I blessed myself, and I prayed putting on my clothes and on my way to the byre, and on my way back, and putting down the fire and letting out the hens and the ducks, and I finished then and looked around me. For that is another thing, take a good look around you in the early morning. You will soon begin to notice things.'

She and Brigid washed up together, and Mary let out the cattle and drove them off the street, and she called to Brigid to warn Tom to get out of bed, for it must be Mass time because Wee Conail was outside, and he was in his dickey. But Tom shouted back that he knew why Wee Conail was in a hurry; he was short two ewes in yesterday's tally, so he would be at the chapel gate early to ask about them and Brigid gave Tom's story to Mary. Mary was soon back again and this time she challenged Tom direct. It was time he was up, for Dan Rua was off to his stable. But Tom knew why Dan Rua was in a hurry; he had to go to the forge for he left a pot out there to get a foot put in it, and it was ready, and he would go for it before Mass, and the forge was a good step beyond the chapel, and again, grumbling, Mary withdrew. A third time she called a warning and now she came to the room door. Mid-glen people, travelling on foot, were off over the hill, taking the near way. This roused Tom. He came to the kitchen in his bare feet. 'It would be a nice how-do-you-do,' he whispered, 'if I had you late for your first Sunday.' He looked at the open doors and shivered. 'My God, are you not an airy pair of people for a frosty morning.' And Brigid told him that this was her doing. She liked the light from the two doors. She found out, by chance, that if she kept the two doors open the light kept the hills out of the kitchen. It would be a great help to her if she could keep the two doors open, until she got used to the mountain. She shut one door so that he might see how the shadows gathered in the kitchen, and then she opened it again so that he might see how the light entered. Mary slapped the black cow with her bare hand to hurry her off the street, her head turned to the talk inside. She watched the cow go in the gap, and she spoke from beyond the doorstep. 'The right thing for you, Brigid, is not to give into yourself, good-bad, about the mountains; even you have to get angry with yourself. The eye will soon stop bothering itself if the mind will not let on it's there.' Tom had to hurry to the stable. Mary sauntered in. 'Above all, Brigid, bear this in mind, not to speak of things that bother you in Tom's hearing, for that man is much given to keeping things in his head. Many a time, long ago, I said a thing and forgot I said it, until one day I would see him up to something and I would know, then, that all the time it was a worry to him. He will be wondering, now, about yourself and the mountains, so be on your guard. Let out a word to make him think you got the upper hand of yourself.' Brigid, feeling a little humble in face of Mary's talk on Tom, tried to make light of what Mary overheard. She told how it all began, on the first night, and how Tom laughed at her and how she had to laugh at herself, and Mary said it was, maybe, no harm for her to talk of this thing, so long as she made a laugh of it and Tom laughed with her. . . .

Brigid joined Tom at the stable, and went over the boreen on the cart, and once they topped the brae Tom saw, from the traffic on the road, that there was no need to hurry and he wondered that the glen people took to the road so early. Brigid rejoiced in this view of the sky, when it was not cut down by a half-door of hills, every way you turned. She noticed that the island boats would have a fair wind to Mass. Tom drew strokes of the whip on the horse's flank. 'You are not to mind me, Tom, when I grumble about the mountains. I'll get used to the mountains. Why would I not get used to them? Your mother says one of these days I will wonder at myself, that I ever let them bother me.' Tom dropped the reins and took out his pipe. It did not seem strange to him that her eyes missed the sea and the wide sky, and the way all that light outside was let inside, through the big windows. That was one of the first things he noticed, the big windows. He turned to her with a lighted match cupped in his hand, and asked could it be that it would be a help to her if they put in big windows, and she grabbed his arm and she did not speak above a whisper, and she said that big windows would be like a vision of the face of God to her, and at that he flung the match from him and picked up the reins, and flicked them and blamed her for keeping such a thought to herself. He knew a man who did such work. He would be at Mass. 'But your mother, Tom, I made a mock of the darkness to your mother. Your mother will think this wrong of you

and she will think poorly of me going back on what I said.'
He cracked his whip and laughed. What his mother would
say was another day's work altogether. The thing now was to
have a word with this man.

It was the rule that horses should be unyoked by the roadside, and led to the back of the chapel wall. Brigid could go
on in, by herself, or she could wait until he tied the horse and
came back to her. She chose to go on in alone for since this
was her first Sunday, she would like a while for prayer before
Mass. Tom helped her down. She passed through a stretch
of open traffic. There was a clump of people by the chapel
gate; men grouped across the road. She looked for the
friendly flash of Briany's dickey among them. She did not
notice the women inside the gate until she was about to turn
in, and then it was the stormy face of Susan Dan she saw.
She knew, now, this was a gathering of the women of the
glen. As she passed them there was a mock stampede, which
caught her and flung her across the gravel path. She all but
lost her shawl. She went in among the headstones and found
a path towards the porch. The women rushed ahead and
reformed, and they stampeded against her a second time,
and she would have fallen but that a girl by a grave caught
hold of her. Somewhere behind her a woman spoke in anger.
'Glenmore bullocks,' the voice scolded, 'Glenmore bullocks.'

Brigid made the Stations of the Cross after Mass. There
were two old women in the porch, as she passed through it on
her way out, and they smiled at her. 'You'll be the new
woman to Glenmore, God bless you.' They shook hands with
her, nodding their old heads in approval of her. 'The world
is outside there, waiting to have a look at you.' Brigid
glimpsed the throng of faces to the right of the door. She
slumped against the wall and shut her eyes, and prayed.
The priest was by the altar rail and one of the old women
beckoned to him, and he came. He was an elderly man, a
frail man with a slight twist in one of his lips, when he smiled.
One of the old women explained that this was the new
woman into Glenmore, and she turned to her companion

42

and they both nodded, and she said they were rough with her on her way into the church, and she faced her companion again and they both nodded, and the priest nodded and he put his hand on Brigid's arm, and he walked out with her, and the women by the porch scattered out among the tombstones at sight of him. He told her he knew Mary; and Tom, too, to be sure; and the glen itself. He would be looking out for her next time he went in there on stations. 'The glen will be strange to you, but you just give yourself time,' he advised, and Brigid told him that was Mary's advice, too, and he laughed at that, and he shook hands with Brigid and he stood on the gravel path until she went out the gate. She met Tom coming towards her. Briany waited for them by the cart and he rode home with them and he told tales of Boston. He and Brigid walked over the casan together. 'A body's first Sunday away from home is, maybe, the most day you think long. I always heard that in Boston.' 'It's not that I think long, Briany, but all this anger around me is taking the heart out of me. You did not see such roughness in Boston.' He interrupted her to tell of a morning in Boston when such crowds gathered to see a couple married that the police had to be called, and the horse police had to be called, or the crowd would put them under their feet. 'You are never short of a story that will make an excuse for the glen,' she taunted at the fork of the casans.

'What kind of a sermon had you?' Mary greeted. 'I was lucky I was able to listen to it, whatever it was, after the stirks of the glen tried to walk over me,' Brigid flared. She draped her shawl over the line in the kitchen, and she told how the women of the glen beset her on her way in, and lay in wait for her on the way out, and she told of the two old women and Mary made her describe them and she named them and praised them. Mary rapped her snuff box. 'They went to the end of their tether this day, Brigid. I let them sulk how they liked, but there is no more length left in their tether to take a stagger out of you, after this day.' She spoke grimly. Tom's steps sounded on the gravel. 'I always like a

43

good long sermon,' Mary began. 'I get no good of a sermon lately unless I am in the front seat. . . .' When their meal was over she reminded Tom and Brigid that they must go across to Peggy. Brigid showed no enthusiasm for the visit. She put the dinner things away and she fed the hens, and Tom said to her it was time they went, and they walked out together. Their way led by Wee Conail's door, and there were sharp voices inside. A startled child fled indoors and there was silence and Wee Conail appeared, and he came quickly to meet them and he walked with them. He noticed a cow in mischief and he whistled for his dog, and two dogs came, and, one seeking to out-do the other they were rough with the cow, and she fled from them and fell heavily and Wee Conail, in a rage, stoned both dogs. He appealed to Tom was he not heart-scalded, that every time he whistled for his dog, Briany's dog came too. Briany had no right to keep a dog. He never rightly named his dog. Briany had three or four names, make-believe names, half-fancy names — Spot, Stumpy, Curly, Fido — but he never could make up his mind to use one of them, so the dog never knew what his name was and, let you call any name loud enough Briany's dog came. There should be a law against a man making an idiot of a dog. It was not to the dog a man should take the stones, but to Briany himself. Tom spoke up in favour of Briany. Briany was a smart man, only people would not listen to him. Only that Briany wrote a letter to Dublin, the glen would still be without a road in over the moor. If Briany got a backing there would be a loop of a road round under the rim of the glen. . . .

'Ah, you and Briany.' Wee Conail made an impatient gesture and turned from them in a gap. Tom chuckled. 'Wee Conail is against the road. Wee Conail is against anything that would cost him a penny. He thinks, if there is a road there will be higher rates; not mind you but Wee Conail is a smart man himself. The teacher gave him a great name long ago. He has the right of it about Briany's dog. Another man that suffers from Briany's dog is Black Donal. Now,

44

here is a strange thing about Black Donal. He never raises his head to call his dog but he roars. You never heard such roars as he lets when he calls his dog, and that draws Briany's dog on him.'

'I'm glad you like Briany, Tom. I would like you always to be good to Briany.' Black Donal came out from his haggard to meet them. 'You are to go in by yourself, Brigid,' he announced. 'She says Tom and myself must stay outside, and that we are to see nobody gets an ear to the door till yourself and herself have your say together. Do not let Peggy's noise upset you, for do you know what I am going to take and to tell you, the regular fact of the matter is, Brigid, Peggy is scared of her life of you. It is your ear-rings.' Brigid looked from Black Donal to Tom. She sighed deeply and went forward slowly towards the open door. Her step was so light, a hen inside the door got no warning of her until she darkened the light, and then the hen flew into the window. Brigid walked unhurried to the window, and caught her and let her down, and she scurried out. Brigid was used to the shadow in the kitchen by now. She could see the face in the bed, a big-boned face in the pattern of Tom's. She moved aside to let the window light bear on the bed. 'Stand where you are,' Peggy ordered. 'Leave the window light on your face. So this is you. So this is what Tom Manus picked for himself.' Her voice was harsh. She tucked back a fold of bed-curtain and moved upward on her pillow. 'Tell me one thing and tell me no more, what made the like of you, with your looks and your blankets, and your ear-rings pick on Tom Manus for your man?' Brigid edged sideways to get a better view of Peggy. 'I want the God's truth now,' Peggy warned, 'let it be the God's truth, no matter what kind the truth is.'

'It was like this, then.' There was a sharpness in Brigid's voice too. 'Tom Manus came stumbling into our boat one Sunday, to take passage to the island. He was all hands and feet and elbows and knees, and everybody laughed at him, and I laughed at him, and I said to myself "that is the ugliest

45

man God ever made".' The dog rose from the hearth and touched her hand with his snout. He went back and lay on the hearth. Peggy rid her throat. Brigid waited but Peggy did not speak. 'He sat on the taft facing me, his legs apart, and his two hands between them gripping the taft, and I looked at him and he looked at me, and I noticed the cliffs of bone above his eyes, and the knuckles of the bones of his face and I thought to myself, God Almighty, there is the strength of a spring tide in that man.' Peggy tried to raise herself higher on the pillow. 'I was up the rocks after him when he landed, and he was the lightest-footed man of them all on the rocks, and I was glad, and I pointed to him and I said to some near me, "laugh now, let you". That evening he came into our house to see did we want lime, or had we a young animal to sell, like he asked in other houses, and I made him tea, and I knew what brought him into our house. He sat by the fireside, and he talked and when he went away I stood in the door looking after him, and I turned round and there was my mother, with her two eyes on me, and we alone. "That is the first man I ever saw. I could say at once I could marry," I said, letting on to laugh. My mother did not laugh. I could never be sure if my mother had any hand in what followed, but Tom Manus came back, again and again to the island, and he bought calves, and he came into our house, and I did not give him much bother catching me.'

'God, O God,' Peggy's voice was gentle now. 'God, O God,' she whispered. She put out her two arms to Brigid, but Brigid did not stir. 'So I married him, and it was near two months later that I came to live among his people, so their minds had time to be used to knowing the like of me was in it, and the night I came in among them they turned on me, and they could not have said worse of me if I was some woman of the roads that everybody knew of. And this day at the chapel gate . . .' Her voice faltered. She went quickly to the bedside and knelt by it. 'It will go hard with me if somebody does not tell me why all this is.'

46

'So you do not know why this is, and Mary didn't tell you why this is. Well, I will tell you the why of it. God o' God, have you no sense? Do you think you can reach into this glen, and pluck out of it the likeliest man it ever reared, a man the women of this glen had their eye on from he got into long trousers, and then expect the women of the glen to gather round you and kiss you for it? God o' God, if the pains would only let me laugh.' She put a hand under Brigid's chin and raised it. 'God in heaven, but you are good-looking. I asked Black Donal what you were like. He said you had a shine in your hair like the hide of a thriving calf, that you had a body like the handle of a whip, and you had the hip of a greyhound. God o' God if only I dare laugh. If only the pains would let me laugh.' She raised her hand against any talk from Brigid. 'Let me tell you how it was: Word came into this glen that Tom Manus was snared by some clip of a woman from the island and the women of the glen rushed in here, on this floor, and they had Mary on their feet with them, and they were angry, and I found no fault with them for that. No outside man comes into this glen with his nose in the wind looking for a woman, so why waste any of the few men we have, and above all such a man as this? They made noise and I made noise, but my mind was only half on what I was saying, for I had a cow at the calving, and whatever strange nature is in her she always calves standing up.' Brigid laid her cheek against Peggy's hand and she laughed and laughed. 'Hell to you,' Peggy scolded, 'you never took a calf from a cow standing up, or you would not laugh.' 'I am going to like you, Aunt Peggy, I am going to like you.' She rose and sat on the side of the bed. 'The devil thank you for liking me,' Peggy snorted, 'for if you are thankful to Tom Manus let me tell you you would never have stretched yourself alongside him in the bed, but for me. What the women had in mind coming to me was to make Mary put a stop to Tom's plans. Oh, the like was done before. It was so. They said Mary should warn Tom if he married, as he had in mind to marry, there was the high road for him, and he could take it and take his foreign wife with him, and leave room for his brother Jimmy who is in Boston to come home and marry, as he should marry. If Mary wanted Tom with her then let her deal with Tom; let her upset this marriage, even she had to dose him with physic in such a way that on the morning when he should be on his way to the chapel he would be in and out to the byre instead, buttoning and unbuttoning; like was done before in this glen. When I think of it now, I have to laugh. Mary stood there, like you always see her stand with one arm across her body, patient like, and no word out of her and her face calm. I suppose maybe my mind was on my cow. As well as that I was angry with Tom, for if I had my wish of the men of Ireland to be in my byre at a hard calving I would choose Tom, and now he was not with me, and it was not away at a fair he was, like I thought, but chasing a woman, so I said to them that Mary would put a halt to Tom's gallop, or I would do it myself, and I said to them to be on their way because all their hubbub was upsetting my cow. I walked out with them, and they went off chattering, and then I took a look across the brae and I saw Tom's cart, and I whipped off my neck shawl and I shook it on him, and I shook it on him, and he leaped off the cart, for he knew about the cow, and he came running.' She searched for her snuff box under the pillow and Brigid found it for her and took off the lid. 'Such a calving as yon was, Brigid.'

'Tell one story at a time, Aunt Peggy.'

'It is all one story, girl. The calving was over and we were in the byre together, and I was watching him rub the calf dry with a wisp of straw, and the great nature I always had for Tom rose in me. I took the girls of the glen into my mind, and I set them beside him, one after the other, and the only one of them I could think fit for him was too sib for him to marry, and a wildness took hold of me and I said to myself "let him have his head"; and it is as true as you are sitting there, it was the calving did it; you never saw such strength and skill in a pair of hands. So, over I goes and sits beside him and I whispers to him about the invasion of women, and what they had in mind to make his mother do to him and he laughs at me. He laughs at me, for, what do you think, does not his mother know. When I think of it, right under my nose, hiding herself behind talk that she had to go to a town-land beyond the chapel, to have a word with a woman home from Boston that is married into the same street as her daughter Cicely, off she went to Carrick to see the priest and Jane Garvey to find out what kind of a family Tom was in tow with. I should have known better, Brigid, for that is how Mary Manus lived her life, for ever on the watch over everything that belonged to her, and she always silent. There never was such a woman for watching. She had a bad neighbour in Nappy, for Nappy never shut a hen-house door and, come harvest-time, Mary had to be out with the dawn to keep Nappy's hens from her oats, and she did it, and she kept her knitting in her fingers and I never knew her to throw a clod at a hen. She would make it her business to say to Nappy, sometime during the day, with somebody listening: "Your hens broke out again this morning, Nappy." For shame's sake, in the end, Nappy would shut them up for a while. Now if yon was your Aunt Peggy, Brigid, the world would hear her roaring — but Nappy's hens would have her oats in the end. Mary is not like me, Brigid, for although Mary will let nothing go, Mary will have peace.'

'You make Mary kind of frightening, Peggy.'

'Mary is a great woman Brigid. She is a woman life beat hard, and it bent her a wee bit, like you see, for she carried a heavy burden, but ever and always there was the calm in her you see now; and the sense. There is something else in her too Brigid; holiness I think. Let me warn you, girl, if you and Mary ever fall out I'll blame you.' Brigid nodded slowly. She stooped quickly and kissed Peggy. 'And now I will put on the kettle, Aunt Peggy.'

'You will put on the kettle, Brigid, and you will call in the two poor idiots outside.'

5

'I HAD Kitty in with me,' Mary announced. 'You will never be at a loss for news while Kitty is in and out, for Kitty misses nothing and nothing rests long in her mind. She scarce had breath enough for all she had to say.' Mary sought in her cubby hole for her pipe. Brigid laid down an armful of turf, and picked up the tongs to build a fire. 'Sean Mor started the talk; I knew how it would be. Poor Sean Mor, he is getting now that he is for ever in the grip of some wonder. I mind when he would sit with you, and go over crops and the growth of your animal and his own animal and tell you of the butt of a ridge of your ground that was going sour, and if he saw that your own hand could not reach it, the first thing you would know, some evening, he would be making a drain or ridding a drain for you himself. He was the greatest neighbour you could have, and you without help; himself and Black Donal. A widow woman with a house full of children gets an understanding of her neighbours. People will be sorry for you but that will not keep them from making use of a gap in your fence to let a calf or a cow spend a night in your meadow fields. I saw Sean Mor, on a Sunday, go over every fence on every field belonging to me. I would not like to have to face God and expect forgiveness if I held anything Sean Mor did now, when he is not at himself, against him in face of all he did for me. God help him, the net was a wonder to him and he had to let his wonder out, and he not only made a wonder of the net but of you, and what you said, so he carried his noise to Nelly and from Nelly to Susan, and across to Bella and round to Sorcha and all they saw in it was you, giving yourself airs, and taunting them that you would teach them how to keep house. It was a bad day for such talk, for they were in half anger as it was over the way the priest made much of you on Sunday, so they roused themselves and what everyone of them said Kitty had by heart; Kitty is not a person that ever holds back a word she picks up. Kitty will bring a story in, and she will do her best to have a story with her out, but she never makes up a story, so you can go by what she tells you. It seems Bella was the one with the most to say. I said to Kitty, fitter for Bella put an odd patch on her children's clothes. Let her carry that. That was enough to let her see.'

'Let them talk, Mary, I could put out my tongue at them now. You should have told me, Mary, what Peggy told me.'

'I would not like you, Brigid, to go too much by what Peggy says. There is over-much noise in Peggy. I said to you, give yourself time, and that is what I say to you, and if you do that one day there will be quietness and you will look out your door and everybody you see around you will be a neighbour; and next to the grace of God the greatest thing in life is neighbours. If you listen to Peggy's noise, and you set out to get even with Susan and Nelly, it will be many a long day before you make a neighbour of either of them; and if you make a wasp's nest of the houses nearest you, what woman is going to come to you and bear the sting of their tongues? If the right thing was to put fight on Nelly and Susan do you think I would not give my mind to it?'

'I will be good, Mary,' Brigid promised. She sang as she lit the lamp and swept the hearth, and Mary held her pipe in her hand and listened. 'I used to sing myself long ago, Brigid, you would never think there was a song about myself, one time.' Brigid turned quickly, 'I would so, Mary Manus. I said it to Peggy, I never saw such a good face on young or old.' 'Thank you girl. If a body is not good-looking at twenty nobody can blame her, but if she has not some share of good looks at sixty she has only herself to blame; if God leaves her the health. I had my share of good locks at twenty.'

Brigid settled herself on a creepy, facing Mary across the fire. Mary had no memory of the song about herself, but she knew verses of a song sung in the glen at every gathering when a new crop of young people were on the wing for Boston, and she sang snatches, and Tom came in on them when they were at it. 'Look ye, Tom,' Mary said, 'there is a nail in that chair that will tear somebody's clothes. Take the shoulder of the tongs to it and beat it down,' and Brigid picked up the tongs and handed it to him, chuckling, and he did as he was bid. A man's step came to the door. It was Dan Rua. He was a bulkier man than Tom, a freckled-faced, red-headed man, in a high-necked gansey. He shook hands warmly, refused the chair Brigid put in place for him, and stretched himself on the floor. Tom took his pipe from his mouth and handed it to him. Dan Rua put out his hand to Mary and she handed him her own pipe and her tobacco as well. 'God knows, Dan Rua, I would miss you. You are the only man in the glen ever fills my pipe the way I like it. Tom there puts his thumb on it and presses it down, or he scrapes the inside of it. . . .'

'A big idiot, Mary, like I often told you. I never thought, in this world, he would find a woman to marry him.' He picked out Mary's pipe into his palm. 'I often noticed the coarsest looking men have the best looking women.' He grinned at Brigid. 'It was a great pity, girl, I never laid an eye on you. Whisper to me, girl, whisper to me,' he invited, beckoning her, and he laughed loudly.

Sean Mor's loud talk came through the open door. 'I tell you, yon is what it is.' He carried his stick under his arm as he came in the door. 'Mary,' he greeted, 'listen to me. In my bed last night it came to me. Do you mind hearing the old people telling of a lame man, a tailor by the same token, who spent a year in the glen, to the great misfortune of the glen and the loss of many a fine beast?'

'I mind hearing the old people talk of him surely. He overlooked the cattle going by the door of whatever house he was busy in, and he did not know himself, the poor man, he had this grudge in his heart.'

'He did not, Mary. Brigid, this is how it has to be on the island.' He waited while Black Donal and Briany, and Wee Conail found themselves seats; he had his own special chair and place on the hearth. He rapped the floor with his stick to get quiet. 'Brigid, there has to be a man in your island — it could be a woman — there is somebody on your island over-looking your cattle, one by one.'

Brigid shook her head. 'The people of the island know fine what kills their cattle. It is something in the grass. They open the animals and they see what it is, and always it is the same thing.' Sean Mor scratched noisily in his whiskers, his two eyes shut tight. 'The island has no belief at all in the Evil Eye,' Brigid went on. 'People would laugh . . .' 'Have a care, island woman, have a care,' Sean Mor ordered, 'such things are not to be spoken of, lightly.' Brigid glanced over the intent faces. She rose to put water in the kettle. They watched her, waiting for her to speak further.

'Away out of here people believe different things from this glen,' Briany put in. 'Take such a thing now as the end of the world, some would laugh at you . . .' 'Ho, ho,' Sean Mor scoffed, 'ho, ho, some people would laugh, if you said the world would end. There was a man in this glen, back from Boston he was, and he had whiskey in him and he denied there was such a thing as a ghost at the head of the Loch. At the fall of the night, coming in from the bog, he had to go by the Loch, and the words he said came back to him in a shout from the dark around him, and he saw the lake itself rise up in a cloud and he heard the whirr of wings and only he had the sense to cry out, "I believe in you, I believe in you," he would be up into the air and dropped into the lake. Let people who deny have a care. . . .'

'Do you know what I am going to take and tell you, Sean Mor, the regular fact of the matter is that man you talk of was a mouth when he said he had no belief in ghosts, and he was a mouth when he told the story of what befell him at the Loch, for the wings he heard were the wings of wild duck, shaking the dusk in a flutter of fear at his step. I would not believe the Our Father from him.' Black Donal turned to Brigid. 'For all that, the ghosts be in it, and such other things as the old people knew of, girl.' He spoke kindly. 'And what Sean Mor wants to know, if he could get it said, is, does your mother safeguard her byre? Has she a bag of darts?' 'Darts?' Brigid said, puzzled. Sean Mor tugged to get a small fat sack, like a pin cushion, out of his pocket. He held it up to her. She looked at Tom for guidance, but he had none to give her. Mary signed to her to take it.

'You see, Mary,' Sean Mor proclaimed, 'that is how it is. The island is dark to such things and, because of that, it is losing its cattle.' Mary nodded solemnly. He asked Brigid if ever, when she drove her cows in or out, she saw a piece of black stone shoot up and strike a cow's leg, or maybe her belly, and Brigid, frowning in thought, nodded and the whole fireside nodded, too, and smiled, for that bit of flint was a fairy dart and Brigid's people should have carried such pieces home to make them up in a small sack to be kept under a rafter in the byre. That was the way to keep cows safe.

At first Brigid was suspicious they were maybe making up a story for her, but soon she was embarrassed, for Sean Mor wanted her to promise she would send the bag of darts to her mother, and she could only shake her head and say she was thankful to him, but her people would not give into such things. 'It would not be right to take a thing from a body that believes in it, and give it to another with no belief at all in it,' she pleaded, handing back the bag of darts, and there was a terrible silence by the fireside. Briany hurried to put in a word; that was the most common thing he noticed in Boston, one putting against what another person believed. Even within the one family you came on it . . . But Sean Mor rapped the floor with a stick. This was a bad business. He addressed himself to Mary. 'I would not let it upset me, Mary. The girl herself is not to blame; she knows no better.' He turned to Brigid. 'Tell me, girl, what word of this glen had you on the island or did you know what

54

place you were coming to?' She straightened herself on her creepy. 'All I ever heard of Glenmore was, mainland people running it down for putting sand into the lime.' That brought a growl and a half. This was more of the lies the world put on Glenmore, and all because of a grudge on account of the lime. One jostled the other to tell her how a stone, that fails to slake, can be missed in the bagging, and how it may crumble later and make itself into the gritty sediment at the bottom of a bucket of lime-wash. Sean Mor rapped the floor again. Let them leave the world to its lies. It was Brigid was in their care, and since she had no understanding of the glen they would have to teach it to her, like she was a child learning her prayers. He scratched at his whiskers. The chairs creaked and men sidled them, this way and that, for comfort, and Brigid could read these signs, and she welcomed them for she liked stories. 'It is right surely she should get a full understanding of the glen, Sean Mor,' Mary encouraged. Nobody else spoke. Sean Mor sat with his eyes shut. 'There is no better person than yourself, Sean Mor, to open her mind to the right sense of the glen.' She turned to Brigid.

'Sean Mor has knowledge of things that happened. Sean Mor has what the old people said, no word put to it, no word taken from it. Let her learn first, Sean Mor, of The Prophecy of Colmcille.' She turned to Brigid. 'He cannot give you the words of the prophecy, for there is a law the old people laid down on that. He can tell how it came that the prophecy was said. Tell her, Sean Mor, and about The Promise.' Sean Mor resting his two hands on his stick pushed himself up and cleared his throat, and in the overtones of a wonder-tale, he told of Colmcille, the near-equal of the High-King of Ireland, and the near-equal of God Himself. Colmcille set himself up against the judgment of the King of Ireland and he fought a battle against him, and overcame the King's army, and God was angry and punishment was laid on Colmcille for the lives lost in the battle, and the Saint would not bow himself to God but walked in anger among the mountains, and he climbed every peak he met to shout his rebellion at God, until he came to the highest peak of all, the grey mountain guarding Glenmore. It came to pass that the men of the glen were abroad that night, on their way back from a foray with victory on their shields, and black pride in their hearts, and it was a calm night and there was a full moon. They knew the voice and they acclaimed Colmcille, and their voices rang against the sky like thunder, and it was then Colmcille saw himself, and how his sin made for sin in others, and he wept, and he wept, and he asked mercy, not for himself but for those others, and refused it for himself until it embraced those others, and God yielded to Colmcille, and behold a great light boiled up from behind the mountains and it spilled into the glen in rivers of music, and birds took the air and they sang and the moon danced and the sky, and the night. And then Colmcille spoke, and like you would clap your hands there was no stir, all the light of the night went into his eyes, and Colmcille saw all the days that were to come down to the end of time, and read out what he saw, and the glen listened, and then they cried out against him because of this burden of knowledge he placed on them above all the men of the world; for life would henceforth have no joy for them because of their fear of what was to come, and Colmcille took pity on them. He raised his hand and let its shadow fall across the seven caves of the glen, and an angel took his stand in the shadow with a sword in his hand, and Colmcille spoke, and he made the promise. And the promise was this. That when, in the fullness of time the days of tribulation come on the world, and men call on the mountains to hide them, and the mountains deny them shelter, then, in that hour, Glenmore will be blessed for there will be shelter for its people behind this shadow of Colmcille's hand across the mouths of its caves.' And when the story was told Sean Mor rested his two hands on the top of his stick, and laid his chin on them. The fireside was silent. The kettle, which Brigid had linked high during the story to delay the wetting of the tea until the end, poured forth a wisp of

56

steam, and hissed softly. 'Behind the shadow of his hand in the depths of its caves,' Mary intoned her rosary tinkling in her fingers. The chairs creaked as men stirred. Brigid rose to wet the tea. 'It is a great story, a great, great story,' she enthused. 'I heard before of Colmcille's prophecy, and his curses too. I always heard that anybody who put an oat cake to bake and let one side bake full, before the other got any fire, got his curse.' She spoke lightly. 'They have a story of the end of the world on the island. Our story is that when the time comes the sea itself will go up in a great blast of fire and consume itself, and then there will be a great rushing noise, only that will not be a storm but the souls of the world through all the generations arriving for The Judgment. They do not tell it much now, for the island has so many men back from sailoring to tell of things they saw in far off parts.' She picked up the tea-pot and went to the table. She glanced back at them, puzzled by their silence. Mary had rid her throat angrily. 'What Sean Mor said was not a story Brigid. It was a thing that happened, the living words coming down from that night.' Brigid poured the tea. The men took their bowls from her in silence. 'And are the words of the prophecy known?' 'Every man, woman in Glenmore has the words of the prophecy on his tongue, like the Hail Mary, but they are never said out loud; except when a woman says them to her child at bedtime. She says them, and says them, night after night until the night when that child starts up out of his sleep screeching that the end of the world is at hand and he cannot find his way behind the shadow of Colmcille's promise, over the caves.' Mary took the bowl Brigid handed her and rested it on her lap. 'And when that happens a woman thanks God, for she knows that child will live, and the story will go on through that child's life to the generations to come.' Brigid sat on her creepy and drank her tea, and nobody put in a word between her and Mary. 'It is laid down that if a woman from afar comes into this glen she will sit down with her own children while a woman of the glen speaks the prophecy to this stranger's child, and the

57

words of the promise too. And so with God's help you will sit by your child one day, and listen, and you too will thank God when the child starts up screeching.' 'No, no,' Brigid said sharply. 'It would not be right to beset a child's mind in such a way.' Sean Mor rapped the floor with the stick, and Mary cried out against her. 'Guard your tongue,' Mary ordered. 'It is not right to deny, nor belittle what you heard.' Brigid turned to Tom. He had his hands down between his knees and he was tickling the kitten with a straw. Brigid took a deep breath. She rose to put the bowls away. 'Anyway we will all be dead before the end of the world.'

It was manners for the men to delay a while after the tea. Briany was reminded of something he saw in Boston and they listened to him. Tom walked out with them, and Brigid sauntered out under the stars. Tom came round by the other gable, and went in and Mary spoke sharply to him, and Brigid delayed on the edge of the street because of the anger in Mary's voice. Mary blamed Tom for not saying to Brigid she must give her mind over to the glen. Brigid would never make a right woman of herself, if every word said in the glen had to be judged against the foolishness spoken in the island. Brigid did not catch Tom's murmur. She spoke to the dog as she crossed the street, to give them warning. Mary let her milk alone, and Brigid shut the byre door behind her so that any argument between Tom and his mother would not reach her. Tom did not wait for the rosary; he had to be afoot early. Brigid and Mary said the rosary together, and Mary was still on her knees when Brigid went to bed. Tom was already asleep.

6

BRIANY rested his wheelbarrow and waited for Brigid to come up and she smiled wistfully as she laid down the water pails. 'You have them making more noise now, and more in one voice, than I ever heard.' He spoke seriously. 'Kitty says Mary is at you too, and Peggy.' 'I am not afraid of Peggy, Briany, nor sorry for her like Mary; Mary is not sleeping. I should have held my tongue, Briany. I let myself get upset. I told Mary last night Colmcille's promise had no meaning to me, with all belonging to me out over the seven seas of the world, and then I said to her that she was forgetting all belonging to her in Boston. I made her angry.'

'Even in Boston, Brigid, women say over the prophecy to their children, and they say it and say it, and the children take to it like here, and have dreams, and the women like their children to have dreams.' He shook his head. 'You will make no headway with Mary, Brigid. It is not you Mary has in mind but Tom. This talk is not aimed at you but at Tom, making out the woman he picked himself is some kind of a daft body. Susan, above all, wants to make a laugh of Tom. Mary wants to be able to boast about you: like when the cows gave in to you.'

'I have Tom in mind too, Briany. I know Mary is at him; every chance she gets. It will be God help him when he tells her of the big windows.' This was news to Briany and lowering her voice she confided in him. He frowned. Mary would not be for such a thing, above all not now, since it would set Susan and Nelly into an uproar of more and more mockery of Tom.

Brigid told Briany how this unhappiness between herself and Mary made her want to put her head out the door, more and more, and look around her at the daylight. She knew Mary saw her at it. She knew it was a silly thing for her to do, and sometimes she set her mind against going out, but it was like holding your breath under water. She wiped her eyes furtively and smiled. She had one great comfort in all this anyway, she was able to talk to Tom about the light for Tom saw into it. It was a great pity Mary could not see into it, for she was making headway in other ways. She often caught the red hen's noise now before Mary's ear got it. Since she and Mary had no ease in their talk there was a thing they did together. She laughed. Mary crumbled turf on the hearth and set them out, like the houses in the glen, and she named them and drew strokes with the shank of her pipe to show how the blood relation flowed among them, and they got so far now Mary would put out questions on Brigid and Brigid had the answers for them. It was Mary's idea that when Brigid was one with the rest of the glen, and a neighbour's name came into the talk in any house, she would know what bearing the name would have on the people listening. It was a pitiable thing, such make-believe. She picked up her pails and went on her way.

Sean Mor stormed across the green, stabbing the ground with his stick, stumbling in his hurry. He had news. The postman brought word to lower glen about the train. Every now and then such word came. The railway was to push itself forward to Carrick village, and Sean Mor always raised a shout against it. The railway was one of the things the prophecy warned the world against. Once the railway came within sight of Glenmore the end of the world was not far away. It was one of the last signs the world would get, the whistle of a train that could be heard in Glenmore. Carrick should be warned to put off this business. People should go to Jane Garvey and warn her they would turn the country against her. In the first shimmerings of his dotage his fears tormented him. He roared out his troubles at sight of

Brigid, and he followed her inside. He pressed the back of his hand against his eyes, and a speck of blood showed on it. Mary scolded him for rubbing his eyes. He shut them tight and beads of red tears tumbled down his face. He gave in his eyes were a torment to him; at night above all. They put him in mind of the roasting heat of a lime kiln. Mary asked Brigid to pour the cold tea left in the tea-leaves into a spoon, so that she might let drops drip from her little finger into his eyes, and Brigid did as she was bid and she stood by Mary and held the spoon and she wiped Sean Mor's face with her apron. Mary chided him for letting himself get upset at town talk. Colmcille said the train would come, so there let it. Trains could come, and no harm would flow from them, for whatever had to come Colmcille knew of when he made his promise. She glanced at Brigid and sighed.

'You have a great understanding of pain, Brigid,' Mary praised when they were alone. 'It is not many can look into Sean Mor's eyes, and nobody could that had no sense of the pain in them, and a wish to ease it. Sean Mor is a pity. He lives with his son Phil, and Bella, the old streel has a down on him: he coughs and he spits and Bella says her stomach gets upset. She says her stomach would turn over if she as much as looked at his eyes, and tried to ease them. The right cure for such eyes is breast milk, but the saying is that the red-hot pain in them would go from the eyes to the breast, unless a woman said the right prayer at the time, and nobody knows the prayer. Some would maybe risk it, but not Bella, and if not Bella, who? This is the story of the cure: A man with eyes like Sean Mor was on his way home from his wife's funeral, and he rested by the roadside above a lake with water lilies in it, and because they were hid from him in the red haze of his pain he wept, and a woman of the road with a child on her breast stood before him in the midst of the red mist and she asked him if he knew her. He said he did not and she told him she was the woman he gave shelter to on a night she named and he said back to her that was his one claim on God, that he never said "no" when he was asked for shelter in God's name, and then she said to him to go on his knees and he went on his knees and she filled his eyes with the white milk of her breast, and she said a prayer and she bade him sit up, with the eyes shut softly while he said a decade of the rosary, and when he did as he was bid and when he opened them the first thing he saw was the white of the water lilies and the clear face of the lake but there was no sign of the woman and when he went home he had no memory of the prayer; only that he knew there was a prayer.'

'There was a prayer surely,' Brigid said softly, 'a prayer to the Mother of God to take away the red mist of pain and drive it to the bottom of the sea,' and she said the prayer for Mary and Mary was excited. This was a tale to tell, the prayer after all the years. But how could the prayer be, when the man who heard it forgot it; unless the Mother of God — for that was who it was — made the cure for others who gave shelter to the poor, and that one of them kept it in mind. She must go abroad with this news. Oh thank God, thank God. . . .

And that night, the talk was on cures. Briany had the gift the cure of the rose, and when Brigid asked him he said the prayer; and it was the only time he ever said it, they knew, except maybe to himself, without being leaning over a woman suffering from the red swelling and he rubbing unsalted butter on to it. 'The Mother and the Son were out walking. They met a cow. The cow had the Rose in her udder. Cure the cow said the Son to the Mother. Cure her yourself for it is You has the power. So the Son cured the cow and He left the cure on the udder. In the name of the Father and of the Son and of the Holy Ghost.' There were other cures and other prayers and they went over them and Brigid added her share. From prayers they passed to curses. A body had to know them, too, for a curse had to be overcome in its own way; prayer could not reach some curses for when God banished the devil He left him the right to traffic in three evils, the evil mind, the evil tongue, the evil heart, and they were beyond the reach of prayer. The talk opened a dark world and Brigid sat in her corner and listened and was afraid, and in the end she put her hands over her ears and cried out against it all.

When they were alone by the fire Mary chided Brigid. These things were in the world and one day they might touch on Brigid's own life, when Mary was not with her to do what was laid down to overcome them. The priest himself would tell her there were things in it he had no wish, and maybe no right, to match his power against. A thing happened one time to herself, and she went to big father Dan. . . .

Brigid insisted that Mary take her turn to Mass and Mary gave in that they should make every other Sunday for a while. In any case she had a wish to go that Sunday, and she would like to be early and have a good while for herself on the grave before Mass, and so Brigid and she hurried through the morning chores and Brigid made Mary wear her new shawl, and Mary was gay setting out over the casan to the old quarry ahead of the cart, and Brigid was sorry when she saw two men of lower glen climb on to the cart with Mary and Tom, for she guessed Tom had in mind to tell his mother about the big windows. Brigid did her odd jobs and she sang at her work for, somehow, it was a lightness to her to have the house to herself and when her work was done she knelt to say the prayers the island laid down for whoever stayed away from Mass. She was well into her rosary when a light, fidgety sound by the door made her raise her head. A shadow touched the jamb of the door, and fingers long, bony fingers that reminded her of a crab creeping from a crevise, appeared. A woman's hand, a faded head scarf, a face. A woman stepped forward into the light of the doorway, her head restless as a bird's. 'Come in, Ann the Hill,' Brigid greeted quietly, 'come on up to the fire.' Ann took a step forward, hesitated, and then, with a queer sideways skip she fluttered up the floor and sat on Mary's creepy, her hands, half-clawed, thrust out in front of her. Her face was worn, grey, lined, dull, almost expressionless. Her ash-coloured eyes were strangely hidden under the lichen-like eyebrows.

She wore a double row of safety pins across her breast. 'I am glad you came to see me, Ann.' The clawed hands opened out slowly and rested lightly on her knee. 'I like to hear you singing,' Ann said. Her manner of speech was strange. Her words seemed to throb in her throat like a bird's song. 'I hid in the byre. I was under the creel. I heard you say to Mary you had no fear of me.'

'I have no fear of you, Ann, why should I have any fear of you?' Ann leaned towards her, her head sideways. 'I have to laugh that Mary did not spot you in the byre.' Ann raised one hand. She rode her creepy across the hearth. 'Kitty is at the back door.' Ann crawled down the floor on hands and knees and lay flat to peep through the space at the bottom of the door. She got to her feet. 'Kitty is away.' Brigid turned to the window, and Ann stood by her and pointed at Kitty on her way to Nelly's. 'You must have ears like a wild goose,' Brigid joked. They went back to their creepies. 'I will make us tea, Ann. Would you like me to sing?' Ann beat her palms together and chortled. Brigid sang softly and later they sat by the fire and drank their tea, and when Ann laid down her bowl she put out her hands to the blaze like a child. She fluttered across the hearth to touch the brooch Brigid wore and Brigid took it from her blouse and set it among the safety pins. Ann placed her hand over it protectively, and eeled back to Mary's corner. She raised her hand cautiously to have a look at the brooch and she put it back and laid the other hand on top of it. 'It was Kitty stole Tom's burden rope. Tom thinks it was Nappy. Dan Rua knocked the gap in our haggard . . .' She tilted her head this way and that, her ear searching and she seemed suddenly to get caught in a storm of words. She told of trespasses, small thefts, things said and seen and overheard from her hiding places. Brigid, interested in Ann rather than what she said, listened in silence. 'Peggy shut in our ducks with her own and she kept the two eggs.' 'No, Ann, no,' Brigid guffawed, startled into laughter. She lay back against the wall and laughed, and Ann watched her puzzled, frowning, her head moving in its restless way. Suddenly, she half rose, glanced quickly at the open door. Brigid, upset that Ann misunderstood her laughter, called her name, and followed her out. There was no sign of Ann. A heavy step touched the gravel by the gable and Peggy lurched round the corner; a frightened Peggy clutching a stick. 'Mother of God, this day, Brigid, my heart was on fire for you.' Brigid hurried to her and put an arm around her. 'Never mind am I ready to faint, it is you, are you all right, God in heaven, are you all right?' She allowed Brigid to help her in the door to a chair. 'Did the life leave you Brigid? Did Mary warn you about her? Did she try to harm you? Wait till I get my tongue at Nelly. I called to her, and I shouted at her to go to you, but she turned her back at me. I was crying for you Brigid, all the way across I was crying for you; and praying. Such a fright I got, but what was my fright to your fright?' She still held Brigid's hand. She saw the bowls, the two bowls by the creepies on the hearth, and she let her stick fall. 'Is this how it was, the two of you by the fire, while I, old fool that I am, drove my bones through a blaze of pain to get to you?' She made to rise but Brigid put her arms around her. 'You are very good, Aunt Peggy. I will never forget this day to you; never.' Peggy let herself be persuaded to sit. 'I cannot make head nor tail of you, Brigid, when a daft creature like that, that will not let the step of man nor woman in the glen come near her but she lets out a screech like a hare in a snare, comes in on the floor to you and sits in the corner and drinks tea.' And then Brigid told the story of the morning's happenings, and how she went on her knees to say her prayers, and how she raised her head at a shadow and cocked her ear at a rustle no louder than the fidget of a kitten playing with a wisp, and how fingers appeared, and a head, and a face and Peggy groaned and moaned, and wondered that Brigid's heart did not fail her. 'Tell me it, leave no word out,' and Brigid told how Ann sat and talked, and Peggy put in a word how the glen thought Ann lost all power of speech, and that all that was left in her

65

was a screech. Brigid resumed her story. Listening to Ann
was for all the world like a body overhearing the glen talking
to itself. Peggy edged her chair closer. 'If Ann has the talk,
Brigid, there is no telling what she has to say, one that hides
and jukes. Will you supple up your tongue and make Ann
of yourself for a minute and talk.' Brigid was not sure she
had her voice under control so she hesitated and Peggy
punched her on the ribs and scolded her. 'One thing Ann
said, that was strange to me, Peggy, was how a woman of
the glen shut in Ann's ducks with her own and kept the two
eggs.' She raised innocent eyes to Peggy, and Peggy gasped
and laid her hands together, and said she thought only God
and herself knew about that, and Brigid, no longer able to
hold back her laughter, laughed loudly, and, in the end,
Peggy laughed too. 'God O God, Brigid,' she enthused,
'this will be the best fun ever, you picking out of Ann
and you and me going over what she says; and not a word
to go beyond the two of us. When she knows about the
ducks she must have ears for the grass growing. This is how
it was. . . .'

Brigid walked with Peggy a bit of the way back and they
rested by a gap and Peggy gestured vaguely to the empty
casans. 'It will not do, Brigid. Mary will not wish you to
draw Ann out of her hiding places into the traffic of the glen.
Mark my words, when Mary hears this story she will forbid
you making a shelter of yourself for Ann to draw her abroad
again. Pity, Brigid: a great pity.'

Brigid told the story to Mary, from the first fidgety noise
and shadow and her glimpse of the faded head scarf down to
Peggy and the ducks, and Mary herself laughed then; not
indeed, she explained, that Peggy had any call to have that
in her conscience for Ann's ducks spent that day of all days in
Peggy's stooks, and Peggy was vexed and she let the ducks in
with her own to teach Ann a lesson. Brigid did not tell Mary
that Ann hid in the byre but she told Tom and they laughed
together.

And right enough Mary's mind worked out as Peggy foretold. She told Brigid it would be best that Ann should be left as she was, out of people's sight and little as could be in their minds. They were used to her now giving out an odd screech, and they had pity for her, but if she walked abroad again it might be another story. There was a time when the children used to hunt her, making it a game for themselves to search the whins and the sallies for her and chase her, and peg clods at her. An end was put to that. But if Ann showed herself again . . . She advised Brigid to put a hard face on herself whenever Ann came her way from this forward. It would be for Ann's own good, Brigid to make her keep back. And when Brigid spoke to Peggy, Peggy was on Mary's side.

Brigid noticed that Mary did not leave the matter to her but circled round her when she went to the well for water or when she drove cattle to pasture, and it annoyed her most that Mary let on not to notice herself acting in such a way, but always having some remark to make as if she was on some errand. One day Ann the Hill appeared to Brigid out of a cluster of broom bushes — appeared was the word for it. The bush shivered lightly and behold there she was, and then again she was not and the bushes were violently agitated. Brigid turned at the tinkle of the handle of an empty bucket and she was face to face with Mary and anger flashed in her. 'There is no need, Mary, no need at all to keep breathing in my ear. I said I would not draw Ann out of her shelter, and maybe get her hurt, but when she shows herself to me I will talk to her. You knew she was here.' Mary nodded. 'I can always tell when Ann is in the bushes or the whins you have to go by; I can tell by the birds, for they whirl and twitter like it was a weasel or a cat they had their eyes on.' They filled their buckets at the well and they walked together in silence. 'The peace is best, Brigid,' Mary said when they were inside.

'Peace is best, Mary, and there will be peace if Ann is let come and go to me, now and then, and nobody lets on she is there. How could any harm come of that?' Mary was silent. 'Look, Mary, every way I turn my mind I am beset. The dark mountains shut me in, the angry minds of the women shut me out, the dark of the kitchen bothers me, you are between me and this poor body, Ann.' Tom's step went by just then. He entered the byre. The two women glanced at each other uneasily. Tom might very well have heard them. At least he likely heard Brigid's voice raised in sharpness. 'I told him he had best look at the black cow's stake,' Mary said, and without any show of concern she crossed the street. Brigid stood in the shadow inside the door. She heard the murmur of voices. 'What she needs is more light in the kitchen. I'm going to put in big windows.' Brigid took shelter in the alcove by the dresser. This was important. She must hear this. She could see Mary's face now. It seemed to her she could see the skin tighten in it, the way it tensed itself on its frame of bones. Mary was silent for a moment. One arm crept up to crook itself across her breast. She did not raise her voice when she spoke, but Brigid heard every word. 'Well, indeed you will not, Tom, and it is for her sake you will not do such a thing. She has a right to her peace in this glen, and she will never be happy in it unless she suits herself to it, and does not think to make it suit itself to her. I warned you already she must not be let make stranger of herself, for ever, in the glen. She has to believe as the glen believes and do like the glen does. She is a fine woman — no finer — and you will have to help her if you want her to make a good wife.' Brigid did not catch Tom's reply. 'If you break out these windows for her you will make an oddity of her, and a laugh and mockery of yourself; like you put her into a hat. What will they think when the story reaches Boston? The graip rasped as he forked dung out the groop-hole. Brigid fled to the bedroom, at a glimpse of Mary leaving the byre and she let on to be busy there, and she even sang a little. She said a prayer on her knees before she ventured back to the kitchen. Mary was on her creepy but she did not look up, and Brigid, at a loss in face of this fierce quiet, thought to say something about a task they had set themselves for that day, but Mary raised a hand, her rosary

68

beads in it, to ward off conversation. Brigid went to the byre but Tom was gone and when she got back Mary was in bed, her face to the wall, her outer skirt turned up over her head. Later, when Brigid made tea and went to her with a bowl, Mary raised her hand again and showed her rosary beads. A man's step touched the street and Brigid, embarrassed, hurried to serve his errand without giving him time to enter. It was Dan Rua, and he greeted her lightly and she could only step aside and let him enter, and when she sought for words to say Mary was not herself, a glance showed her Mary in her corner at her ease, and she greeted Dan Rua with talk as light as his own, and she gave him her pipe to fill, and Brigid stood at the door and bantered with him when he left. When she turned to the fire Mary was back in bed. She did not stir as Tom came in, and he said nothing of what passed between himself and her.

Brigid asked Mary about the churnings which were due that day and Mary advised her to leave it over till the next morning. There was no anger in her voice. Brigid spoke of other tasks and Mary added her word in the same friendly way, but she initiated no talk between them. She drew her neck shawl out over her head and she sat in the corner and she held her beads in her fingers, and it seemed to Brigid that the gloom deepened in the kitchen; and deepened and deepened until it bellowed out to meet the frown of the mountains, and the two glooms buffeted her. But gloom, and beads, and shawls and all, it was Mary heard the lap of the cat at the cream in the spare room. It was Mary caught the soft pad of a dog going by the door, and she raised her head to warn Brigid of Briany's dog, on the sniff for an egg in the byre. A hen cackled. 'That's a new hen, Brigid. That's a hen I did not hear, so far, this year.' And she went outside and Brigid watched her hurry to the hen-house, and she was between laughter and tears.

And day after day it was like that, gloom and silences by the fireside. Tom went his way without change of gait or word. Mary often followed him out. Brigid was unhappy that there should be conflict between Tom and his mother. She could not bring herself to tell him she knew there was a battle in progress between them, although she caught gusts of Mary's angry talk. Once going by the groop-hole when Tom was cleaning down under the cows she got its full blast. 'Then is it such a wonder a woman to marry you that you must tear down your house to please her? Is it airs you are giving yourself, like the Yankee in Carrick . . . ? I warn you, Tom.' Brigid hurried on her way and she hoped Tom would say something to her, but he did not and that was a thing that frightened her, and it was an ease to her that she could speak to Briany. It was wrong that Tom should have to carry this burden of his mother's anger, and it was a terrible way he did it, without a cross word to Mary or the need of a soft one from his wife. If he would only talk to her. Once when a neighbour went out and Mary withdrew back into her gloom Brigid turned on her. 'Maybe you think the glen does not notice that you are at Tom over something. Let me tell you, the glen is not blind, and one of these days the laugh will go up.' Mary was taken aback. 'It is the last thing I would wish, the glen to get its ear to what is going on in this house, and it is my one prayer that Tom will come to his senses before he throws his name for good sense to the winds. In this matter he should have sense for the two of you.'

Briany came to Brigid with a story. There was talk in the glen. People did not know what was afoot but their eyes were more and more on Tom and Brigid and Mary. They saw Mary making errands for herself, that made no sense to their eyes, across to Tom when he was at work at a fence or in a field, and they read more sharpness into her heels than would be in them if she was not at him about something. His advice to Brigid was speak to Peggy. But Brigid did not go to Peggy for Peggy swept down on herself and Mary. Brigid saw her come over the green, and she warned Mary that Peggy was angry over something, and Mary pushed back her head shawl from over her face and took up her knitting. 'Whatever errand Peggy is on, she is letting the world see its nature, there is such anger in her step,' Brigid announced. Peggy marched in and shut the door behind her. 'Not indeed that I need bother to shut the door,' she barked, 'for the whole glen, it seems, knows there is some trouble in this house.' She got a chair for herself and sat erect on it. 'All that I have to say is this: if I go out that door without hearing from one or other of you what is the trouble among you all, then I'll never darken this door again, as long as I draw breath.' She folded her arms. 'Well, Mary. Well, Brigid,' she challenged.

'It is Mary's story, Peggy. Let Mary tell it.' Mary told it. She told how Brigid said to Tom she would not be happy in the house unless he broke out the wall and put in big windows, and how Tom gave in to her that he would put in big windows. She told her tale and waited. 'God O God,' Peggy breathed. 'God O God, is there that man's equal in the whole world, for what man but himself would have so much sense of a woman's ways that he would do such a thing? You must be a great joy to one another, you and Tom, Brigid. You must so.' She found her snuff box. 'This glen will make a laugh of it, a man to be said by a woman in such a way that he tears down his house.' She turned to Mary. 'So that is your bother, that the glen will scorn Tom. Little you know, for once, what the talk is. The word that is out through the glen beats that. Nelly said it to Susan, and Susan gave it to Kitty, and Kitty gave it to the world, and it is this: That there is more of a pimple on Brigid than is decent considering how short a time it is since herself and Tom got married.' Mary jerked erect in her corner. 'That's the story that is out through the glen and it is your heels it runs on; you racing around after Tom everywhere he goes with a rap of anger in your heels. What they are saying now is that you are at Tom to put her away.' She took a long pinch, her eyes on Brigid. 'God O God, so all you do is laugh.' She brushed her apron. 'That is my mind too, to laugh. We will let them talk. I'll go back now, and I'll put such venom into every step they will be in the door after me to see what word they can draw from me.' Brigid helped her to her feet. 'I said it, and I say it, Brigid, it is the mercy of God it is not into me you came, for I wouldn't thole you as Mary tholes you. The glen would not have to have its hand behind its ear to catch words between you and me, that I will swear.' She paused in the doorway. 'And another thing, it is a great wonder to me, and if anything could shake my faith in him this would, that Colmcille gave no hint that the like of you was to come.' She gestured Brigid to remain indoors. She rid her throat aggressively as she tramped across the gravel to the gap. Brigid and Mary faced each other on the hearth. 'I will bring the priest in on them, Brigid . . .' But Brigid's laughter interrupted her. 'You will do no such thing. God O God, when I think of Peggy ready to go out to do battle with them for me, not caring what the truth was, so long as she knew what the truth was . . .' She dabbed her eyes quickly. 'You will not go next or near the priest, Mary Manus. Leave the glen to Peggy. Let Peggy have her fun.'

And then, one morning coming in quietly with a basket of clothes from the bleach field in her arms, Brigid found Mary asleep by the fire. She laid her burden on the chair noise-lessly. A live coal smouldered on the hearth and its smoke came out through the kitchen. Brigid kicked off her boots, so there would be no trip, and she went on one knee to brush the coal back with her hand lest the tinkle of the tongs might waken Mary. She slept with her head rested against the side of the bed, her rosary entwined on her fingers, and there were beads of tears on her cheeks. This was a new Mary, not bossy, nor stubborn, nor angry, but hurt, and Brigid was defenceless before her. Mary opened her eyes and Brigid was embarrassed, too. 'I fell asleep,' Mary said shyly. 'They say that is a sure sign that the world is nearly through with you, when you nod every time you sit down.' Brigid re-mained on her knees. 'You fell asleep, Mary, because you are not sleeping at night; I hear you. It is too bad that you have to cry yourself to sleep like a child, and if the big windows do this to you then I will do without them. I will do without them should I smother.' She rose wearily. 'And let you go now and tell Tom, and let us have the last of this so there may be peace. Go now let you.' Mary rose slowly. She drew the door shut after her. Brigid slumped on her creepy and wept.

Tom pushed the door open. He stood inside the door and she rose to face him. 'I said it, Tom, and it will have to be so. It would not be right for me.' He came up the floor with long strides and he seemed taller than ever at that moment and there was a hardness in him. 'But I told her she was not to bring his matter up between the two of you.' 'And she did not, Tom. It was that I came in, and she was asleep, and her head was resting against the bed and I knelt down to brush back a coal and I saw her tears.' 'But, Brigid, if we let her get between us and the big windows we will be a pair of children to her for ever, and we will never get past her. I cannot let you stop me now.' 'Oh Tom,' she murmured. 'Tom.' Her body trembled. She took his hand and she led him into the bedroom. 'I'll be terribly good to her, Tom. From now on I'll be terribly good to her.' She remained behind in the bedroom when he left and she dozed.

Mary started up, as Brigid crept softly back to the kitchen, and she wet tea. 'I waited for you, Brigid. I made up my mind not to waken you. Like myself you were not sleeping either.' Brigid was puzzled. 'He was angry with you, Brigid?' Brigid nodded. 'This is how it was. He was kneeling on a bag in the mouth of the pit — that is one thing about Tom, he always takes care of his clothes — and he looked up, and he saw I was glad over something. "Brigid said to tell you she no longer has any wish for the big windows." He made that cutting move with his hand that was a habit of his father's. "She has no longer any wish for the big windows, I said, and told me tell you let there be no more talk about them." He keeled over and sat on the bag and he put his fist out. "You and Brigid can take turns now, nipping and nebbing, and muttering, but I have the big windows in mind, and not you, nor Brigid will get between me and them;

things as plentiful outside this glen as daisies." He got up and he shot past me and stormed over the fields and I was sorry for you.' She sipped her tea thoughtfully.

'And yourself, Mary, you have no mind to go against Tom?' Mary shook her head slowly. 'The way it is now, Brigid, it is his own doing and if there is noise it is over something of his own making.' Brigid stretched out her legs and rested her bowl in her lap. 'So, if it is Tom's own doing, Mary, it is all right, but if it was my doing you would get between me and the windows.'

'I would not like you to make Tom stand up to be a cock-shot for their talk, for Tom would have no backing in himself for what he was doing and he might get angry. He will not get angry now, he will only laugh at them.' Brigid put her bowl away. She sighed as she got to her feet. 'If life was like this on the island, Mary, I grew up blind to it.' 'People get angry everywhere when they are at odds with themselves, Brigid; like Tom would get angry if the windows were not his own doing, and he would not know why he got angry, and now he will laugh.' She poked back a strand of hair. 'I was thinking to myself, Brigid, sitting there waiting for you to show yourself, that it would be a nice thing for you to go back to your people, for a day or two, and tell them you are happy with us. They would like to hear that.' They were both on their feet. Brigid had a besom in her hand and she laid it aside. Mary was fingering Tom's socks on the line over the fire. 'If you went by the mail car to Carrick you could light a fire, like I heard you say.' 'I could light a fire, Mary, or I could borrow a boat.' She laughed. 'I tell you, Mary, I can go back to the island with a light heart, and I can leave it again dancing.' And then, for the first time they embraced.

And so a morning came when Brigid left the glen for her first visit back to the island. The bustle of spring was in the morning. There was traffic of horses under creels loading out manure, and men's voices were loud among the fields. Dan Rua called out to Brigid on her way across to join Tom in the cart. 'We will examine you when you come back, so we will, and if Tom will not give in to rear it for you I will.' He roared his lusty talk. Women peeped out of doorways. 'I cheated you out of a wedding,' Tom gave back, 'and however I come by it, I will not do you out of a christening.' Brigid beat at him and he waved his whip and gave back shout for shout to Dan Rua.

Nelly was the first woman to walk out into the open and raise her voice. She scrambled up the humped flag at the gable as soon as the cart started off on its noisy way over the boreen. She wore a bag apron and it was short for her, so that it was out-thrust from the great mound of her belly. She rid her throat noisily, and Wee Conail glancing back, delayed on his step and rid his throat as if to call out to her, but he changed his mind and went on his way. Nelly trumpeted again, and Susan Dan went up on a mound and faced her, and Kitty showed herself. 'Hoi, Susan.' Nelly called so loudly it was clear she was calling the world at large to listen. She called again and Susan raised her hand. 'Is this the last of her, is the glen rid of her for good?' One of Peggy's roosters clapped his wings and crowed; she kept two and one or other was for ever showing off. 'Shut up, rooster,' Peggy ordered and her voice was like the Angelus Bell, 'shut up, rooster, don't you know it is only hens crow in the daytime.' Nelly swung round to accept the challenge, and she staggered. Peggy paced up and down her street, arrogant as any cock. Nelly turned again to signal her audience and she named Susan and she named Kitty and Sorcha, and she was about to speak a message when Dan Rua's donkey brayed; donkeys often bray when any commotion starts up near them. Wee Conail's donkey joined in, and another, and another, in the way of donkeys, and Nelly could not orate against them, and twice when she thought she had a space she got caught in a new bray, and when the silence did come Peggy got in ahead of her. 'Did anybody ever hear the donkeys of this glen in such a heat? Hoi, Susan,' Peggy's voice was sharp and urgent, 'do you hear me, Susan, run to your cow. Your cow is at the pit.' Susan let on not to hear, for Nelly had her hand raised and Susan wanted to stand with Nelly, but Peggy would not be gainsaid, and she thundered her warning that Susan's cow was in danger, and Dan Rua raised his head and he whistled, and Susan had no choice but to do as Peggy bade her, and she called her dog, and because she was angry, she called him loudly, and the dog came with a great rush and Briany's dog came, and they frightened the cow, and they put her in danger for she had a potato in her mouth. Dan Rua left his work and his whistles and curses paralysed the dogs, and the cow lumbered to a halt, and she stood with her head drawn in and she frothed at the mouth, and a shout went up that Dan Rua's cow was choking, and everybody within sight and sound gave heed. Susan beat her hands together and wept in fear and guilt, and her children were scared too, and they wept. The cow stumbled to her knees. She coughed and the potato shot out, and before anybody could stir, she went nosing her way back to it. Dan Rua whipped off his belt and beat at her, and he turned, with the belt still in his hand, and his children fled and he shouted out angrily that the women of this glen were running so much to talk they had no time for their business. He strode back to his work, and the gathering of neighbours fell away. Nelly, who stayed back on her flag, offered herself as a rallying point, and Susan waited, too, and Kitty stood with her and they wore check aprons of the same pattern. A few women of houses further down, on their way to the commotion, turned to Nelly and she came down from her mound to meet them, and Susan and Kitty closed in too. 'You did a wrong thing, Nelly, to raise your voice this morning when Peggy was abroad, and it plain to the world she was waiting for you,' Kitty grumbled. 'It was Peggy sent this woman out of the glen. Peggy wants Tom's wife out of the way so that she may outface us all, with the men listening. Peggy wants noise.' 'You did a wrong thing, Nelly.' 'Let me tell you I will outface Peggy,' Nelly boasted, 'and I will double outface her, and why would not I?' 'And I will outface Peggy,' Susan proclaimed, 'and a good right I have, this day putting Dan Rua in a rage; of set purpose she did that. . . .'

'There has to be some end to this business Susan, and you Nelly, let you see to it that there is some end to this business.' It was Sorcha spoke. She was a young woman, tall as Susan and as fair. 'The rest of us withheld ourselves because of the two of you, but we are not blind, and we see now it is not she who is afraid of you, for it is you keep out of her way. She has the casans and she goes her way with her head high, and it is you take to the open fields and keep your heads stooped. So there has to be some end to it. We listened to you, and we are still of your mind that it was a pity she ever came in among us, and that she is a danger to us and that she will likely do her best to bring in other girls of the island, but she is here and she is Tom Manus's wife and there has to be some end to it.'

'And I know the end would be to it if we were the women we should be,' Bella stormed. She was a tall woman, worn, bare-armed, with a streeling skirt, and a cut-down Paisley shawl for a neck shawl. 'My sister is married at the other end of the parish and last spring when hay was scarce men from afar came with carts and no money was too high for them, and people could see there was going to be a scarcity, and the men grumbled. But the women, they rose out and they turned on the strange carts with stones. I am sick to death of her; living under the same roof with Sean Mor, like I am. I have her name for my breakfast, and it is the last thing I hear at night time, until I could brain Sean Mor, and kick my own backside for marrying his son.'

Nelly brushed Bella aside. She faced Sorcha. 'It was from your side of the glen the word first came that she made a convenience of Tom Manus when it suited her,' Nelly charged; 'that was your shot at her.' Sorcha got to her feet. 'We said what we heard, and we were said by you in what we did. She is here against all our wishes. There has to be an end to this business. She has Mary for her, and she has Peggy for her.' 'And she has Ann the Hill for her,' Susan stormed. 'Don't forget that, she has Ann the Hill roused out. And Ann the Hill is not only walking the casans. Ann the Hill is talking. A nice thing if she is going to make herself a shelter for Ann the Hill; and I don't believe Mary is for her.' 'There has to be some end to it,' Sorcha sulked, turning away.

Mary was on the street when Wee Conail's mother, Eilis, came round the corner, a frail old body in a white bonnet, leaning on a stick. Mary went to her quickly and murmured her welcome, and she helped her in the door and drew a chair up to the fire for her, and seated herself in her corner. 'I do not wonder at you, Mary, to make me a stranger.' The old voice had a faint quiver. She leaned on her stick. 'I wanted to come to see you, Mary, every day I wanted to come to see you, but Nelly forbade me. Now she sent me to see what I could pick out of you. Are you in any trouble, Mary? You need not be afraid to say it to me, Mary, because Nelly will not hear it from me.' 'I am in no trouble, Eilis, and if I was in trouble I would say it to you, and I would know you would be sorry for me. No, Eilis, I am in no trouble. I think I am going to have a good life with her.' 'God owes you that, Mary. You made a great fight, Mary.' 'We all made a great fight, Eilis. I wish you had more happiness yourself.' 'Ah, what about me, Mary. It is no matter about me. It is Wee Conail. God help him, the hardest working man in this glen and a thrifty man. You know that, Mary. But Nelly has no softness in her, Mary.'

'You have to be patient with Nelly when it is near her time, Eilis. You did the right thing not to upset her when she forbade you this house, an upset now might do her harm. You know yourself Nelly's mother had the same strange nature.' 'And her grandmother, Mary. I never wanted her, Mary. I blamed Wee Conail for marrying her. Wee Conail tholes too much.' She edged her chair nearer. 'In the morning Wee Conail sits down to dry bread, but Nelly has her egg. And maybe, she has another egg in the evening, but Wee Conail gets no egg, and you know, Mary that is not how

I reared Wee Conail. And then, Mary, his socks. Only that I darn his socks and keep buttons on his clothes he would be worse off than the tramp that goes the roads.' Her hand shook on her stick. 'You are sure you are in no trouble, Mary. It is good you to be in no trouble. Wee Conail is my trouble. You know yourself, Mary, a man needs eggs.' Mary nodded. Eilis would not delay. 'Nelly said to me to go over to you, and that if you would not open out your mind to me, I was not to sit with you. I am not going to make up a story for her, Mary, so I will be on my way. There is a lot of noise, Mary.' 'Foolish noise, Eilis. There is no more sense to it than the barking of a dog at night at the sound of a neighbour's step. You just tell Nelly that I said I thank God for the woman Tom got.' And Eilis said she would say just that, and she chuckled and said Nelly would not believe her, for that Nelly and Susan and the others had a tune of their own, and they would not be put off it. 'We looked after our men, Mary, while we had them, and if there was an egg going it was not we ate it; only maybe we let on we had our egg too.' Mary saw her half the way home. When she got back Dan Rua's mother was in the kitchen waiting on her.

'I suppose, Nappy, Susan sent you over,' Mary greeted. 'I had it in my own mind to come, Mary. I had so. As soon as I heard you were in trouble I wanted to come. You were happy, Mary, when you had the house to yourself; like I was happy. I hear there is trouble between the two of you, Mary.' 'No, then, Nappy, thank God there is no trouble between us.' 'I said that to Susan. I said you would not give in about any trouble. It will come to it, Mary, that you will not be able to keep it to yourself. You made this a good warm house, Mary, like I made mine, now I have to sit in the corner and watch it being squandered.' 'You are not fair to Susan, Nappy, I always said you were not fair to Susan.' 'Then listen to me, Mary, and see am I fair to Susan. Do you know how long a seven-stone sack of flour lasts Susan? I could give you ten guesses and you would not guess it. Do you know how far she makes a full half stone of sugar go? And as for

tea, it is tea, tea, tea night, noon, and mōrning, tea and sugar.
But can I get my one ounce of tobacco out of her? I cannot.
And Dan Rua, the big soft lump — he takes after his father —
he sees what is going on, and he will not raise his voice to
her. Tell me, Mary, what is the trouble between you? Now,
mind you I said to Susan, I said, catch Mary letting Tom
marry this woman, only she knew all about her. The thing
is, Mary, let it be one trouble or another trouble, you will
have trouble. She will get between you and your cows, and
your hens, and the tea canister, and the flour bag, and what
you gathered she will scatter. If I had it all to do over again,
Susan the lassie, would not pull the house out of my hands
as she did. I blame Dan Rua. He sees the waste and the
robbery but he will not forbid it. He has no cutting in him;
soft, soft like his father. I am not to sit, Mary. I am not to
wait for tea. Susan is waiting for me. Eilis was in with you.
You likely told Eilis what the trouble was. Oh, God help
you, Mary, and everyone like you in the world. It will be
with Tom like it is with Dan Rua, when I raise my voice,
instead of biding within, and laying down the law to make
her look after his house instead of scattering it, it is what he
puts on his cap and goes out. Keep a firm hand on her from
the start, Mary, that is where I made my mistake. God help
you in the trouble you are in.'

Black Donal came round at dusk to leave in turf and do
any other jobs Mary might set before him. He stayed on
after lamplight and Peggy joined him, and Mary told how
Eilis came to see her, and Nappy next. Briany came in and
let on he was on his way to mid-glen, but Peggy made him
sit for she had a question to ask. She wanted to know from
Briany whether he saw sense in Tom's talk of big windows,
and Briany said he saw sense in it, and he thought the windows would be no sooner in one house than everybody would
find they had big windows in their minds. And Peggy cried
out at that. 'Wee Conail has this woman sized up, Briany.
Wee Conail says, if this glen begins giving itself airs it will
not carry half the people. Wee Conail is a man with great

sense.' 'I have my eye on Wee Conail too,' Mary agreed, 'and I think it would be a good thing if other men had more of Wee Conail in them. Wee Conail is making himself a new field. All the time Wee Conail works and works and watches the half-pence. I know myself Wee Conail will be one man that will not like the new windows; I would be sorry Tom to shoot past Wee Conail.' 'There is one thing I know,' Peggy threatened, 'whoever makes noise against the new windows will draw me on them.' She offered a round of her snuff box. 'This glen has a lot on its stomach and that is one thing I see. It always does this glen good to work itself into a noise. It will maybe get help from me. . . .'

7

As soon as Tom crossed the shoulder of the brae his dog barked and people raised their heads and they saw the stranger on the cart with him. Susan hailed Nelly, keeping her voice down so as not to rouse Peggy. 'I said when he did not get home last night, take care but some of her people would be back with him.' Kitty trotted up. Whoever was in the cart, he must be a stranger for no man of the glen was abroad to ride back with Tom; could it be the tailor, for she had word the tailor was coming to lower glen but this man had too much bulk to be the tailor? Peggy called her dog noisily, as if serving notice that she had her eye on things. Nelly ordered out a flight of children to surround the cart and bring back word if they could pick up a word who this man was. If Tom was drunk, it could be that it was only a tramp. The cart halted and the stranger stood up on it, and climbed out over the wheel and they knew now, this long-legged, round-shouldered man, the carpenter. Ho, ho, the carpenter in the horrors with drink likely, on the hunt for a wife like always when in drink. Tom must be at peace with himself, when he could set out to make fun like this. It was the first time ever, for all their tales of him, that the carpenter headed for the glen. Who could it be within the glen, that the carpenter had in mind? One shouted to the other now. Dan Rua ordered Susan indoor proclaiming aloud that he heard the carpenter himself threatening to come after her, one fair day. Tom himself must be well on in drink when he let the carpenter climb into his cart at all. This would be fun. It was a good time for fun, idle days, and the hour itself an idle hour. But suddenly it was clear to them all that the carpenter was sober, for he set out over the casan with the air of a man in full control of himself. So now what — what use could Tom have for a carpenter; not a cart body noryet a wheel barrow. A cradle? Ho, ho, a cradle. They were in clusters now. Some of the children raced back. They had a look into the cart. There were windows in it, big windows. They all stood and watched, and they saw Tom hand down the windows to the Carpenter. He laid them on the grass. Dan Rua slipped the bit out of the horse's mouth, and let him go, and he waited for Black Donal to come up to him and they crossed the green together, and Wee Conail joined them and they walked in silence. Wee Conail stooped and set the windows up on end. 'This looks like a bad business, Tom; a terrible cost this and for why, Tom Manus? Is this her doing?' 'It is not then, Wee Conail.' Wee Conail turned to face Mary. 'It is not at all her doing.' Wee Conail turned again to Tom. He wanted to understand this thing. A thing Tom Manus did, must have some sense in it. Tom put a match to his pipe. 'It is not her doing, Wee Conail, in one way and in another way it is. You would have to see the island with the sea back of it like the reflector of a lamp, to see into this. They have windows like this in the houses. I noticed the brightness myself. I know she missed it.' Wee Conail rubbed his chin. 'The thing about this, Tom, is one starts it but who ends it? This glen cannot stand such things.' He waved aside the pipe Tom offered him. 'I am burned smoking,' he explained turning away.

'I have something ready for you before you begin work,' Mary said. 'Come in and have a sup with them,' she invited Black Donal, and Dan Rua, but they thanked her and they went back to their work. The carpenter and Tom followed Mary indoor. There was a thing Mary wanted Tom to bear in mind, the nail below the lamp. His father always hung the looking-glass on that nail when he went to shave. It was in deep, and she could not pull it out. She would like it kept and put back again; there would be a blessing in it. In a way many a laugh she got from that nail. Manus was the easiest going man in the world, children could tumble the house around him and he took no heed, but once he took the razor in his hand to shave you could not sneeze in any part of the house but he let a growl out of him. She would be lonely now without that nail. Tom promised to take care of it when he knocked the wall, and to put it back. Mary got to her feet. She would as soon not be in the house when they began on the wall. Somehow she would not like to see the wall giving way under blows. . . .

The neighbours saw her go over the path to Peggy, and Nelly took a meaning out of that. Mary was not for this thing, and it was a poor how-do-you-do, Tom to push past his mother at the bidding of this harum-scarum from the island. They should tell Mary not to give way. It was her right above all to tell Mary not to give way, for the man who built that house was her great grandfather as well as Tom's. So she ran up on the hillock and hailed Mary and told her to stand her ground, and at that Bella hurried to Sorcha and urged her to come with her to Nelly, until they would nag and provoke Nelly into an uproar, and Bella shouted to Susan, and Susan came and Kitty and others and they clustered around Nelly, elbowing and winking, inciting her into a frenzy so that she hopped up and down stiff-legged and screeched above the chorus of their mutterings. They were taken aback when Mary came quickly around the side of the turf stack, and spoke sharply to Nelly and ordered her to bethink herself of her condition and to quieten herself; and, when Nelly paid no heed, they were scandalized and enraged that Mary should walk up to her and slap her sharply in the face. It was even stranger to them that Nelly should crumble in front of Mary, and they found themselves without speech when Mary faced them and told them they ought to think shame of themselves, and they knowing Nelly's nature. And then Mary took out her knitting and she sauntered away and she left silence behind her; except Nelly whimpering like a child. Mary went out of sight again behind the turf stack and they saw Peggy drawing on them, with an angry stride, and they were willing to face Peggy, but she seated herself at a distance and called Susan and said she wanted to have a word with Susan and Susan gave back that she wanted no word with Peggy. 'I wish I could leave it like that, Susan.' There was no anger in her now; that was strange. 'I wish it could be like you say, but this has to be, Susan.' She raised her head and called Dan Rua. 'Stop it, I say,' Susan stormed. 'Stop it, I tell you.' But Peggy called Dan Rua a second time, and he handed the reins to his child and he headed towards her. Susan hurried forward too. 'Listen to me, Peggy,' she pleaded, 'say what you like to me and I will listen to you, only leave Dan Rua alone.' Peggy took out her snuff box and she looked beyond Susan to other women, moving closer. 'Is there no cutting in you? Did I not tell you I want this word with Susan and Dan Rua?' They withdrew grudgingly. 'It was a shame for you, Susan, for all of you, not to try to quieten Nelly. Last time she was this way she took a down on Wee Conail, and the second time before that she almost brained Eilis.' 'We know about Nelly, it is not about Nelly you want to talk. I am warning you, Peggy . . .' but Susan kept her voice low, for Dan Rua was at hand now. Peggy held out her snuff box to him and he poked out a pinch. Susan waved the snuff box aside. 'You have something to say to me, Peggy,' he said quietly, a shade sternly, and Peggy, sighing deeply, nodded. 'It is not my way, Dan Rua, to choose my words so what I have to say let me say it in my own way.' 'Come on home, Dan Rua,' Susan moaned. He did not as much as turn his head to her. 'Tell me, Dan Rua, you mind the day long ago there was the fight between your father and Black Donal?' 'I mind that day.' 'It must be nearly your longest memory, Dan Rua.' He nodded. 'It was a fight beyond reason. It never left my two eyes nor will it ever.' 'What under God is all this about?' Susan moaned, 'let us go home, Dan Rua. Leave Dan Rua be, Peggy.' But Peggy did not seem to hear her, nor Dan Rua. 'And I suppose the story you heard, Dan Rua, was that they set on one another over their dogs.' 'On account of their dogs,' he agreed. Peggy shook her head. 'That was the story the world got; that the two dogs made at one another's throats and that the men came running, and that one said the other did an unfairness to his dog and that the other made a liar of him, and that then they set on one another.' Dan Rua was puzzled. 'Well, let me tell you the truth, Dan Rua. Hear it you, Susan. It was not the dogs put the match to their anger.' Susan was crying quietly, whimpering at Dan Rua to come home. Peggy took notice of her now. 'It is not without good cause Susan, that you are scared.' Dan Rua's eyes did not leave Peggy's face. She found a seat for herself on a boulder. He went on his hunkers before her. 'I never knew, Dan Rua, if the men themselves thought it was because of the dogs they broke out in such madness and I will never know, for I will never ask the one of them that is with us still, Black Donal, to tell me. Your mother knows like I know that if our men's fight was of the dogs' making the dog-fight was of our making.' Dan Rua went down on one knee for better balance. 'All that spring your mother and I would not break breath with one another. Let the why of that rest. We thought to keep how it was between us to ourselves. We could have sworn only God and ourselves knew of the anger that was between us, but we were wrong. The dogs knew. So one day we passed one another, one going to the well and the other coming back from it, and we rid our throats at one another and the dogs flew at one another, as no two dogs ever. Then the men came. Maybe, for all our cuteness, the men knew.' She bowed her head and was silent and when she spoke again her voice was harsh and dry and strong. 'Maybe I was the one to blame, maybe your mother had her good share of the blame, maybe the world was to blame; two women and the world hard on us. Anyway that is how it came about, Dan Rua, all because of your mother and me not speaking.' She loosened the shawl around her neck. 'Now it is your woman, Dan Rua, and Tom's woman that will not break breath, so one day it may be the dogs or it may be a clod flung at a hen or a duck, but of one thing you may be sure, it will be something, and you and Tom Manus will raise your fists to one another. It will be a great fight, Dan Rua, and whoever sees it will talk of it for ever. But it would not be right that Tom's woman should be here to see it, for she has not hand, act, nor part in this business.' She looked from him to Susan and back. 'Maybe you know, Dan Rua, that Susan had most to do with what took place the night Tom's woman came into this glen. Maybe Tom Manus knows. I never said it to him, and Mary never said it to him, and the thing that is stranger than that, Brigid never said that anything happened but she knows too it was mostly Susan's doing. There it is for you, Dan Rua, Brigid and Susan like they are, and you touchy and Tom touchy, and a great gift for anger in both of you. So, if it has to be, let it be now while she is out of the glen, and if the glen has a heart at all in it, it will hide the story of the fight between you and Tom from her for ever, for, like I said, she is innocent of it.' She struggled to rise and he helped her. 'That now is what I had to say, Dan Rua, and God bless you, and God bless Tom and I would wish it was any two in the world but the two of you.' She did not glance back. Susan made for home, half running. The glen watched her race over the fields. They saw Dan Rua stand like a man in a daze, and then turn and look after Susan, start across the fields with long, strong strides, and go inside and shut the door behind him, and it was a great wonder to them, and they ran out from their doorways, calling to one another and there was no laughter in any of them. They kept their eye on that shut door, and nobody dared to send children to listen. And then the door opened and Dan Rua stepped forth, his pipe was in his mouth, and in the calm they could see the puffs of smoke rising; it was as if he was cheering. He picked up a shovel and sauntered over to Tom Manus, and he took the hammer from Tom's hand and he struck blows that were heard half the length of the glen, helping Tom put in the big windows.

8

WHO knows how a townland at odds with itself, over some sudden departure from pattern, strives to find its way back to peace; if a townland cannot have peace it cannot survive. It whispers to itself, recounts its experiences, measures itself against this new reality and thus promotes its own growth, disowns, discards, accepts, while all the time it is uneasy and easily roused to noise. It was a little thing that a man should go out of view to find himself a wife and they could easily have accommodated her within their pattern. It was a widening of the world but it was not altogether new. The thing was, the glen had not made itself ready. Nobody pictured them arriving in the dark. Nobody foresaw that Susan would go back in on herself, and somehow rouse in the glen its old, old dislike for strangers. Thinking back on it all next day, they could laugh: So Susan had it in for Tom Manus all the time, for not turning her way when she let him know she was looking round for him when Dan Rua began shaping up to her. Ho, ho, all these years all this grudge. If people kept at her she would give them a vision of herself they could all laugh at. Will you ever forget what she said? Keep at her; egging her and shouting with her . . . And then there was this talk that Tom Manus was only a convenience for Brigid, or else that she made a trap of herself. Serve him right; not that they could greatly excite themselves over this rumour. They were too near relatives to life to make any story over the like, now that a marriage had taken place, unless they chose to make noise of set purpose. There were moods and anger but mostly it was horseplay, but one thing above all they could not make a stranger of this woman for ever. Every spree had to have an end, and Dan Rua hammering the wall alongside Tom Manus was a signal that this one was over.

Briany, sitting by himself smoking, watching and listening, laughed and put his pipe away. Mary, driving a donkey out on to the rough communal pasture, looked towards him and halted and turned his way. She reached him her snuff. 'Susan made a wasp's nest of herself and the others were afraid to go by her. Susan has to make a change in herself, Briany.' He nodded. 'Tell me, Mary, did you ever know man or woman of this glen to go to another in cold blood and say "I was wrong, forgive me"? Can Susan put out a hand to Brigid now and say "you are welcome"? Can Brigid put out a hand to Susan and say, "let us be neighbours"?' They both sniffed their pinch. 'I was thinking back, Mary. Dan Rua's father was five years without darkening my father's door, or my father his and it was not until the gauger all but caught my father, and Dan Rua's father put the keg on his back and ran with it, that they got drunk together and became friends. Something has to happen; a thing like that, a cow in a bog, a death, God save us, some excuse so that people can find themselves together without one having to say to the other, "I am here" or "you are here", "I did wrong", or "you did wrong".' Mary nodded. 'My own mind is at the same kind of work,' she confided.

'The glen knows there has to be a change, Mary. I get news from Kitty.' Mary smiled. 'Sorcha blames Susan for it all. Sorcha threatens Susan that she, for one, will not withhold herself, when Brigid comes back. Listen to them now.' He picked up his creel and strode off to the turf stack to fill it. Mary made an excuse that she must see how it was with her two cows over by the Loch. She did not look back when a group of women, with Sorcha at their head, moved forward from Nelly's door to bandy talk with the carpenter. How was it, Sorcha taunted, that at no time no matter how drunk he was, did he come roaring into the glen? They had a woman for him. They would put her on a rope and stake her out till he got time to raise an eye to her. The carpenter made no attempt to hold his own against them, so Dan Rua entered into a bawdy tussle with them all. They came closer. They caught Dan Rua in among them, bustled him on over to his own house, and somehow, with all the roaring and the jostling the glen so wrought on him, he cried out in anger against all that went on round him. 'Choking to you,' he roared, 'choking to you. What hell odds what happens the carpenter. It is myself I have in mind. I want to drink, and drink. What this glen needs is a celebration, a wedding, a wake, a christening.' 'Ho, ho, a christening,' the women chanted. If that would do, that was one thing they could let him have. Was not Nelly due? 'Nelly,' he scoffed, 'is it hungry Wee Conail to stand the glen a christening? Now if it was myself and Susan — what delayed you, Susan.' They shouted at him, and Susan taunted him, too. It was God's own pity this rumour about Brigid had not more truth to it, for Tom Manus would have the heart for a christening. Why did they let Tom's woman out of the glen. What hell got into you all to make idiots of yourselves over her? Tom Manus and his woman. God's truth, Tom to give a christening; Tom and his woman. Why not give them the first child ready? Why not Tom and Brigid give a christening, no matter whose child? Tom owed them all a big night . . . Who put one word with the other during all that shouting and laughing and elbowing, God alone knows, but suddenly, there it was, an idea that the glen could use — Tom and Brigid to be sponsors for Nelly's child and the christening to enlarge itself into a dance at Tom's. They burst forth from Dan Rua's giving out the news. A blast of women swept across the field to Peggy and they thundered their plan at her, and Peggy roared a welcome to it, and swore that Tom Manus would do the manly thing and bring in a decency of drink for the christening. Let them leave it all to her now. . . .

Peggy undertook to fix matters with Mary. Mary was

cautious. Would not all this come too sudden on Brigid? It was easy for the glen that wrought this change in itself, battling its way through noise, to give over its mind to this business but all this took place apart from Brigid, so how could Brigid's mind feed itself into these ideas? But Peggy would not listen. If Brigid had the head and the heart Peggy thought she had, she would see in all this a miracle straight from the hand of God. How could she hope to become one with the glen, except for the glen and her to clutch at one another in some such moment as this? Briany had the right of it. The glen could not go to Brigid and humble itself to her. Brigid could not go from house to house and cadge people to be neighbourly to her. If two families had a fall out in the glen how did they make it up, was it not that when something happened that gave one an excuse to run in on the other's floor they caught hands as if nothing ever estranged them? It had to be this way. . . .

The carpenter put in the big windows and departed. The glen set about making itself ready for what was coming. Susan Dan and Mary walked together as if there never had been a shadow between them. The whole glen badgered Nelly for her delay; a woman always in a hurry before to be holding back now. Was there no other woman handy in lower glen or upper glen? After all it did not have to be the birth of a child, any excuse would do. If a donkey was to drop a foal. . . .

Nelly took it all in good part; which was maybe the best proof of how ready the glen was for the celebration and the pacification. She said she was willing to be put on a horse and galloped up and down the fields to hurry herself. And then, at mid-day, two days before Brigid was due back from the island the shout went out that Nelly's time was come and that Mary was with her and that Mary called in Susan to help her. Ho, ho, so it was on Susan that Mary's mantle was to fall. . . .

Nelly did not keep them long in doubt. She gave birth to a boy and that suited the glen fine. But now Wee Conail pushed forward through the noise. He was not going to give over his child to them to make an excuse for a burst of nonsense. Why should Tom Manus spend money on a child of his? And there was one sure thing, none of his money would go into this spree. Could it be that any of them had hope to put part of this cost on to him? But his voice was too thin a sound to make headway against the lusty roar of the glen.

Tom drove out to meet the mail-car, and Brigid saw the red-wheeled cart pulled in off the roadside and she waved. The mail-car driver had news and he was slow to go on his way. Tom hoisted Brigid into the cart and climbed in beside her. She pointed to the hills and laughed. She said it looked to her that they had lost bulk since she left. She glanced at him shyly. She beat at him with her hands. 'They are in,' she chuckled, 'I know by you. Speak can't you? They are in?' He nodded. 'I think I would have burst out crying if anything got between you and them. I could see clearer and clearer on the island that they are what I want.' They were at the cross-roads now. Tom pulled up. He poked back his cap with his thumb and she turned to him puzzled. 'Do you believe in miracles, Brigid?' he asked seriously. 'I believe in us anyway,' she said sharply, 'in you and me. With God's help we will make a go of things. I am surer than ever of myself now. Whatever it is, say it. I can see there is something.'

'What would you say if I told you we are to stand sponsors for a child and that not the father nor the mother alone wished that on to us, but the whole glen, and that it is an excuse to give you a home-coming?' 'I would be glad to be welcome. I am free to stand sponsor for a child for I have not stood sponsor for a child within the year; you know it is not lucky to stand sponsor for a second child within a year. Is it Nelly's child?' He nodded. He flicked the reins and sent the horse on his way. He told her that Peggy and his mother had brought the child to the chapel and were waiting. Peggy came because she would not trust his mother not to try to make him some little bit tight-fisted when it came to buying drink for the christening. 'Peggy says I am to look on this as our wedding.' 'Then I will marry you, Tom Manus,' Brigid chuckled, 'it would only be decent.'

Mary was at the chapel gate waiting for them and she would have greeted Brigid as on the first night but Brigid embraced her. The priest's housekeeper had the kettle on the boil and Mary was to bring Brigid in. The priest was on a sick call but word was sent after him. Tom and Wee Conail could go across to the public house, a wee while. Mary warned Tom to take no drink. He would need full power over his tongue to give out the Apostles Creed at the baptism. It was a prayer a body could trip on, if he had a sup of drink in him. Indeed, drink or no drink, there were spots in the Apostles Creed you could stumble over. If a body's tongue did stick on a word the right thing to do was not to work on it, but to go back to the beginning and come up at it again with another race.

When the baptism was done they all rode back together in Tom's cart, Wee Conail's horse trailing behind. The moon was up now and the sky was as clean as ice. The upper reaches of the hills had no more shadow on them than under the hardest sunlight. They crossed the brae into the glen. The big windows swaggered forth amid the winking lights of the other houses, all three of the big windows alive. The horses drew up on the quarry floor. Withered gorse was set alight and other fires were started and a throng of people swept in around the cart. 'Mind the child,' Peggy shouted, 'mind the child.' The crowd took up the cry and roared out. 'Mind the child.' Mary called men and women, by name, to make a shelter round Brigid and the child, and so a procession was formed and it bustled across to Wee Conail's door and the door was open and Brigid entered, and she closed the door behind her.

Brigid sat with Nelly and she told her of all that passed at the christening. The crowd outside became impatient and shouted for her, and Dan Rua strode in. They would all be in through the house, unless Brigid led the way over home and started the dance, and she must dance the first dance with him. He bantered Nelly gaily, linked Brigid and swept her out the door past Susan. 'That's for you,' Susan shouted, 'I best keep on her heels in case she needs help; that is, if she would like help.' She caught sight of Tom Manus and drew his arm through hers. 'Ho, ho, Tom Manus, Dan Rua took the bread off your plate again. You will have to content yourself with me this time.' She spoke to the crowd around them. 'The devil is in him, when we used to be footing turf together long ago I used to be mad with him for being so easy to put off. I wonder did he get any nerve since.' And they all laughed and the night rang with their shouts, 'Mind the child.'

Nobody bothered to name the neighbours as they came up to Brigid to shake her hand. They just reached out to her and she reached out to them and they became neighbours, and she matched them in all things and joined in the cry when somebody roared, 'Mind the child.' The thronged kitchen was at peace with itself, eager, gay. Tom, with a mug in one hand and a bottle in the other, circulated among them, offering drinks. The mug was for the women. His measure for the men was five bobs of their Adam's apple. It was Sorcha who saw that if Tom was left on this job he would have the men off their feet before the night was half through, and she spoke to Susan, and Susan rallied the others and they fought Tom Manus for the bottle and they made Black Donal steward. But before Black Donal would take up office he must have his ceremonial dance, his one dance of the night. He took off his coat and he rolled up his sleeves and Peggy roared out for the floor for Black Donal, the man among men, the greatest among them. She ordered the fiddler to his feet. He must play a tune worthy of Black Donal, and she cheered him for the tune he struck up. Black Donal stood, his two eyes shut, his body swaying gently. He leaped into the air, landed with strange lightness and tripped off round the space made for him on the thronged floor. He set out in the first of the series of steps that made him famous throughout the hills, and at the end of each step Peggy whooped and challenged the world to show the equal of Black Donal. He ended his dance and Susan handed him the jug and they all acclaimed him.

Brigid sought shelter from further dancing, in Mary's bed, with Peggy on guard before her, the tongs in her hand threatening to brain any man who would drag Brigid back on the floor until she got her breath. Peggy nudged Brigid and whispered to her to keep an eye on Wee Conail. A minute ago she caught the sound of his voice outside. He was angry. Wee Conail changed himself according as the drink took hold of him. In his sober senses he was a civil, sharp-spoken man. If anything upset him he would walk out. In the first stage of drink a word could anger him. Give him back an angry word and his fists would be up. Next thing you would know, he was past that stage and into the hiccoughs. Once he got into the hiccoughs he would laugh all the time. Ho, ho, there he goes now. Listen to him laughing. 'Mind the child.' She raised the tongs in her hand. 'Mind the child,' she whooped.

'What change does drink make in Tom?' Brigid asked. 'Is it Tom Manus?' Peggy roared. 'Let me tell you my girl, that man could drink whiskey till he pissed punch and give out the rosary as solemn as the parish priest at the end of it; a head on him like pot metal; a man my girl, an iron man.' She raised the tongs again. 'Audience,' she shouted, 'audience. Audience for Sean Mor.' For Sean Mor had come to the stage where he wanted to sing his one song, Mary's song, the countryside's lament for a boy or girl going into exile. Youths around him were holding him in check, drowning his efforts in their noise. Peggy threatened them name by name and forced them to silence. The old voice fluttered up shakily. Brigid slid out of bed and made her way to him. She drew his arm across her shoulder and she added her voice to his and her voice was a wonder to them, for although there were many better on the island, the glen was not much given to song. With the breeze of her voice blowing through his own,

Sean Mor's song found appreciation. They cheered him when he finished and they cheered Brigid and she had to sing a song of her own. 'You are good, Brigid,' Peggy greeted, 'but you are not a patch on Mary here. I would rather hear Mary Manus lilting, than any music I ever danced to. Ho, ho, there goes Sean Mor now. This is the end of Sean Mor.' He stood very erect, a fine frame of an old man, his head high, tears trickling down his cheeks. It was a weird thing to see this big hulk of a man crying. Words came. 'Parnell. Ah Parnell, Parnell, my poor Parnell, what did they do to you.' The fiddler ceased strumming the strings. Sean Mor took off his cap. 'Parnell, Parnell,' he sorrowed, and men near him took off their caps too. Tom and Dan Rua went to him and they oxtered him out. Peggy spoke softly to Brigid. 'That is how it is with Sean Mor always; ever since I first knew him. He will drink and he will drink and always he will be civil and you will see no change in him, and then, like the lid might rattle on the kettle at the boil, he will make a great sound in his throat and then the tears will come, and no one knows until that minute what sorrow is on him. It comes out then, and he will speak, and when that is done he will just lose all power over himself and he will have to be carried away. This is his sorrow, like it is all our sorrow, Parnell. Ah Parnell, Parnell, many a sore heart turned to you in your day.' She raised her stick and waved it at the fiddler. 'Where do you think you are, sir, at a wake? Strike up a tune. Mind the child.' They took up the cry afresh and danced. The fiddler brought the tune to a close and got to his feet. He put the fiddle under his arm and hopped down from his chair on the table by the lamp, near the room door. The night of the christening was over.

Black Donal and Peggy were the last to leave and Brigid went a bit of the way with them. She listened to them cross the field together, linked and staggering, Black Donal calling for cheers for this person and that, and the last bellow she heard from him was to call for cheers for the moon. She turned her head at a rustle. 'Ann,' she breathed, 'Ann the

Hill,' and Ann rushed in out of the shadows to her, and knelt by her and clasped her knees, and Brigid raised her and embraced her. 'I brought you a necklace. I have it in my pocket. All night I carried it in my pocket.' She fastened it on Ann's neck. And Ann, hearing steps, fled.

Mary was in her corner, her beads in her fingers. 'Brigid, you have your shoes on you, will you run out and see did I close in the ducks. And will you put your head in the byre door. Oh thank God, thank God.' She went back to her prayers.

9

SUSAN made a gay entrance into Tom's the next morning before Mary and Brigid were finished with their morning work. 'Such a night,' she cheered, 'will I ever forget it: I was near the first over to the old quarry to wait on you coming in. Next thing I knew the world was gathered. I never saw Dan Rua on such a lead, in all my life. It was Dan Rua made ready the fires. Not a fire or fire kind would there be only for him. Then he got a half pint bottle of oil — where he got it, or how he thought of it I do not know but he got the half pint of paraffin oil — and he put a lit rag on a wire and he held the lit rag in front of him and he took a mouthful of the paraffin oil and he blew it across the lit rag and he blew it straight at us. That started the fun I tell you. That was the beginning of the whole devilment. Dan Rua was the head and tail of everything. . . .'

Susan went and Kitty came and Kitty's entrance was like Susan's. Last night's carry on would be talked of for ever. Since the day he came back from Boston Kitty never saw Briany outside his skin like last night. It was he showed Dan Rua the game of the lit rag. Briany had another trick too. . . .

Kitty told the story of Briany's doing within the general uproar of the evening and when Kitty was gone Sorcha came. Sorcha had no story of her own man but she had tales of other people and then Sorcha added a word. 'It will be God's ease to us all now, Brigid, to be out and in to you, and you out and in to us.' And having said that Sorcha went on her way.

That evening a firesideful of women came to talk and they told Tom to get out and they shut the door against him and all the men for that night, and they told their tales of the christening, going over the things that were done, name by name, and they jostled one another and snapped the words off each others lips, and Brigid made tea for them, and when they had left she turned to Mary in some anxiety. What kind of a carry on was that, noise and foolishness that could be clowning or could be jeering? Why should grown up women think they had to make noise for a whole night like children playing games? But there was no bother on Mary. It would take them a while to get used to her, and it would take her a while to get used to them. This noise would pass and soon they would come to her in quietness; one by one they would come to her. But next day Brigid met Susan at the well and she was still noisy and her talk was of the christening, and it was so with Kitty, and Brigid grumbled to Peggy and Peggy laughed at her. 'God bless us, girl, there's nothing harder in the world than to make quiet talk when there is any strangeness between people.' She offered Brigid her snuff box. 'There's no woman ever married a man but finds that the hardest thing of all, to sit with him and talk. You can make your own of him in every other way but you'll be at a loss for talk when there's no one there but the two of you. I mind when I married Donal — I was maybe feeling a wee bit guilty for if I had my choice it's not him I would have. I was going by him one day within the first week of our life together. He was cutting a lintel out of a block of stone and he stood up to talk to me and I had to find talk so I says to him: "How will you manage to cut a lintel out of that big stone," and he went down on his hunkers to point out the grain on the rock and I went down on my hunkers beside him, as if all that was a bother to me at that minute was to learn how the grain ran in that rock; I knew as much as himself about the grain in granite. You see we were strangers with one another notwithstanding all that had happened between us. I have to laugh now to think of it.

99

So put manners on yourself, my girl, and do not be in too big a hurry to put this noise past you. The women need the noise to beat a casan to your door. They have to make it look like the night of the christening was your first night ever in this glen. No talk is ever to dig below the floor of that night of the christening. Bear that in mind.'

And then one afternoon Susan came in on the floor to Brigid, without noise or news on her lips, and she asked Brigid could she spare her a cup of sugar till she got in her own supply of sugar, and Brigid asked her to sit and Susan sat and Brigid made tea and they drank it together and they talked of brands of tea and found fault with one, and praised another. Mary sauntered in, and as soon as she darkened the door Susan burst forth again to tell her story, how she took no heed at all of herself using up her sugar until there was no more sugar, and Mary raised her hand to stay Susan's talk. She herself could bear witness how easy it was to get to the end of your sugar, or your tea, or even your flour, unbeknownst to yourself. Brigid and Mary together saw Susan off the street and then Mary nudged Brigid and Brigid followed her inside. 'A cup of sugar, no less,' Mary chuckled, 'that now is what I was waiting for. All this time I was waiting for Susan to walk in on this floor to say she wanted this or that. Now it will be your turn to go in to Susan's and say to Susan you ran out of cream-o'-tartar. Susan will know you have no shortage of cream-o'-tartar, but this is the only time there will be any need of let-on between you. The be-all of neighbourliness is to ask and to give. Susan knows that. You will show her you know that, too, when you go to her.' Sorcha came. Sorcha had sewing to do and the pup had carried off her number forty spool of cotton thread; the devil was in him. Brigid had a spool and she gave it to Sorcha, and Sorcha noticed that Brigid had just made a churning and Brigid offered her a can of buttermilk and Sorcha blessed her for it. She met Mary on the street. 'That's more than I would get, Mary, if it was you had sway on the floor,' she joked — if it was a joke — holding up the gallon can.

'You did the right thing, Brigid, to give Sorcha a can of buttermilk. The like is a fine thing where there are children. Sorcha is a good woman. She is the one among them I would like you to make most of, but for all that learn to keep an eye on yourself, Brigid. It would be a bad habit, a habit of being too plentiful with your share. To be a neighbour you have to give and you have to take, but you have to keep an eye on yourself not to over-give. Give in your turn and ask in your turn and to be too soft is as bad as to be too hard. I often think of the sapper's wife. She made a great mistake. She brought a riches of things into this glen. She showed people this, and she showed them that, and if you praised a thing she would force it on you, but she never asked anybody for anything. So they all took and they took and the more she gave the lighter they spoke of her, and it was not long till they were laughing at her. They ended up stealing everything they could lay hands on belonging to her, one afraid the other would get ahead of her, and in the end she had not a friend among them. You have to keep your eye on your neighbour — good watching will make good neighbours anywhere — and you have to keep your eye on yourself.' They talked much together, and neighbour women came on them laughing together, and that was a strange thing for it was not what people thought would take place between Mary and whoever came in to share the floor with her. And so the days passed and the weeks and Brigid travelled on neighbours' carts on a Sunday and neighbours travelled with her and Tom in turn.

Susan, resting on the stick on a gap, watched Brigid gathering clothes off a bleach field and Brigid, laughing, held up Mary's chemise for Susan to see. 'Would you ever think, Susan, that Mary Manus would like embroidery on the sleeves of her shift? I found she likes it, and I did this for her and sometimes I see her rubbing her hands on it, like a child.' Susan climbed through the gap. 'Brigid it is in this you make yourself the greatest puzzle of all, you and Mary all but playing wee horses together.' Brigid made little of putting a spot of embroidery on the sleeves of Mary's chemise. What was it altogether but pastime when a body had a free hour. 'Then tell me this,' Susan challenged, 'why should it be so between you and Mary, when with me and Nappy it is like this: if I have to wash Nappy's shift I pick it up with the tongs and I drop it into the suds that the other clothes came out of, and I rummage it round and round with the tongs or a stick, or maybe I put one of the children in to tramp it, and then I lift it out with the tongs and I put it on the bush or the grass and I never lay a finger on it that I can help.' 'God bless us Susan, you hate her.' 'I hate her, Brigid. I do not deny it. I'm waiting for the day she dies. You need not cry against me for, as I hope to see God and that He will have mercy on me, it is the truth. She is my cross and I bear it badly. Sometimes I hope she is my Purgatory. She sits in the corner and she watches me. She has a mark on the tea and on the sugar and on the flour, and every time the fit takes her, she goes to one or the other and mutters to herself at the waste and the cost, and says we are on our way to the workhouse. I will eat the roof from over Dan Rua's head and leave him on the high road. It's not in nature to stand it. It's in no woman's nature to stand it all, yon gurning, night, noon and morning, and her eyes on me and her mind on me, and she talking to herself about me.' Brigid stood with the washing in her arms, too startled to find words of blame or comfort, watching Susan on her way home.

Susan told the story of the embroidered chemise and it was news and it went through the glen. Peggy gathered some of their comments and she brought them to Brigid. The chief wonder among them was that it should be between Mary Manus and the woman who came in to her that this should be, for always it was their talk that the woman who came in to Mary Manus would be a woman to pity, beyond all women in the glen. And then there was this: if Brigid and Mary got on well together it was not that Brigid soothed down Mary by letting her have her own way. They went over among themselves how Brigid got between Mary and the cows and how she got past her with her big windows. 'And I may as well say, Brigid,' Peggy growled, 'that in the end I was angry with you myself, for it is true as I sit here that it is as big a puzzle to me as it is to them, you getting your way with Mary like you do, until now you are going to tumble her hen-house and put up a new one, and all she does when a body casts it up to her is offer you her snuff box. Upon my soul, Brigid, if it was in on my floor you came I would put manners on you. I said it to Mary, and she did nothing only raise her head and look out past me with a look on her face that made me shut my mouth and makes me say to myself that from now on I'll keep it shut. But let me tell you if I do, I'll still keep my eye on you, and when I see the need of it I'll take the edge of my tongue to you.' Brigid made a face at her. Mary came in and they talked of other things.

Nelly came to Brigid heavy-footed. There was trouble between herself and Eilis. Eilis's people were from lower glen and now that there was a trickle of traffic up and down to the quarry Eilis had an eye out for one or other of them, and she had a story on her lips. Wee Conail was not getting his fair share of the food of the house. By Eilis's story Wee Conail never got an egg. Nelly had her egg and the children could get eggs but not Wee Conail. Nelly blurted out her story and it overpowered her and she wept. She wept because she did not keep the story to herself but made a storm of it to Wee Conail, and he got angry and he raised his voice to his mother and his mother took a weakness and Wee Conail got a fright and he did not get right back to himself. Nelly tried to comfort him saying that the way things were between her and Eilis was how they were everywhere that a young woman and an old woman shared the floor, that up and down the glen there was this taunting and arguing. 'If he had to get angry with me, say, Brigid, it would be better, but he did not. All he did was sigh and say to me that it was a queer thing that it was only the woman from afar that could be heard laughing with the old woman she came in to.'

Brigid gestured Nelly further away from the door and they sauntered out on the green. 'Is there something we have to learn from you Brigid? Why should it be like this with us — search the glen from one end to the other and you will find it is like between me and Eilis, while it is as it is between you and Mary?' But Brigid had no answer to give her, and when Nelly wept because of the sadness she had brought on Wee Conail, Brigid wept a little with her. Mary was waiting for Brigid inside the doorstep. 'You will have to put a stop to this, Brigid,' she said sharply, 'do not let them unburden their hearts on to your heart. It is not right. Nelly is not the only one. They come to you dragging their legs and maybe you are singing when they come and they go away with a light step and they leave you without your song. Yesterday it was Sorcha.'

'Yesterday it was Sorcha,' Brigid agreed, 'and if Sorcha has not due cause to be angry who has? Her man's mother, Ouida, takes to her bed. She has to be lifted in and out of the bed, and only her son can lift her in or out. But she can eat and talk and when she is out of the bed she can walk. She lost the power of her legs, and of her arms, so that she has to be lifted in and out of bed, and it is all because one day when her son came back from the fair and she put out her hand for the money and her son's wife, Sorcha, put out her hand for the money, he preferred his wife above his mother. Is not that a cross for Sorcha to have to bear this tantrum in the old woman?'

'It is a cross surely, Brigid, but it sits lightly on Sorcha. There is plenty of noise and fun in Sorcha. And in Nappy and Susan. Take Susan and Nappy: they have their hours of ease together too. They are both of a lumpy nature, and every now and then they would be sure to turn on one another, for there is a thing between them that can cause a sting like a toothache. Susan did not want to marry Dan Rua. If Susan had her way she would be off to Boston rather than marry Dan Rua, and Nappy knows that. How could they be at their ease all the time, with a cross dog like that in their minds ready to start up at a cough? But they have their fun together. It is worse between Eilis and Nelly. It is bad that Wee Conail should be upset.' 'You see everything, don't you?' Brigid challenged. 'The heart is a good watch-dog, Brigid,' Mary said quietly. 'Don't let them air their troubles to you, just because you are a stranger and you don't gabble.' She went to her corner and Brigid, watching her, rapped a tooth with the nail of her thumb. 'I suppose you think I have no need to go to them to ease myself of any burden.' Mary, who was stooping on her creepy, rose slowly, a protective hand creeping up to her breast. The bone structure of her face seemed to bare itself. 'I said to Susan the other day' — Brigid spoke hurriedly — 'I said to Susan the other day to look at your shift, how I had to put em-broidery on it for you.' Mary's tobacco-stained teeth showed in her smile. 'They want to know why it is you and I never spit at one another; they all seem to be of that mind, to wonder that there is no sharpness between us. They want to know why we do not make noise.'

Mary settled herself on her creepy. 'I always prayed that when Tom married it would be like this.' Brigid took her place across the fire from her and drew her darning from her private cubbyhole. 'It was God did it.'

'If it was God did it, Mary, Tom was a good help to Him. I would never get over a longing for big windows; even after I got them every now and then I had to make a race to the door, but let the mountains and myself get on or not get on, once the big windows were put in, there was no shadow be-tween the two of us. If I had to be smothered in the small windows we might laugh less together.' Mary found her knitting. Brigid darned. 'When I came in on this floor, Brigid, there was an old woman on it, and she stood between me and my own way. Still, I think I took no hurt from it. Everything was work, work, work. She set work before me, and I could see sense in it and I did it.' Mary laid her knitting in her lap. 'There was one thing she did. Is it not a strange thing, I did not think of this earlier? I brought a lamp with me into this house. His mother never took to it. People would come in, and I would turn up the wick and she would bide her chance to turn it down; let there be but one wee corner of smoke and she would be out off her creepy to turn it down, using that excuse even with people in. As soon as we were alone together she would put it out. I think now I used to laugh at her from the start. I could not be sure of that. She was a hard woman; it was a hard world. She was always afraid that food would get scarce. She used to say to me that if I got the children's stomachs into the habit of small meals they would not widen themselves out and get greedy; she thought you could train children not to have a craving for food. I do not know of any one way that I had the upper hand of her ever until Manus died. I became the man of the house then, and I said to her do this and she did it, and she worked herself to the bone and I got a great liking for her, and I cried my heart out when she died. . . .'

Wee Conail came for the loan of Tom's axe to shape a stake for the byre. Brigid was fixing new curtains on Mary's bed and he watched her at it. He pointed at the curtains with the stem of his pipe. 'That, now, Brigid is the one thing I'm all the time afraid of, the island in you breaking out in such ways as that. I make it no fault in you, Brigid. You have to be like you are. I can see now it was the island in you made you need the windows, but, once you put in the windows, the windows will spread from one mind to the other; like enough they were there all the time only people did not notice them. That puts new cost on people. You will do a thing like this, and that will spread too, and that will be the destruction of the glen Brigid. The glen cannot give itself such airs without some hurt to itself.'

'But, Wee Conail, there is more money in this glen than on the island. There is more money in this house than in my father's house. How is it then that the island has a greater conceit in itself?'

He drew a chair to him and straddle-legged it. 'You said something like that to me before, Brigid, and I went over it in my own mind, why should the island spend and not be afraid to spend and why should we scrimp and scrape and be afraid not to save and scrape? It looks to me like you are more easy going, like there was less fear of things in you and that is a strange thing in face of an uncertain world like the sea.' He puffed his pipe. He pointed out the open door at the tilled fields. 'You could be looking out that door, Brigid, at a field of blossoms giving promise of the best potato crop in all your day, and a fog might come with a smell in it, and you would know it was death and when it passed your very blossoms would be a stinking mess.' He turned to her. 'Tell me, what stories of the Famine have you on the island?'

She took Mary's creepy. 'The island has no story of its own about the Famine, that ever I heard, beyond mainland people coming to it for fish; I always heard it was a great year for fish. Anyway, it is not right for you, Wee Conail, to keep the Famine in mind, you that has sheep on the mountains and cattle. It is the fault above all faults I have to find with this glen, Wee Conail, all the fear in you. Every way the mind turns inside this glen it has to face some fear.' He rose quickly without speaking. She reached him down the axe from the top of the canopy over Mary's bed. 'Let me tell you, Wee Conail, it was touch and go between Mary and me. If we get on well together, it was touch and go.' He turned quickly to her. 'Touch and go,' she repeated. She let him go out alone. He was not right clear of the doorstep when Nelly ran in. 'What was on his mind, Brigid? Do not hide a word from me. If he said something to you, tell me for I know he has something on his mind; something more even than Eilis. Sometimes I think he has a mind to go away for a while, but it's not that alone. He is upset. He is not sleeping. He is short with the children, and that is not like him. He makes no use at all of me, and that is not like Wee Conail. I am praying, and praying and I'm doing my best to make up to him, to take the soreness out of his mind that I put into it that day when I made him angry with his mother. . . .'

'Look, Nelly, why don't you all get together, you and Susan and Sorcha, and most likely every other young woman in the glen sharing the fireside with an old woman, and let you go to the priest and say how it is, for he is an old man and no end of women have opened their hearts to him and he must be wise. Let you all go.' And Nelly went forth with Brigid's message and when she told it she laughed, and as it came to the others they laughed and that night they gathered into Brigid's and they talked in such a way as if the battles between themselves and their old women was the one fun they had in life. They even planned new battles. Susan declared that one of these days she would walk into Nappy and say to her she was going to make herself a sup of tea, and if Nappy as much as coughed, she would pitch the canister of tea into the fire and the sugar after it. She would so; some day when Dan Rua was out of the glen she would do the like of that. And the others shared her mood of bravo; even Sorcha. One day Sorcha would put a battle of straw under the bed and put a light to it, and there was great laughter, and in the days that followed there was brightness in them.

Anyway the days themselves were brighter now. Men were abroad in the fields and there was a roar in their voices, and the sky itself throbbed with bird song. The island had no such riches of bird song, and Brigid lamented that all the birds that thronged the strands of the island should have so little music in them. The mountains, too, made headway with her, and she often idled, watching them change their draperies. And the breeze was unlike the breeze over the island. She put her face into it to pick out the scents it carried, and almost without noticing it, she shared her enriched day more and more with Ann the Hill, as she watched the cattle feed by the edges of tilled fields. Ann and she played games together, for Brigid discovered by chance that Ann could imitate bird calls and she became Ann's pupil. Ann would not just appear now. She would give out a call from her hiding place and Brigid would make her call back, and sometimes a startled thrush or skylark would take wing excitedly and chirrup. Brigid made Ann a dress. One day Andy went out of his way to meet Brigid on her casan. 'I would like to thank you,' he said simply. 'I would so.'

But Brigid and Ann's game did not go unnoticed. Peggy sent for Brigid. 'God Almighty is there no end to the rascality in you. One thing I always held, that it is not right for a Christian man to let on to be the brute beast. There was a man, let me tell you, in this glen one time and the tongue God gave him was put to such use. When he wanted his dog, he would not call him, like a Christian, but he would bark. People said to him he better watch out, but he laughed so people withdrew from him. The priest spoke to him. He put no heed on that. His end came. He took a weakness abroad in the field and a neighbour saw him fall and the neighbours ran to him, and they had to stone the dog away from him. They carried him inside, and they put him to bed and they bolted the door against the dog. They sent for the priest. They sent for the priest and the messenger was no sooner on his way than the man himself began barking. There it was, the man inside barking and the dog outside barking. The priest came and the priest could not stop the man from barking, so he said to the men to take away the dog, but they could not take away the dog so they had to kill the dog. They killed the dog and the man's voice fell away with the dog's and he died, and the priest never said what passed between himself and the man.' She handed Brigid a bowl of tea. 'I listened to the two of you making fools of the birds, but when I heard you giving a bleat like a sheep, Mother of God, says I, the next thing she'll have you making a screech like a hare in a snare.'

'I know what's wrong with you, Aunt Peggy,' Brigid scoffed. 'I am not carrying any stories to you.' 'You are not carrying any stories to me surely,' Peggy agreed. 'You sit on that flag in the long field, where you can see all round you, so that no ear can get near you and you listen; and little good comes to me of it.' She took a long drink. 'What does she say to you?'

'Will you tell me something first, Aunt Peggy. I often draw up Tom's name and Mary's; I do it for fun. Like a person fishing I draw the names across her mind and it always seems to me I can see her shutting her mind in, and I wonder to myself, could she be that wise.'

'She has no need to shut her mind in on Mary's account. I do not believe God Himself has a mark in His book against Mary; if He has it will be a big strain on His mercy to let the rest of us in.' She held her bowl to her lips and looked over the rim. 'Tom stole a ram.'

'No,' Brigid bellowed, 'no.' Peggy nodded. Brigid flung out her arms and laughed.

'You will hear it, if you promise I will hear the stories Ann the Hill gave you.' Brigid promised. 'This is how it was: Tom drove into this glen, drunk to the world, asleep in his cart with his two arms around a ram's neck and the ram asleep. It was the dawn of the day and only Briany had a cow at the calving nobody would have been awake to notice the horse coming to a halt at the end of the road, and only Kitty was on Briany's heels no word of the ram would have got out; for Briany is like that with Tom, and drunk as he was Tom disowned the ram as soon as he saw it. In his sober senses he had no memory of it. By his money he could see he had not bought the ram. He went out over the same road but he could get no word that anybody lost a ram. Tom took the ram with him and he set him free on the stretch of mountains that was the most likely place for him to catch up with him on that day, but the next time he went out on his own mountain to look at his sheep there was the ram; and I think Tom got scared for he never tried to get rid of him after.' Brigid took the story to Tom himself, and Tom made a face. 'That is not the whole of the story, Brigid, for like it was a judgment on me, every second lamb I look at since has that ram's face. When he got old I took him in near the house and I made a shelter for him. He died inside in the kitchen and I was with him when he died. I buried him, hide, wool and all, and I never forgot him.'

Around the fire that evening, after the rosary, they talked of the ram and they laughed that Ann should have sense to withhold the story from Brigid. When Tom and Brigid were alone they talked further of Ann. 'I had a bit of a notion of her myself at one time,' Tom confided. Such a thought had come to Brigid already. She was glad Tom had no word to say against her wish that Ann should come and go to her freely when she was in that part of the glen. Ann served as a topic between them and their conversation ranged outward in a way that was unusual between husband and wife in the glen, and now and then Brigid chuckled to find that Tom had almost as sharp an eye for things as his mother. 'Don't let Susan play on you,' he advised. 'Susan lets on to be at war with Nappy, but any trouble she has with Nappy is of her own making. Nappy lies in wait for me for a smoke. If Susan wants peace between herself and Nappy let her put her meanness aside and buy Nappy a regular bit of tobacco. In a way maybe, Dan Rua is to blame for he should see Nappy got her tobacco.' Brigid laughed. She told him how Mary was for ever lecturing her that the troubles between women should be hidden from men.

The time came to put up the net and Brigid spoke to Tom of it. 'This is one time when you will have to make your own way,' he said, 'and I will only laugh if my mother gets the upper hand of you over it.' Mary grumbled in his hearing, that the hens would wear themselves to feathers, racing round searching for a hole to get out, and he put his cap on his head and winked at Brigid and went out. Mary gave Brigid no hand when the day came. She stood inside the door and she grumbled when she saw Briany cross the field, his dickey shining more than ever that day. Briany gave Brigid a hand and children gathered, and they were eager to finger the net, and they were a help. The enclosure was outward from the hen-house gable where there was an opening that the hens would come through in the morning, since the door would be shut, and food would be awaiting them within the enclosure. While they fed, Brigid would go in through the door and collect the eggs. Mary tried to take a stand over the red hen. The red hen would never give in to lay an egg anywhere but in the byre. Brigid would not give way. The red hen would have to be like the rest of the world. She would have to make the best of things that she could not change. And on the morning when the hens hopped out through the opening in the gable, one by one, into the enclosure, it looked as if Brigid was going to have her own way without any trouble. The hens finished their food, and moved away from the feeding boards to peck and scratch, without once raising their heads to the net. Some settled down to sand-bathe and among these was the red hen. Susan found time to come to watch, and Nelly came and Sorcha, and Brigid told them she had not at all been as easy as she let on, over the red hen. If the red hen had to make any noise and hurl herself at the net, Mary might go back into a cloud of bad humour over it. As she talked, the red hen ruffled her feathers and raised her voice. She shivered herself free of dust and sharpened the chant that often carried the news into the kitchen that the byre door was shut against her. She disappeared into the hen-house, popped out again, and spreading her wings to ease her to the ground, she raced to the net, her neck outstretched. She probed the meshes. She raced along, pecking and peeping. She took wing, searching for an exit higher up. She cackled angrily. Mary came out on to the street. She saw the cluster of women and went back in and shut the door behind her. 'If she has sense to leave the door shut and if we will walk away so that the red hen sees nobody is heeding her, she will go inside and lay her egg like another.' She gestured the others to move away with her and they went, disappointed that Mary had elected to shut herself in. The men's voices were loud in the fields. Brigid sauntered a bit of the way with Sorcha.

The kitchen door was still shut when Brigid came back. She looked for a sign of the red hen but she was not in sight. She hurried to the byre and pushed the door open slowly.

The red hen's comb glowed like a live coal amid the straw in the black cow's stall. Brigid closed the door gently, and went into the kitchen. Mary was in her corner smoking. 'A touch of toothache no less,' Mary explained. 'It is that old stump.' Brigid went to the window and looked out. She heard the rasp of Mary's creepy as she pushed it aside and stood up. 'I just could not stand it, Brigid. I went in to bed and I turned my skirt over my head but I could still hear her.' There was no word from Brigid. 'You're not angry with me, Brigid?' And then Brigid turned to her and her laughter rose in gusts. She put her arms around Mary, and Kitty, going by, looked in and she spread abroad the story of what she saw, and heard.

10

A MAN from the lower glen stormed down from the mountain in the first hour of the morning's work to charge that he got sight of a dog that harried a ewe and that the dog headed for upper glen. He had a long story of how he came to be abroad at such an early hour, and how the haze of the morning made it easy for the dog to get out of his sight. It was not his own ewe, but a neighbour's ewe that suffered and it could be there was no great harm done, but this dog was at large, and that was harm enough. He could give no clear description of him, beyond a white splash on his shoulder, or it might be his rump. He was loud-voiced but he was reasonable. He doubted whether he could pick out the dog. His own dog had a white splash. Black Donal spoke up. He had a dog that could answer to that description, but his dog was not abroad last night. He was shut into the stable. Last night above all nights Black Donal remembered shutting him into the stable, and that morning, of all mornings, he remembered seeing him at his heels on his way back to the house after opening the stable door and, since then, his dog was within call. Nobody doubted Black Donal's word. The man went on his way, crying aloud his message and warning.

Nappy was first to raise her voice. She had her suspicions. This could be Briany's dog. The man could be wrong about the splash. She heard Briany's dog one night make a cry, and it was not good that a dog should raise a cry like yon at night. The white splash might be tufts of wool. Yon crying was a sign. Such a dog had something on his mind. Then, too, there was the strain of the dogs of the other glen in Briany's dog, and in that other glen many a dog had the strain of a fox. She could tell such dogs by their ears. A man told her, the way this came about was that, every now and then, they had a habit of staking out a bitch in heat for a dog fox. Great working dogs, they said, came of such a cross; and great rogues. The roguery would come out on top in Briany's dog for he got no training; no work to put sense in him. Let Briany's dog be examined. She would hate it should be Briany's dog, but better that it should be Briany's dog, that was no better than an orphan, than any other dog. It was a poor story to carry to any door, their dog to be accused of killing sheep. It could be the work of a young dog, a playful dog, chasing things because they ran, with no mind to hurt them; it could be that. Again, it might be Andy the Hill's dog.

Towards evening, that same day, Andy the Hill strode across the field with a creel on his back and a purpose in his step and he headed for Wee Conail and Wee Conail came to him and lifted down the creel off his back, and everybody within sight knew something was afoot. Wee Conail turned over the creel and, when he drew it aside, they could see a dead sheep on the green, and then they ran. Andy the Hill told his story. The bleating of a lamb caught his ear and he at work on his turf-bank making it ready for cutting. There were plenty of lamb bleats in the air, on spring days, but this one made a place for itself among them all, and he turned his ear to it and it kept on and on and he became uneasy. One time he stuck his spade in ground thinking to go and see could it be that a lamb was in a drain but, at that moment, it stopped and then other things got on his mind and maybe his ear was unheeding for a while, but later, all at once, he heard such a bleat he stuck his spade and he ran and he found the lamb, lying bleating by the dead ewe and he knew it was Wee Conail's brand.

Wee Conail remembered this ewe above all his sheep. She was one of the triplets. She was the one that was reared on the bottle and it was likely because of that she had less fear of dogs than other sheep, and so, when the other ewes bunched together at the sight of the dog, this bottle-fed ewe held her ground and the dog got her by herself, cut off from the others. As Wee Conail talked somebody brought a wool shears, and then Tom and Dan Rua dug a hole, a deep hole so that dogs might not get at the carcase, and when that was done the men stood in a silent group, for this was a serious affair. Tom's dog sat on his haunches and he yawned, and Tom called his name sharply and the dog, not knowing what to make of it, slunk towards him with an air of guilt. He lay at Tom's feet and when Tom stooped over him, he turned on his back and raised his paws. There was no trace of blood on his chops, his neck, his breast. Tom drew the dog's mouth open. There was no trace of wool caught between the teeth. 'There is talk of my dog,' Briany said quietly and he led a group of men across the fields and he called his dog and Tom went over him and there was no trace of blood nor other sign of guilt on Briany's dog, and it was so too with Dan Rua's dog. Andy the Hill whistled up his dog. Andy's dog was bedraggled. There was no wool on his teeth. This might well be a long search. A patrol of men would have to go out at night.

They scattered out over the casans. Black Donal trudged into Tom's. He stood on the hearth. 'It could not be that my dog was abroad, Tom? I shut him in last night. I opened the door myself this morning. The first I saw of him was that he was on my heels when I walked back to the house. But for all that I mind this: the white patch on his chest had a dark stain on it. I wondered at it, but not enough to bother about it. I said nothing about the stain on his chest over there for, since this could not be his work, what sense would be in pointing a finger of scorn at him? He was shut in, Tom; that I know. He was on my heels on the way back to the house after I opened the stable door; that I know. It would not make sense Tom, and yet there was something strange . . .' He rubbed his chin. 'Even there was wool on his teeth Tom, he had a busy day and he nuzzles sheep. A fine working dog, Tom.' 'I'm afraid it could be your dog,

Black Donal. A thing came into my mind too. Do you mind I told you how, one night, a moonlight night it was, coming into your house towards bedtime, I wondered to see two pairs of eyes looking out at me over the top of the stable door? It was a warm night and the upper part of the door was open, like you often leave it. And the two levels of eyes were the dog standing on the horse's back. There is a pile of manure in front of the door and the dog could well jump off the horse's rump on it. 1 am afraid of what we will find, Black Donal, when we take a look at your dog.'

'I would not know, Tom, did he come out when I opened the door or did he sneak up on my heels from the back of the midden.' Black Donal sighed wearily. 'Peggy will take this hard, Tom.' 'This could be taken care of in such a way, Black Donal, that Peggy need never know.' Black Donal shook his head. 'For forty years I never hid anything from Peggy. It's not likely I will begin now. The only thing is to be sure.'

As soon as Black Donal and Tom started across the fields people recognized they were on an errand. Tom signalled to Dan Rua to join them and he called Wee Conail and that drew women and children after them. Peggy saw them coming and she stood on the street, silent, and her dog stood close to her until the men drew near. He lay at her feet and pressed against her legs. Black Donal called him and he started to his feet, wagging his tail hopefully, and Peggy felt his body tremble and she sorrowed over him then, and she asked him what came over him, at all, at all, at all, and the dog licked her hands and she gave him her hands to lick, and she called him pet names. 'I had him judged already,' she announced, 'half an hour ago I judged him. I was angry with him at first and I beat him. Now I am sorry I beat him. Ach! what came over him? It is not like he had an excuse. He is not a dog was ever hungry. He was the most dog I liked.' Black Donal dragged the dog out on the green where they examined him and condemned him, and, as soon as they released him, he crawled back to Peggy's feet and lay flat with his nose between his paws. 'Come on then. Get this over,' Tom said. Black Donal nodded. The thing now was to get the dog to the Loch and put a rope on him and tie a stone to it and throw him in. Black Donal called the dog, and his voice was friendly, and the dog wagged his tail and followed and he kept at Black Donal's heels, and the others held back and let them go on ahead. They followed slowly. On the rising ground overlooking the Loch, the dog halted and he trembled. He lay down. Black Donal called him again, coaxing him to follow, and the dog wagged his tail but he did not rise. Black Donal spoke sharply and the dog half rose, the hair bristling on his shoulders. The link between him and Black Donal was broken. Tom came up and put the rope around the dog's neck and the dog leaped to his feet in panic and he struggled wildly and snarled. He was rapidly becoming dangerous. Dan Rua had an idea. Let Tom pass the rope through a hole in the stone fence and let the dog be dragged close against the fence so that they would stone him to death, but Peggy, standing back by her gable, demanded to know what was the delay and they told her what they had in mind and she forbade it. He must not die in such a way, she decreed. He was not a dog to die in such a way. Let a stake be driven into the ground and let him be staked out and let word be sent to lower glen for the gun. Black Donal said that it would have to be as Peggy laid down, and two children were sent on the message to lower glen and the people sat around on the green and waited. Peggy sent a child with a bowl of milk for the dog and he lapped a little of it, and when his hour came, he neither whimpered nor whined, but rose to his feet, and he did himself honour in dying.

'If ever I was frightened of this glen it was this day,' Brigid confided to Mary. 'I never saw men act in such a way. Nobody had a thought to save the dog. What sense has a dog? Surely there is some way to cure such a dog . . .' 'Is it the dog you have on your mind, Brigid? Ach! The dog. It is Black Donal and Peggy should be in your mind. There was nothing to do with the dog but to kill him, but it takes a body a while to get him out of your mind. I dread changing from one dog to another. There was no excuse for Black Donal's dog, of all the dogs in the world; no excuse. Peggy is upset. Black Donal, too, wondering was it some mistake he made. . . .'

A gust of men's laughter came from the hillock where the dog was shot. Susan halted on her way home to call Brigid out on to the street to ask her if Tom had settled yet on what day he was to cut his turf. She had no talk of the dog. 'Sometimes I think it is on purpose you do it,' Brigid stormed at her. 'You do a thing I would not give a spit for, and you make the end of the world of it, and you do a thing takes the breath off me, you make as light of it as a spit.' And Nelly, who overheard her, joined Susan in a light-hearted jeering and Brigid withdrew. Mary had a further word to say. 'You will have to get a right sense of such things, Brigid. There are not many things in this glen can set it on edge like a dog to be loose savaging sheep. I saw great harm come out of such a thing. Great harm. It was the first thing that separated Andy the Hill's house from the neighbours. On such a day as this a dead sheep was found and children saw a dog, and they said it was Andy the Hill's dog; Andy's father was of that name too. The men of the glen gathered at the house and they asked him to fetch the dog to them, and he did, and there was no blood on him but he was wet, like he was swimming in the lake. The children said it was Andy's dog they saw, and the men said to drown him but Andy would not have it so. The men withdrew. It was their habit, at that time, to gather into Andy's on Sunday nights to play cards so, the next Sunday night, they went there and one of them had the leg of a chicken, and he held it down between his knees until it drew the dog and then he closed his knees on him and his hands and he was a powerful man, and, when the card school left the table that night, they left the dead dog behind them. And next Sunday night they went there again but there was no light in the house and they did not go in. They never went back. That was before the sickness came on the house!'

Although the season for visiting was over, a group of neighbours gathered into Tom's kitchen that evening, and Black Donal came and Peggy. They talked a little of the dog. 'He was always a bit odd, that dog,' Peggy explained. 'He was a dog that never took his food like he should. It's not a good sign that a dog should have a sour against food, now and then. Such an animal separates himself from his true nature. Maybe the great mistake was, when he was a pup, and I noticed this oddity in him, that I reared him. The one thing above all for a dog is health.' But Wee Conail had a wish to talk of other matters. It was time, and past the time, to settle what roads men were to spread themselves out over, now that the opening of the lime season was near at hand. And another thing. A man in lower glen last year fired his lime kiln with turf that went into yellow ashes, and that was not a thing that should happen. The great merit of Glenmore lime was its whiteness; that was a matter of the turf more than anything else. The rogues below in Carrick would bring in lime from far off, like they did before, and Glenmore would not hold its own against them if they did not take care to burn only turf that gave white ashes; if it could hold its own even then, for if the train did come, who could tell what weight of lime that would bring?'

'When the train comes let not the lime be on your mind,' Sean Mor advised, 'for the end of the world will be at hand . . .' They drifted into an argument on the meanings to be taken out of the old people's sayings about the time allowed the world from the coming of the train until the day of judgment. The prophecy itself was not clear on the matter. . . .

Let the train come this year, next year, let what will follow, it was all the doing of Carrick town and every town like it; all these changes; blame the rogues and robbers, rascals and thieves, of Carrick for trains and all such changes; Wee Conail scolded. Black Donal was not so sure. He told how he worked for most of a year on the making of a railway near Boston. It was a mortal sin he was not within reach of the glen then. You could take away hammers and crow-bars — anything. If yon railway had been within reach of the glen, the glen could give itself tools of all kinds. If it came to pass that the railway must be built, that would be the glen's chance. Let the glen have that much satisfaction . . . But Wee Conail could not agree to that. No use thinking to steal tools. If any robbing could be done, the town would do it. Glenmore would get little. Ho, ho, the towns . . . Briany thought Wee Conail misjudged the town. The country would do poorly but for the town. Where did the country get oil, and buttons and thread only for the town. It was all very well to belittle the town, but the town was always making changes. Now take Boston. . . .

'To hell with Boston!' Wee Conail exploded. 'What did you ever get out of it beyond a dickey? If the women that's spent a while in Boston had only your sense and came back wearing hats and kept on wearing hats, where would the glen be . . . ?'

'What harm would it be, a woman to keep on wearing a hat?' Brigid challenged, sheltering Briany. 'If a woman thought well to wear a hat, what harm? Take care would it be like it was on the island when a woman came into it wear-ing a hat. She was a Carrick woman. The man she married was a good man too, but nothing was right with his people either unless it was like what went on always. If it caused talk it was wrong; there are plenty men like that. Anyway he married the girl and on the Sunday she got ready for Mass. She came down from the room wearing a hat. His people, his mother, and his sister — the father never said a word — they got angry. This would be a thing for laughter. The whole world would laugh at him. She must be like the next and wear a shawl. Well, she wore the shawl. She walked up the street of Carrick village before her own people wearing it, and she kept her head stooped and, after Mass, she went back to the island without a word. The next morning she was afoot early and it was winter and it was a while before she was missed, and then it was seen a boat was gone. Another put out. They got news. By the mercy of God the tide favoured her, and the wind, and she got to the mainland and she was seen crossing a field. That was all the news ever. That was the last seen of her. I mind people laughing at him, making fun of him.' They argued the case seriously, blaming her mostly. What did a woman want with a hat, anyway. . . .

'A good riddance, that woman,' Wee Conail judged. 'Tell me, are we going to fix on a price for this year's burnings, and is every man going to stand by it and not be like last year, one cutting the other's throat . . . ?'

II

THERE was traffic of men, children and youths, from mid and lower glen to the quarries for the raising, napping and burning of lime. There was a growing bustle as the kilns were loaded up and made ready to fire, all building up towards a somewhat ceremonial day when the midday meal was cooked in the quarries, to be followed by the lighting of all the kilns. Upper glen women had little part in the throng life around the open fires on that day, for their men fed in their homes. Some mid glen men went to their homes too, so that lower glen made it their day and they elected to show noisy scorn of upper glen life, mocking the men, taunting women; noisy, joyous, rough spoken. Upper glen women considered themselves just a little more refined but, for all that, when lower glen women finished their day's chore and scattered out among upper glen houses, they were welcomed, and indeed matched, in banter and abuse.

'I'm wondering Kitty is not on the trot down to mid glen, Brigid,' Mary joked, pausing in the door-way. 'If you met her on her way she would have a story as long as the day and the morrow why she had to make the journey. Every year it is so; not, mind you, that I greatly blame her, for lower glen women get more and more shameless. They sit that long you have to make them a second tea often. Kitty takes care they do not plant themselves on her.' Mary interrupted herself, and, with her finger to her lips in warning, she went to her corner. Kitty rid her throat noisily as she approached. She paused in the door-way and spoke her blessing and Mary blessed her back. Kitty took the chair Brigid set in place for her. She poked herself a pinch of snuff from Mary's snuff box, speaking leisurely of the great gathering of lower glen people at the quarries that year. 'I hear they are thinking of crowding into this woman,' she confided to Mary, jerking her head towards Brigid. Mary straightened slowly on her creepy. Kitty turned to Brigid. 'Mary always made this day a day of oat-cake only, like turf-cutting day is the day for currant bread. They were arguing among themselves would that be how it will be the day.' She glanced from Brigid to Mary. She brushed a trace of snuff from her blouse. 'I mind when nothing would do Briany but he must have the ould teacher over to us every Sunday throughout the summer, for his tea. "What is it," says he, "but an extra drop of water in the tea-pot." But yon old fellow had to have an egg, and, when a stranger has an egg, everybody has to be a stranger and have an egg. Three eggs every Sunday. I put a stop to it. And if upper glen had any of me in it, lower glen would not have a holiday for itself out of our sugar-bowls and tea-caddies every year.' Her sharp face felt the air around it, the nose twitching and sniffing on the doorstep. Brigid and Mary stood well back from the door and watched her cross the green. 'I have to laugh when I hear her coughing and ridding her throat when she knows you see her coming . . .' Brigid laughed. 'She has the right sense of this business of lower glen women setting on people, plucking and eating like crows on a field of stooks,' Mary said sharply. She put her hands on her hips; an attitude so strange, Brigid turned to her in wonder. 'You could not be expected to know they were going to swarm into this house. You go over to Peggy and leave them to me.' Brigid laughed. 'I will give them nips of the oat-cake and bowls of tea in their hands and as much saucy chat as they want. You go to Peggy yourself Mary.' Mary's protective arm crept up to her breast. She laughed easily. 'I have to take Peggy a sup of buttermilk anyway.'

Brigid chanced to be coming out of the byre when the

clustered lower glen women came through the gap. She smiled her welcome. 'We will come in,' a woman announced, 'and we want to go in to you, if you will give in not to bother making tea for such a shameless congregation of us. I'm Big Mary Donal Brian.' She was almost as burly as Peggy, a youngish, red-faced, gawky woman. 'As far as a cake of oat-meal goes, if it is only a nip a piece,' Brigid greeted, 'you are welcome.' She shook hands with them. 'To tell the truth, I heard you were coming and I was half scared. . . .'

'Ho, ho, upper glen for you for ever, with its mockery and its short laughs,' Big Mary Donal Brian scorned. They found what seats they could, using two flat sods of turf where nothing else offered and thronged the floor. 'We heard that much about you we wanted you to ourselves. They spread talk enough about you when you came; a heathen woman with no belief in anything but God. That was what we heard.' 'The devil is in you all, tell me what stories they put out.' Big Mary gave the recital and she made a good fist of it. They drank their tea and they were light-hearted and friendly. 'We of lower glen said, when you came here first, it was God's charity, you to come into this end of the glen and make little of some of them,' she ended. She raised her hand. 'Not mind but we would be as bad to come in among. God knows a woman came among us . . .' A screech, so sharp and piercing, that it brought them all to their feet, arose outside. Brigid recognized it as Ann's voice. She was first out the door. Youths of lower glen having come on Ann the Hill in a patch of whins, made a noisy attack on her with clods and shouts. Finding themselves with an audience, and mocked-at by children of upper glen for holding back, the youths pressed their attack. Ann held her ground, leaping stiff-legged and screeching her screech that was like a hare in a snare which she had found hitherto an adequate defence. At that moment, Susan, for some lumpy reason of her own, chose to shout encouragement and the throng of women joined her, clapping their hands, hooting and laughing. Ann was moved to greater violence than she had ever manifested before. She was never known to wield a weapon, but she had one now, an old reaping hook. It suited the mood of youths and visiting women, Susan and all, to let on to panic — in part the panic was real — and fly before her. Andy hurried over from the quarry and she turned in anger on him. He took the reaping hook from her and she kicked and shouted as he carried her home.

'Now you see it for yourselves,' Susan shouted. 'Like some others, maybe you thought we had a down on her. She should be put away.' Lower glen women agreed she should be put away. They would not sleep in the same end of the glen with her. Ann's screeches were not of this world. They knew Ann's story . . . Somebody noticed Brigid sitting apart, weeping quietly. They turned to her. Some flung themselves down on the grass by her. Susan stood in their midst, calling on them to add their voices to hers and make Brigid agree Ann should be put away. 'Andy's one cry all the time is, he promised his mother Ann would have a roof overhead while he lived. Let her have a roof; there is a roof on the Big House. . . .'

Brigid spoke quietly. There was a simple body like Ann on the island; a man. She often saw the whole island in flight before him, when something or somebody roused him. There was no talk ever of putting him away, only anger at whoever upset him. 'Will you listen to her'? Susan appealed, but the lower glen women were silent. Big Mary spoke angrily to her boy, and ordered him home, and the others shouted at their sons and ordered them home.

Ann made her appearance next day again, but this time there was no regalia beyond the safety-pins and she circled round Susan, who was spreading out a washing, and she raised her voice and she was overheard and she taunted Susan that the ground under her feet did not belong to her, and that Dan Rua used other ground which did not belong to him, and that Dan Rua stole their cart-way and made a ridge of it. Andy came for her and took her home, but the harm was done and nobody could catch up with it. Ann appeared on other casans and she spoke and everywhere there were those who were hurt and those who whispered and laughed. Peggy sent word for Brigid and Brigid went to her and on her way she met Sorcha and she brought Sorcha with her. 'You will have to go to Andy, Brigid,' Peggy urged. 'Let you go to Andy and say to Andy to put her away. And it is no more than what you should do, to go to Andy, for if Ann is abroad it is your doing, and murder will come of it.' But Brigid pleaded that the glen had a right to have sense, that Ann's talk was of things that had been done; footy things that need cause no noise among neighbours. If people feared Ann it was because of things they did. What harm is it if Ann casts up at people what they know they did and the whole glen knows they did. . . .'

'You have been listening to Briany,' Peggy scolded, 'Briany tells of people that roared out their own sins in Boston. Is not that what you are saying, only we are to let Ann do the roaring for us? It is easy for you, that is new to come among us, for no word out of Ann's mouth can touch you.' But Brigid would not have it so. Some of the things Ann said touched her closely, she pleaded with mock seriousness, and Peggy drove her forth and Sorcha with her and now Sorcha took Brigid's side. 'Then, for heaven's sake,' Peggy taunted, 'this is what you will do. Go out to the priest, the two of you, and tell him to come into the glen to hold a station only let the whole glen go on its knees round him and leave it to Ann to make all our confession. And when that is done let the priest serve out the flails of the townland to the men and let them do like the Fianna Saint Patrick saw in hell are at, let them wreck, murder all round them with the flails till the gads break. . . .'

Tom came in out of the field in the throng of his work. He was worried. Dan Rua would get drunk on the first day of the lime carts. It was a thing men did on the first day, but if anything was on Dan Rua's mind when he got drunk it came out in him then, and he could be a wild man in drink. And there was a thing on his mind; that ridge of ground, Andy the Hill's cart-way that he delved into his own land. He would not give back the piece of ground. It was not in his nature to give back a spadeful of ground, for there was a wild hunger for land in Dan Rua. He just could not help himself, but must shave every mearn. Tom sat straddle-legged on the chair. 'I had a mind to go to Andy, Brigid, and say to Andy maybe he should put Ann away.' Brigid, leaning against the table, wept quietly. 'I did her harm, Tom, when I wanted to do her good. I would not be said by Mary, and, because of me, she has to be put in a cage.' She dried her eyes. 'And it is not right, Tom. This glen will do no good to itself if it puts Ann away, for one will whisper to the other what Ann said and some day, when there is anger, one will shout it at the other.' He pushed the chair away from him. 'Ann's talk will be like the ram's face so, it will go on for ever.' He smiled at her, lit his pipe, and went out.

The carts left the glen in a noisy procession and the children and the women cheered them on their way, and then as if it had been a thing agreed on among them, the women gathered round Brigid and Sorcha spoke for them. 'Here is a thing that is in all our minds, Brigid. When your child comes, will you have any fear of Ann's eye for him?' Brigid shook her head. 'Is it that you have no knowledge of the evil eye?' Sorcha probed. And Brigid told them that the island knew of such a thing but it was like they knew of a story, and she had no fear of it and she would not mind if every woman of them all turned it on her; she would but laugh. She could not tell them why her mind should be so unlike theirs, unless it was because the glen was unlike the island in some ways. 'I wish we knew better what to say to one another,' she lamented. 'I had little liking for this glen, until Ann the Hill began telling me what people did to one another, and then I got to like it.' They stormed at her for this was the first time she told them that Ann the Hill emptied her mind out to her, in their talks together. 'It will be God help us all, if your tongue should ever break loose so,' Sorcha laughed. 'Let Ann the Hill go to hell anyway, now that we have a day to ourselves to stretch and yawn. I hope when the men of the glen come back drunk, as every single man of them will, that Tom Manus is the drunkest man of them all. We want to pick talk out of him.'

And when they were alone, Mary told Brigid it was friendly of Sorcha to say she hoped Tom would come back drunk. Men had a few days for drink and one of them was the first day of the lime season. There was a time, long ago, when on that first night of the lime carts, there would be fighting as well as drink. The two ends of the glen used to fight. She herself had a hand in putting an end to it. It was the year Manus died and two men began to fight by the gable out there, and they were two fine men and she got angry at the waste it was, two fine men doing harm to one another, and she took a bucket of water and she dashed them in the face with it, and while you could cough, every woman that could get a bucket was sousing them with water and the next year the women of the glen gathered at the quarry and they all had buckets, and the buckets were full of water, and somehow the men had word of it, for they leaped off the carts and they swept down on the women and every man took a bucket and he emptied it on the nearest woman to him, and there was never such a night in this glen, and, from that day forth, there was no fighting. She found her pipe. 'Some say maybe it was a mistake, that it does men no harm to fight when it's a thing they are celebrating and showing off.' She spoke lightly. 'I always heard it said that there was no harm in drink for a man if he took to it, once in a while, when he was happy. God help the poor man that pours it on his sorrow.' Later Peggy had a word to say. She looked forward to the noise, and the fun, and the squealing. 'In my bed last night I was giving you a going over in my mind; scolding you in dread that you would be a sour woman for a man to come home to, drunk.' She offered Brigid her snuff box.

'The first day her man comes back to her drunk·is a day a woman always bears in mind, Brigid. Some people wonder will Tom be himself, will he come back like he always did, with drink in him or will he be so afraid of your ear-rings and your airs that he will come back sober; why would not they talk like that when I lay awake saying the very thing to myself? The glen keeps an eye on a man when he is drunk and tries to pick talk out of him. When Briany gets drunk he calls Kitty Mrs. Conaghan; Briany is a bitter man, Brigid. Briany cannot bear to go to bed to Kitty when he is drunk, and somebody has to watch him or he would sneak away somewhere and go to sleep outside. The glen would like its laugh at you and Tom, be it something Tom will say in his drink, or just that he denies himself and stays sober; a body has to wait. Say a prayer he will bide by his own nature and drink his fill.' 'Tom will be himself and he will come home as is natural to him,' Brigid said sharply.

The carts trekked back, and Brigid was among the throng that gathered on the quarry floor when the word came that they were in sight and she found Peggy's eye on her and she made a face at Peggy. Tom was the second cart in the convoy. He got down quickly and went to the cart following him to help Black Donal, and they jostled their way through the throng linked together stumbling and cheering and Peggy went in between them and linked them both. Brigid watched them go through the gap. A gust of people were on their heels and she was within it. Black Donal fell and Tom dragged him to his feet, and Black Donal, freeing a hand, waved his cap and cheered and Peggy cheered and Tom cheered. 'Tom's drunk,' Black Donal proclaimed, 'Tom Manus is drunk.' He called for cheers for Tom Manus. He must put Tom Manus into bed, before he would set out for home. Tom suddenly lost the power of his legs and Brigid had to help Peggy oxter him over the field and she helped Black Donal and Peggy take off Tom's boots and pile him into Mary's bed, and when that was done Peggy and Black Donal went on their way and Mary went with them, and she advised Brigid to bolt the door after her.

'Is he gone?' Tom pushed the curtain aside and grinned at her and Brigid stared at him startled. Tom swung his legs out of the bed. 'Nothing will do Black Donal every year but get it into his head that he has to put me to bed.' Brigid came forward slowly. 'Do you mean to tell me, Tom . . .' She came closer to him. 'Do you mean to say you're not drunk?' He caught her hand and drew her beside him on the bed. She freed herself angrily. 'Am I never going to get any understanding of this glen? I watched you cross the fields and I thought you did not even know I was in the world.' People going by called Tom's name. They got into noisy arguments on the street. Brigid turned down the lamp light. Tom took a chair by the fire. 'What kind of a journey had you?' Brigid asked dryly. 'I travelled with Briany, Brigid. Let me tell you it is a great thing to travel the roads with Briany.' His words came slowly. 'This glen misjudges Briany. Let me tell you this, there's no man goes over the road out there as much thought of as Briany. Let me tell you something, Brigid, Briany should be in Parliament.' She went to him quickly now, and put her arms round him, and laughter gurgled in her. 'I declare to my God you are drunk, Tom Manus.' She skipped to the door and flung it open to the squal of women demanding to be let in. 'He wants to make a member of parliament of Briany,' she proclaimed gesturing towards her man struggling to his feet by the fire.

12

THERE was a good gathering of men at Tom's on Sunday evening to go over their experiences on the roads of the townlands; Sean Mor considered it the most important 'discourse' of the year. There was first of all the market for lime itself. The men found it good, and in that they found cause for wonder. What was it gave townlands, with no clear way of earning money, the heart to white-wash and make changes that cost money? The new sharpness in the price of cattle was not a good enough answer. It was not money from America, for the townlands outside were no better off than the glen in that, and yet some of the townlands put Wee Conail in mind of the airs men gave themselves in the town of Carrick. There had to be some other sense in things, else men he named would never give in to the changes he saw in houses and byres. He could see no hidden things beyond the earnings brought home from Scotland, for therein alone the parishes outside differed from the glen. The men went to Scotland and they came back. They must bring money, a fair fistful of money. That must be the meaning in things. Households were mentioned, families known to the glen for years and years, friendly households, and gradually news of births, deaths, marriages, were added, kindling into stories until the discourse crumbled into gossip and stories. Towards bedtime they were back to their speculation on Scotland, and next day Susan came to Brigid and Mary, uneasy over Wee Conail's hints that it might be a good thing, glen men to take the roads with the men outside and see what would come of a season in Scotland. She was afraid that Dan Rua might heed Wee Conail, for Dan Rua was not a man to keep teasing a thing in his mind. If any two men left the glen they would be Dan Rua and Tom. Brigid made light of it. Men went out from the island and they came back. There were some who took to a wandering life, men of idle ways, or a daftness. But why should Tom go, or for that part Dan Rua? There was no hardship to send Tom away. Tom had no talk of it.

Wee Conail came in to light his pipe and Brigid joked him about it. He told her it was his wish to go to Boston. If Nelly would give in he would cut his stick for Boston in the morning, and put in four or five years there, and gather money to bear the burden of his young family. He sat and when Mary came in he let her in on what he had in mind. 'You will stay where you are, Wee Conail, if you listen to me. Your growing family is on your heels. Turn them on to your own land. That is all land needs, the strong hands of a growing family; many hands make strong hands quick. Let me tell you, Wee Conail, when Manus left me, his land was in a fine healthy state and the health in that land was what stood to me at first. When the land began to lose heart in my weak hands I began to lose heart with it. I could see the mountain making a face at me, raising its ugly features within my fields. I used to pray for more strength to hold my own against it, and one day I mind I wept. Then before I knew what was happening the children were alongside me, and they went past me and they beat the image of the mountain out of their land. You're now in your worst days, Wee Conail, when your family is all eat, and tear and wear. But, look behind you, Wee Conail, and thank God for what you see, hurrying up to help you.' When Wee Conail went on his way Nelly hurried in and Brigid gave her the news of what he had in mind. She carried the story to Susan, and they brought it to other women. Brigid brought them and their talk back to Mary. Mary, thinking back and naming men, told of such as did like Wee Conail said. It would not be her mind to let men loose like that. They would murder themselves working and saving, maybe, neglecting their food and their clothes and come back skin and bones. If a man had a mind to turn his back on his land it must be he was unhappy. That was a poor way to leave home. Let people be rich, let them be poor only let them be together with their children. That was how it should be. Take care was Nelly herself at fault. Mary's talk started a storm, for Brigid said with her. It was true enough, Brigid argued that the glen was a friendly place, so far as one family and the next family were concerned, but what about within the families; Eilis and Nelly; Nappy and Susan; Sorcha and Ouida? Take even Black Donal and Peggy. Black Donal would like young Donal and his wife to come in there but Peggy had no wish to have young Donal and his wife with her. How could people be settled if they were at odds by their firesides? 'Young Donal made poor picking,' Mary argued. 'Well! Under God, Mary Manus, you above all women who had to put up with a pick you had no say in yourself.' Mary shook her head. 'Tom was a sober man, Brigid, and Tom was a conceited man. From the first day ever Tom had a conceit in him for himself. . . .'

Peggy descended on Brigid. 'Listen here to me, you clip,' she stormed. 'I hear you found fault with me over young Donal. Tell me one thing. Did Black Donal talk to you or how did you come to know he had a wish that young Donal should come to him?' 'I like Black Donal, Peggy. Maybe the thought was of my own making.' Peggy, sighing, offered Brigid her snuff box. 'I had my reasons, Brigid. I have my heart set in Hugh coming back, the harum-scarum of my family. Donal is the good boy, but when Donal married a girl across the mountain with a place of her own, even it was a poor place, I thought to get Hugh back. If Hugh came back to me and he married a tinker woman out of a ditch I would put my hair under her feet if she was good to him.' 'God bless us, Peggy, God bless us, a body should never talk.'

And Mary and Peggy and Brigid went over the talk and

the rumours together. Brigid found fault with Dan Rua for the way he put on his cap and walked out when words arose between Nappy and Susan. She walked abroad and spoke freely, blaming the men for how things were between the old and the young and, on a day when they washed clothes together on a flag by the stream, half the women of the glen went over such things with her. Sorcha argued that no blame rested on her man anyway. Brigid thought Sorcha should bring the case of Eilis to the doctor. It looked like something a doctor would have a cure for. Sorcha shook her dripping arms. 'I heard of many cures, from the smothering of live cocks in a hole in the ground to help a woman in labour, to thorns as the cure of warts, but I never heard of any cure for bone laziness. If there is such a cure, who has it?' Brigid wiped her arms in her apron. 'If I were in your place, Sorcha, I would send for the doctor,' she said stubbornly. The other women drew together. 'What kind of talk are you at,' Sorcha demanded, 'or what doctor?' 'The man in Carrick,' Brigid said. Their puzzled looks puzzled, even bewildered her. 'What kind of carry-on is this?' she demanded, 'that you make a wonder of talk about the doctor. You know him?' 'I saw him twice on fair days going by in his gig,' Sorcha said grimly. 'Then what doctor comes in here?' Brigid asked sharply. Sorcha seated herself on the warm flag and the others dropped down beside her until only Brigid was standing. 'Do you mean to tell me the doctor was never in this glen?' They shook their heads. 'No doctor ever?' They shook their heads. Brigid sank on her knees in the grass. 'What under God brought me here? Why did Tom Manus have to live in a glen that is back at the beginning of the world?' She rose quickly. 'Why does any woman have to live in such a glen? Let me tell you,' she stormed, 'you have come to the end of that story for I will have a doctor.' 'No Brigid,' Sorcha said sharply, 'no Brigid.' She rose and the others rose with her and they closed in around Brigid and they told her not to let such a thought into her mind. She could put her trust in Mary.

Mary might not be a woman they had a great liking for — they thought her hard — but she was a good woman, and she was a lucky woman and nothing ever frightened her. They chorused their praise of Mary until Brigid raised her hand against their clamour. She would have the doctor. 'Then if that is your mind, Brigid, here is my advice,' Nelly said, 'betake yourself to the island in good time, for no man in this glen will ride out of it for a doctor. Betake yourself to the island, Brigid.' 'But I cannot go back to the island,' Brigid moaned. 'The island says it is not lucky for a woman to go back to her own people for her first child. She may go back for any time after that, but never for her first child.' 'Ho, ho, the island.' They jeered her now. So that was the kind of place she came from, a cute, crafty place. They didn't want a woman back for her first child, because the first child was a woman's greatest danger, and the island did not want to take the risk that she might die and leave her people the burden of rearing it. For no man would want a first child in his way when he began thinking of a second wife. Now they were seeing the island, the crafty, cute, mean island. So after all her talk this was her island. She turned from them wearily. They were sorry for her. Her case was worse even than their own. She would not have her way with Mary, and the island would not change its ways for her.

They argued among themselves and they grew short-tempered. Children herding cattle on the inner reaches of the mountain got a glimpse of Ann the Hill in hiding, and they set on her with clods and she broke cover and stood on a high ground above the women and screeched her rage beyond anything they had ever heard before. And Andy came and he scolded the children and they, drawing courage from the women close at hand, jeered back and Andy lost his temper and he chased them and he caught one of the boys who struggled so violently it became almost a fight, and the women shouted and the boy's father came and Andy and he exchanged threats, and they would have to blows only for Black Donal. 'God help the people if this is how it's going to be; if Andy is now going to take a stand alongside Ann, from now on, every time she screeches,' Susan scolded. But when the men got the story sorted out they blamed their children, and here and there a belt was used. They blamed Andy, too, and they blamed themselves, but, say what they would, they could see no way past the trouble but to put some end to this business of Ann herself; unless Ann chose to go back into hiding for a while. But she did not. She raised her voice daily. Brigid tried to speak against the growing storm and Peggy helped her. It was a new thing for the glen, Peggy scorned, that it should let itself be moved into quarrels over children. Whatever else caused trouble between households in the past, the glen had a proper sense of the mischief in children. Andy was wrong to lay hands on a boy, but Andy was a man in great trouble; a civil man so far. The root of it all was, the glen was not itself. There was some bad drop at work in the glen. . . .

This was Mary's view, too; only the bad temper of the glen was not a wonder to her. She often noticed that this was the time of the year when men lost their tempers easily; between the end of the spring work and the cutting of the turf. In the spring when the land was at work in them, men were all roar and rattle, and again when it was time to go to the mountains to cut turf they would be all roar and laughter. In the weeks in between their minds were neither on one thing nor the other, and she often noticed it was the most time they lost their tempers. The turf-cutting was at hand. The turf-cutting would bring peace. . . .

Tom fixed his day for turf-cutting and he got a team together and Mary and Brigid made ready to feed them. They would breakfast in the glen, but at such an early hour that a second breakfast would have to be made for them on the bog. Their dinner, too, would be cooked on the bog, and later on in the day they would get tea again. At night they would come back for their supper. Mary had memories. Turf-cutting day was changing. She remembered when men would think it a shame not to have their coats off on the turf bank by the time the sun rose. At that time a woman might find it was not worth her while to take off her clothes and go to bed, when she had everything ready on the night before turf-cutting day. Many a time she herself stretched out on the hearth. That was the time you got a big day's work done. Sean Mor always came to her, and Black Donal came, powerful men, and they saw that nobody idled. 'Ach,' she sighed. 'Ach.' She leaned towards Brigid. 'Do not let this upset you Brigid. It is maybe your last cross, turf-cutting day. It is the habit here that at her first turf-cutting, after her marriage, a woman has to give a meal to all the women that care to gather round her, and that they make it a special kind of an affair. They do their best to anger her. The year it was Nelly's turn she ran from them, and they chased her and they caught her and they beat her with heather.' 'No, do not tell me, Mary, I have to put up with more of their children's work.' 'It is children's work, maybe, but it is of a great age and it is only fun. It is a kind of a court the women hold, and one woman is picked to ask questions and two to stand over you with heather besoms and to beat you on the legs, if you boggle at a question, and if you run they will all follow you. They warned me not to tell you but it would not be right.'

Peggy sent word for Brigid, and she told Brigid who was chosen to put the questions to her; Bella, a useless big lump from mid glen, with an arse on her like the end of a rick of hay from idleness; no spirit nor spunk in her but plenty of talk. She had it in for Brigid because of all Sean Mor's boasting about her. A lazy strap, Bella. She had a sister, Winnie, who lived with her and was her donkey. At one time Winnie had a mind to go to Boston and she wrote to her uncle, and her uncle sent her the passage money, but Bella got the letter and Winnie never sniffed it, and Winnie left it at that for she could see her sister's children would need her. If Winnie came Brigid's way she would know her, because one eyelid was like a broken wing the way it fluttered and fell. 'What made me send for you, Brigid, is to tell you things you can throw back at Bella. You can say this. . . .'

Brigid had a word with Briany and she asked him about the court of the women on the turf-cutting day and what he knew of it. But Briany knew little of it; men knew little of it. The women gathered on a height, so they could have a view of the ground around them. Always boys watched and wanted to overhear talk, and one year a youth crept up a gully and the women let on not to see him until he got close, and they made a rush at him and they caught him and they stripped him naked and they beat him. To the best of his knowledge the court of the women was a kind of a game. It began long ago and the story was that a man married a woman from the far end of the parish, and that it turned out that she was with child already, and his mother left it until the day of the turf-cutting to cast it up at her, when she was out on the mountain. All the women had word and they came and they made her tell her story, and there never was any more sight or light of her. Some said she ran away. Some said another thing. The court of the women had its beginning that day. It was a game like Hallow Eve, and, like every game in the glen ever, its aim was to make some-body angry. A game was no game unless it angered some-body. On Hallow Eve the children picked on some one house and they kept at it, to see could they make you mad. For the last two years they picked on himself. He tucked his dickey into place. 'I often wonder why you wear it, Briany.' 'To spite myself, Brigid. I never forgave myself for coming back from Boston. It was my two brothers did it. I went round with a pack selling things and they said to me "you go Briany and when she dies sell the place and that will make it up to you". So I came, and I had a mind to sell the place, for we were a family that never took to land; our father was a cobbler mostly. When I came back I took to drink, and after I married Kitty I kept on the dickey so that she might be uneasy that any morning I might be missing; it was her mother's doing that I married at all. It was not that Kitty was not far too good for me, but in my own senses and of my own will I had a mind to marry nobody. It is not, mind you Brigid, but I am as well off in the glen as in Boston.' He laughed. 'I made no money going around with the pack, for all I wanted to do was talk to people. I saw me tangling in talk in a house, and the end of it would be we would sell things out of my pack to buy us all a meal. I met some grand people.' They were both silent for a while. 'I thought one time I would put up a stall at the chapel gate out here, during the missions, and sell things. I never did. Maybe I would not stay at all, only people came to me to make the cure of the rose, and that brought me here and there; like in Boston.' He fondled the bowl of his pipe with his palms. 'Then I began to notice the glen, and to laugh to myself and make ballads; if you want me to have everything in them tell me about the court of the women.'

'Every last word, Briany.' She promised. She turned on her heel, back to him. 'Tell me, Briany, was there a hen on the roof that day?' He grinned at her. 'The hole she made for herself by the chimney was there, and I had to put a patch of thatch on it some day so I chose that day. It was not all a lie.'

Tom's team gathered early, and Mary sent the needs of the day with them in creels and Brigid herself put such other things as she needed into a creel for herself to carry later. It was a day of light breeze and brightness within a spell of good weather, and the ground was dry. Ann the Hill waited for Brigid at the edge of the mountain and they sat together on the heather and Brigid gave Ann slices of the turf-cutting bread. Children raced by, and Ann crouched low and gurned angrily, and she walked with Brigid until the men were within sight. There were many fires on the mountain. Brigid's fire was already lit. The men greeted her noisily, letting on to be hungry. It was the first time she saw Briany without his dickey. She made the second breakfast and the men fed hurriedly and smoked leisurely, arguing over rival claims to the greatest feat of turf-cutting by any one spade in the glen's annals. They spoke seriously and no one made a mock of the other, and Briany and Wee Conail were as much at their ease together as the others. All the time she worked by the fire Brigid was attentive to their gay voices. She made the midday meal, when the time came, and they praised her for it and sprawled on the heather afterwards and smoked.

The time was now come for Brigid to make ready for the women so she prepared the meal and the time ticked on and there was still no sign of them and she began to hope. They came round a turf bank in a body, in their Sunday aprons and Sunday skirts and blouses, and Brigid was suddenly nervous. She waited for them to seat themselves. None of them stirred to help her hand round things. She took her time, and they laughed loudly at jokes that were obscure to her. She served them in silence. 'Would you fill this for me again?' Bella spoke sharply. A rustle of expectation stirred the cluster of women. Bella got on one knee to raise herself above the others as Brigid came to her. 'Well, God knows, you're a brave woman, island woman, to show yourself to us without a bother on you, in your shameless appearance.' Brigid poured the tea and returned to the fire and a jabber of bawdy talk assailed her, and she started up. 'You should get new words,' she said sharply, 'because this is only going over what I heard before, oh ye woman of one tune.' 'That'll do you,' Bella shouted, 'you are to humble yourself, and say what is asked of you.' Brigid seated herself. 'What have you to say for yourself?' And the others asked her what she had to say for herself. 'Let you give in, and no lies about it, many a roll you had in the mouth of a haystack before Tom Manus got as far as you.' Brigid sat erect her hands in her lap. 'And let me tell you,' she mocked, 'you have to put up a good wrestle in the mouth of a haystack on the island, if you are to hold your own, for it is the men do the courting and the picking on the island; not their mothers.' They roared at her and the two women by her got to their feet and raised their heather besoms. 'You made little wrestle with Tom Manus and for good reason,' Bella charged. 'I made no wrestle at all,' Brigid confided. 'Well damn his blood,'

Susan stormed, 'he went through this glen like a cart, and many a one would be glad to give in without much of a wrestle.' Bella signalled Susan to be quiet. 'Tell me island woman, is this his doing? Did you set a trap for him?' Brigid leaned forward. 'This is how it was.' She confided. 'He said to me "will you marry me" and I said I would and he said "hold out your hand", and I held out my hand and he slapped it and said "sold". It was all the same for him by that time, for I had made up my mind to marry him.' She sat back, solemn faced, mocking. 'She's foxing,' Bella cried, 'she's foxing. That is not how it was. You set yourself out to trap him.'

'Don't I tell you, I had no need, and if I had need to put myself in his way I would put myself in his way, and is not that enough for you? And what is wrong with you all anyway, with your children's games? It's no wonder, God knows the men never bother to bring you a doctor.' 'Stop foxing,' Bella shouted, 'stop your foxing.' But Sorcha was on her knees now. 'Let her fox so that she tells us about this, for this is what we want to hear. Did Tom say he would?' ·'Let all such talk wait,' Bella ordered, 'she is foxing her way past us, and if you let her get by us it will be the end of the court of the women.'

'Let it be the end of anything, so that it be the beginning of this,' Sorcha gave back, 'for this thing has a meaning and we want to know of it. Did Tom give in he would go for the doctor?' Brigid was silent for a moment. She waited until the angry hush of the others forced Bella to silence. 'I said it to Tom and he laughed.' They stirred uneasily. 'He laughed. Says he to me, "I wondered when you would talk of this. Your mother made me promise her, I would go for the Carrick doctor".' Bella hooted her scorn but the others cried out against her and they got silence. 'If Tom said that to her she can depend on it,' Susan declared. 'She's foxing you,' Bella scolded, 'foxing you she is.' She tried to gain control of the proceedings but the others shouted her down. 'I lost a child,' Sorcha said. ('And I' 'and I'). They laid their bowls aside and they crept closer to Brigid. 'If only we could believe, Brigid, that this could happen to us,' Sorcha worried. 'To tell nothing but the truth I'm scared after what happened to me the last time.' Bella got to her feet. 'I wash my hands of you. Good luck to her for foxing you.' They watched her go. 'Tell us Brigid, what makes you think he would come to a place like this? Would people have to white-wash and make ready for him like the priest was coming to a station, would there be all that cost?' And Brigid told them of his simple ways, and how he came to the island through storms. Bella shouted her last challenge from the top of the hillock but they did not even turn to look her way. They helped Brigid wash up, and they would have taken a share of the burden of the things she carried to the mountains, only that the men had a spare creel. Sorcha spoke all their minds as they left. 'We have our hearts in this thing, Brigid, and if it comes to pass through you, you will have our prayers. But you will never have other than the sharp end of our tongues and the harsh thought, if it turns out that Bella was right.' Brigid made a face at them, 'You made a poor fist of your morning's work,' she bantered. 'The island has a better day. The women boat themselves out to dangerous rocks on a day in the year, and they gather dilsk and then they withdraw to high flags, and they make themselves a meal, and they go over things of concern to themselves. I know because we sneaked up on them.' And now they shouted for Bella and they told her come back and teach this woman a lesson, but Bella was gone and Brigid turned to the odd jobs still awaiting her, and she sang at her work.

There was still a bright heel of an evening when Brigid, on her way home, let go of Ann the Hill's hand within speaking distance of Mary who was herding the two cows on the grassy selvedge to a patch of oats. As soon as Mary caught sight of her she beckoned her, and Brigid knew that news of what had passed on the mountain had reached Mary. There was no sign of any other woman around the open doors, except Nappy on an upturned creel at her own gable. Mary sauntered to meet Brigid and awaited her in the middle of the field holding up her knitting as if she had delayed to count the stitches. 'They have their eyes on the two of us.' She laughed quietly. 'Since they got back, Bella is at them, bleating that you took a hand at them. They're not sure should they be angry with her, or with you, or with themselves.' 'I ought to have told you first.' Brigid sank down on the dry grass and Mary found a seat near her and took out her snuff box. 'I had it in mind to say to you, and I kept saying to myself, it would be time enough tomorrow.' Mary offered her snuff box and Brigid poked out a pinch. 'Are you doing all this, Mary, to make out it was no news to you?' Mary took a long, leisurely pinch. 'Bella got no satisfaction out of me. I saw her coming and I knew there was some scud in her heels. "So you're not good enough for her, not that that is any wonder, for your house was not good enough for her, or do you know about him at all?" "I suppose I do not know about him, what would I know about him unless maybe you would tell me who he is?" "The doctor," says she, sticking her head forward at my face. "Oh him," says I, "I hear great praise of him." "And are you going to give in to her, to put that cost on Tom, and to make little of yourself at the same time?" "Many a time, Bella," says I to her, "in the past twenty years ever since my mother told me I was the best fitted to take care of women in her place, I wished for a wiser pair of hands than my own, and many a time, when something went wrong, I lay awake and I used to cry out of pity for us all."' Brigid looked up quickly. 'It's true, Brigid, every word of it is true.' She took up her knitting. 'I think you best keep an eye on the cows here, and I'll make an errand in home, for if you go in now they will be after you, and you would have to make tea, and you had a long day and they got their share. Let them come to you here.' She sauntered on her way and Nappy waddled out from the haggard to cross her path. Susan peeped out from the corner of the gable, and when the way was clear she ran to Brigid, and Nelly came and women of mid glen who delayed with

Sorcha to see what would come of this meeting, hurried up, too, and they all sat on the dry ledge of the ditch and Brigid told them her story. 'There is a power of enlightened understanding in that woman,' Brigid said earnestly. Peggy hailed them and Susan called one of her children to take Brigid's place with the cows, and Brigid went with them to Peggy. 'What under God do you want to make of me?' Peggy scolded as they came up to her, 'when you keep me dancing on my toes here, watching you with your heads together talking, like ducks, and Mary off over the green by herself like she was a banner at the head of a Saint Patrick's Day procession. Am I a stick or a stone, or some kind of an enemy?' Sorcha told her what was to do, beginning with her story of the mountain, and ending it where Mary gave in to Brigid that the doctor would be sent for, and Peggy blessed herself when the story was told. 'So this is what it's coming to now. We will make this townland the laughing-stock of the glens. There was a woman out there by the chapel, a gentle woman, God bless the mark, because she was a hired servant to the bishop's brother. Well, when the doctor gave out that he would hold a kind of a station three miles away, every month or two, so she walked every step of the way there and she walked every step of the way back with the bottle he gave her in her hand, and she told everybody where she was and there's not a woman along that road but put her tongue to the bottle to taste it, and she never let the doctor's station pass her but she made the journey. When she got home she emptied the bottle into a drain, for not a thing had she in mind but to give herself airs. Now we are to have the like of her.' 'Peggy Manus, if you make a mock of this,' Sorcha stormed, 'you will be a blister on all our hearts. For the one bother will be on all of our minds, from now on, will be to make ourselves believe that this man will come in here.'

'Why, under heaven, is it on me it should fall to say the word of sense any one of you, young women, could say'? Peggy upbraided. 'Do not you know fine what this is? A notion Brigid got, like a woman often gets, only mostly it is something she would like to eat. I mind me racing across stubbles looking for wild carrots. I would waken up in the dead of night and I could cry there would be such a hunger on me for them. Mary knows, and Mary is wise, and Mary said with Brigid knowing this is such a notion. Well I am not of Mary's mind. I would not like you believing in such a thing, and I knowing it cannot be.' They were all intimidated by Peggy's seriousness; all but Brigid. She smiled at Peggy. 'The way it is Peggy, I picked a good mother for my man.' But she went out the door alone, and left them in a gaggle around Peggy.

13

WHEN it came Black Donal's turn to have the team of turf-cutters for a day, Brigid and Peggy went to the mountain together. Brigid would have taken all the work on herself but Peggy had a wish to make this last trip, to say good-bye to a scene that had many memories for her. Black Donal mocked her. That was her tune every year, he assured Brigid, every turf-cutting day for the last twenty years; every such day was the last trip she would ever make to the mountain. And on their way to the bog when Peggy prophesied that this would be her last year Brigid laughed at her. It was a long slow journey and they had to rest often. A girl went by riding a donkey, the basket of food for her men resting on her knee. 'That's Winnie,' Peggy said, 'sister to Bella's man. Did you get a good look at her? That one eyelid that you saw drooping like it was a broken wing, can fly up and you never saw a thing that makes such a change in a body. A good girl. Bella did her a great wrong. She is Bella's donkey, but she is willing to stay and rear the children, for the world knows it is not Bella rears them.' They got to their feet and Peggy hoisted the creel on to Brigid's back. 'If ever you think to get Andy the Hill a wife — and if Andy ever has the chance or the mind to marry a wife it will be your own fault if she is not your choice — keep Winnie in mind; unless you think to take in a girl of your own people from the island.' Brigid jerked the creel upwards on her back and turned to face Peggy. 'I do think that a woman would be a great help to him with Ann.' Peggy made a face at her. 'There you go, Ann, Ann, Ann. It would be my hope that if Andy got a wife she would whisper it to him to put Ann away; when the shouts of the glen won't move him a whisper from the bolster might.' 'Ach,' Brigid scoffed. 'Ach.' They trudged on their way in silence. When Peggy cried again for a halt she eased down the creel and they rested on the heather together. 'Not so much of your "ach",' Peggy scolded. 'That's how it is with you always, "ach", "ach". You have to have your own way. The cows had to give in to you, and it is God's own pity one or other of them didn't plant you in the sink with a kick to teach you manners. Andy has a good place. All that's standing in Andy's way is Ann.'

'If Andy gets a wife that has any feeling for him, she will have feeling for Ann. If she has any sense she will never breathe a word to him to put Ann away, for if she should get the best of him on that Andy's mind would always have an ache in it, and that would be a poor thing, a man all the time to have some ache in his mind; or would you pick on Winnie, thinking Winnie would play the cuckoo scaldy on Ann for you, and tumble Ann out of the nest with no thought of Andy?' 'I had Andy in mind when I spoke of Winnie, indeed it is myself had.' She beckoned Brigid closer to her. 'I saw them, Andy and herself. His turf mearns hers and Winnie foots turf, and Andy foots his own. Well, we have a bog there, too, and I was footing and I got lazy and I fell asleep, and woke up, and there they were the two of them. They thought they had the whole world to themselves, and indeed they needed it. I didn't move. I held in the laughing. There I lay, and not one hand's turn did I do till they went, so they would never know I saw them. Somehow it came to my mind afterwards that maybe it was a sin on my soul not to make some sound and I told the priest when I went to confession that year, and I asked him did I do wrong. "Did you hold your tongue," he said. "I did," says I. "It is no harm at all to leave God some of his own business to mind, now and then," says he. That is the thanks I got. He gave me the fifteen decades of the rosary three times for my penance, and it was the least year I had sins to tell. I think

he was laughing at me. He is a strange kind of a man anyway. I mind one time. . . .'

'If Andy was to marry Winnie he would have to burn down
that house he is in and build himself another.' 'Well,
Mother of the Good God,' Peggy roared, heaving herself to
her feet, 'Mother of the Good God, there you go. A body
talks to you and there is understanding in you, and a body
thinks there is sense in you and then all at once the devil
breaks out in you. Burn down his house.' She blessed herself. She lifted the creel on to Brigid's back and lurched on
ahead, her hand thrust back to forbid talk. When the rush
died in her she turned slowly. 'Is it that you think there is
some curse on the house, and that the fire would consume
it?' 'I think there is a disease in the house, when, one after
another, a family die of the decline. There was such a house
on the island and after a while the doctor got to know of it,
and he said to them to burn it down, and they did not and
soon there was nobody in it and nobody ever went into it,
and one bonfire night it was put on fire and I always heard
it was big people did it, because there was talk of a boy and
girl going to marry and live in it. If ever I had any say in the
choice of a wife for Andy it would be after he burnt down
that house.' Peggy made another angry sweep of her arm
and trudged on and when they halted to rest again she
grumbled at the state of her bones and the state of her mind.
'Sometimes, Brigid, I say to myself, I'll keep my mouth
shut and listen to you talk, like I might listen to a child
talk, only the way it is you never start with wild talk.
Promise me you'll not say to anybody Andy to burn down
his house, promise me, and I'll pray to God for Him to help
you to get some hold on yourself.'

'It would not take the men of the glen long to build Andy
a house; and he could easily buy himself the things for the
new house.' 'Ho, ho, more of the story. Andy now is to burn
the house, beds and all. Then he will bring a woman in to lie
down with him on the ashes. Ho, ho; ho, ho. Ask Ann herself to start the fire. Let the two of you go out some night and

start the fire, so we could get the two of you put away and we would have peace.' She helped Brigid take the creel on her back again, and this time she kept lumbering along ahead and she was silent.

The fire was lit and Black Donal was just leaving it when they arrived at the bog. They had work to do and they did it in silence, and when the men had their meal over they sat down together by the fire and drank tea. 'There is one thing, Brigid, that you have to bear in mind. There is talk through the glen that Mary says with you in all things, because she took a liking to you, and that because of that liking you can twist her round your wee finger.' Brigid frowned. 'That is the talk. Black Donal heard it, too, and Black Donal agrees with me that it would be a hardship on you if such a thought got a hold on you. Mary said with you about the doctor; I was wrong about that; I know it was not that she gave in to you but said with you. Mary has not the same belief in herself, now, when she wants above all times to be of help to a woman, for Mary's heart, to be sure, is in Tom's child and that child has to be a boy.' Peggy laughed. 'Mary has you in mind, and it would be a heartbreak to her anything to happen you, and she has Tom in mind, and she has the child that is coming in mind, but more than all that she has the land in mind. Tom has to be on that land and on Tom's heels there has to be a son. Mary is like a man in her feeling for land, for her body and her heart and her strength went into that land. Nobody in this glen knows Mary Manus like I know her, and Mary Manus frightens me; the goodness in her frightens me.' 'She had a hard life, Peggy.' 'She had a saint's life, girl, and a saint's life is not a hard life, for how could it be? It would be hard for you or me. It was heavy on Mary, and it gave a bend to her body, but Mary had God in her all the time.' 'I am fond of Mary,' Brigid said hastily, 'you do me wrong if you won't believe I'm fond of her.' Peggy nodded. Brigid turned slowly. 'Mary made no grumble to you Peggy?' 'Mary made no grumble to me, Brigid. It's just that I would be afraid Susan saying to you

you can do what you like with Mary, and Nelly saying it and
Sorcha and all the rest of them saying it, would maybe give
you notions; you are young.' Peggy sighed. 'There was a
girl in this glen one time that set herself out to get round a
man's mother and she did it and his mother liked her and
made a match for her with her son and that was the woman
that married Hughie who was Black Donal's brother, and
the man I had my heart stuck on only his mother had a down
on me. So she had her way, Hughie married her his mother
picked for him, and Hughie had no more feeling for her than
a donkey, for it was myself he had in mind. Black Donal was
in Boston at that time. Hughie took to drink, and the more
he drank the more the two women came together to scold
him. Within the year he was dead. He fell off the cart on a
night of snow, and he drunk, and he was dead in the morning, the big hailstones like bird's eggs in his mouth. And by
this time there was a daughter. You would think these two
women would turn to one another more and more now, but
that was not how it was. Hughie's mother turned against
this other woman, because no land could last in such weak
hands and she was afraid of a strange man coming in
through the widow and she beat her out of the house and
she sent to Boston for Black Donal, and Black Donal came
and he married me; a good man, a better man than Hughie,
but where I would run to Hughie with a laugh in my heart,
I had to pray to God to make me a good wife to Black Donal.
And God was good to me and I got to like him, and in the
end I got so I did not hate her. Always bear that in mind
Brigid, you and the land, you and Tom and the land must be
going in the one direction, if Mary is to breathe out and in
with you.'

'And what became of the woman Hughie married?' 'Oh,
her. She went to Boston, what else? Her daughter is
married in lower glen.'

'It would not be like that on the island for the island is
used to the sea taking a woman's man from her; and his
mother would not make any noise if another man turned to

her.' 'Ach the island. There's no shape to anything on the island, how could there be, a new cow every other day; land that no more knows what to do with itself, than Briany's dog. Anyway, nobody makes the sea, nor sows it, nor crops it.' She busied herself around the fire. She straightened slowly. 'You blame me about young Donal's wife. Well, a change has come over me; so here I am, this year, to say good-bye to the mountain in earnest, for I am going to tell young Donal to come home and bring her with him.' Brigid murmured praise. 'At the close of the day you will have to let me go aside there, and cry my fill. I will maybe get cause to cry later on, only it's not any fear for what is to come I am crying now. I suppose I have cause to be afraid, for this woman will likely hold it against me that I did not let her in earlier, but so long as she is good to Black Donal I will thole my share. If she slights Black Donal in his food, or in his place by the fire, I will stretch her with the tongs.'

'It would be fun living on the same floor with you Peggy. Young Donal's wife will have to like you.'

'If God lets her Brigid. I earned the rod, for I was a heart-scald to Black Donal's mother for a while. Looking back at it now I think maybe I was out of my mind. Look at me, Brigid, would you ever think I would go over to a row of eggs on the dresser to pick out the smallest egg among them for her, whenever I had to give her an egg? She liked to cook potatoes for herself in the coals — she said that was the only way they did not give her wind — and I stopped her. I said she was destroying my fire, poking out the coals; that, mind you, in this glen that is full of turf. She gave in to me like a child. I knew she was afraid of me, and I knew why she was afraid of me; that I would say she killed Hughie. That is one thing I have to thank God for, I never said that to her. All the time I was praying to make myself a good wife to Black Donal. Black Donal himself was a great help to me in that, for there was a power of life in that man. I think now he always had a liking for me. I got to like his mother, and I cried my eyes out when she died.' They worked together in silence for a while. 'There was great heart in this glen at that time, always great noise and laughter; that was a help. There was sure to be some old body, doting, that people could make fun of, or some simple body, without badness in him, to make angry. Then there was dog-fighting. The Sapper put a stop to that. He was the one man ever to join the soldiers; a great man for drink. The word in this glen before him, when it came out that the new house in lower glen was for him, was that he was above himself with conceit. People were waiting for him to see what fun they could make of him; a conceited man with a strange wife. He had a big dog, a lazy lump of a powerful dog, and the men brought the pick of their dogs one Sunday to belittle the Sapper and his new house by beating his dog. He came out, and wanted to stop the fight but the other dog's people squared up to him and everybody shouted at him, so he quietened himself and he watched for a while. He turned on his heel and back into the house with him and the people all jeered at him and at his dog and they cheered the other dog. The next thing, out with him, the gun in his hand. All of a sudden there was not a sound but the yelp, yelp, of the two dogs in their anger. He raised the gun and he shot his own dog and then the other dog, and nobody's breath could come or go. "It is not the dogs I should shoot," says he, "and it's not the dogs I will shoot the next time I come on the like of this." He stood there and they went away, all of them. Now, the strangest thing was, that instead of getting angry with the Sapper for what he did, all at once everybody said that it was long past time to put a stop to dog-fighting; although, mind you, it was hard on men after their week's work to have no dog-fighting on a Sunday. The men made friends with him. I mind that year. It was the year that the great flood of young people left this glen; it was the first year the Garveys began paying the passage for people who wanted to go to America and this was the most place they trusted. That was how this glen got such a grip on Boston, there is always work waiting for a glen man there. Your children will not be among strangers when they go to Boston, Brigid; or would you rather they went with your people? You are thinking of the woman Hugh married?' Brigid nodded. 'Then let me tell you something. If Tom was to die, which God forbid, what would happen to his farm of land? Would it not founder in your weak hands, fall asunder field by field into a neighbour's grip? Do you think Mary would let the like happen, and she with two sons in Boston·and you young enough to lift your head and look around you for another man? Let me tell you how it would be. Everything you brought in with you you could bring out with you and a fair share of the animals on the land if you had mind for that and Mary would grudge you nothing, and she would cry to see you go and I would cry, but let you try to take root in the corner and Mary would turn on you and I would have to be on Mary's side. Land has to be in strong hands.' Peggy looked around her. 'I came out here Brigid to cry myself, such a load of pity I have for myself, having to stand aside in favour of this other woman. Now I just could cry for everybody. There is a great wrestling match between the world and the people in it, and people are not always much help to one another. You gave me courage to say I would bow before young Donal's woman. It was thinking of you, out and in to me, that gave me the courage, for, like the Sapper put an end to the dogs fighting, maybe you could put an end to old women and young women snapping at one another. For that, above all else, is the great talk of the glen, how does it come about that the strongest minded woman in the whole glen, for that is what Mary Manus is, and the young woman that is most set on her own way, for that is what you are, you young clip, should be able to laugh together. Now, how does that come?. I would like peace in our house.' Brigid had no answer for her.

'Black Donal is not swallowing enough raw eggs lately,' Dan Rua shouted from the turf bank, 'for the roar is dying in him. He has no name in his mind for the new dog to follow Kruger but has to fall back on Oscar, the first dog I ever mind in your house.'

'It was Oscar was in the house when I came and it is a name I like and I'll give Oscar a welcome,' Peggy said eagerly. 'Did I tell you all, that I'm sending word to young Donal and that woman of his to come home?' Black Donal staggered, so quickly did he turn. He grinned at Peggy. 'Now what in the world put Oscar in my mind?'

14

PEOPLE were back from Mass, their dinners over and at their ease, when Peggy shouted to Tom to come over to help Black Donal load her on to the horse, and Dan Rua was at hand and she shouted at him, too, and Tom and he hoisted her up behind Black Donal for her ride over the mountain track to the next glen to ask young Donal and his wife, Grania, to come to live with them. The glen had word of what was afoot. Brigid was already with Peggy, and she would stay and look after things around the house, until Black Donal and Peggy got back. 'I am giving the floor over to you this day, Brigid,' Peggy announced, 'and you can call in the world and have a feast if you like, for this is likely the last time I will ever have the giving of this floor to anybody.' She laid a hand on Black Donal's shoulder. 'I am a fool Black Donal, for all I know we are two old fools.' He thumbed out his pipe. 'It would not be hard for you to slither down off the horse and take off your shawl and go back to your corner,' he said earnestly, but she struck the horse a slap and ordered him on his way, and the neighbours within shout came out to wave to her and pray a blessing on her journey.

Tom and Dan Rua came back in with Brigid, and while she did odd things about the fire they sat and smoked, and they talked of this errand of Black Donal and Peggy, and they agreed it was high time Black Donal got young Donal's help, for already his land was showing signs that it was going back on him. Black Donal was a great man in his day but his day was over. He was a man could not be happy, looking at the heather creeping in on him. It was a right step of his to send for young Donal. They went out together and Brigid, hearing women's voices in banter with them, went to the door. Sorcha and Nelly were making their way to her and, from further back, Susan shouted at them to wait for her. 'I was just saying to myself,' Susan greeted, 'thank God the like of this happened. We will have something to talk about now, if it is only to wonder how long it will take Grania and Peggy to begin a war with one another. Once it begins we will have more and more fun, wondering how every battle is going and what will be next.'

'Peggy is my aunt,' Nelly orated, 'and I would not want to have to put up with her for a week.'

Brigid led the way inside and they found seats for themselves. Nelly touched Sorcha with her elbow. 'If you had a hand in this, it is likely some of Peggy's noise will have your name in it. I would not like to be the one Peggy could lay the blame on for this day's work, when she wishes it undone.' 'If Grania has any sense she will have a good life with Peggy.' Sorcha, who had the tongs in her hand put it away and sat up. 'Look, is it of set purpose you make friends with old people, is it some anger in you all the time over how it was when you first came?' Brigid frowned. 'Get angry or not, hear what is going on. Eilis goes to you, and Nappy, and they come into Ouida, and all I hear is, "Brigid gave us tea," "Brigid gave us eggs," and I sit there and I wonder and I get mad, and then I begin to wonder again.' She rid her throat sharply. 'And let me tell you it's not so long since they had as much to say against you as the next, in case you are good to them by mistake.'

'What would you want me to do,' Brigid challenged. She pushed the fire together under the kettle with her foot. 'The old people are as much a pity as young people. Sometimes Nappy gives out to me, mixing me up with Mary, for Nappy is on the edge of doting and her mind goes in and out of clouds. Sometimes she will say to me: "You let her have too much of her own way, Mary," her mind is in such confusion. Sometimes she says to me: "You are to be pitied, God knows, living for ever under the watchful eye of Mary Manus."' She stood by the dresser. 'Will I put you down an egg apiece for us? Peggy said not to go easy on anything, this being the last day of her rule on this floor. She said us to have fun. And that is a thing Peggy said and Eilis said it and Nappy, that long ago they all used to have fun in this glen, when they were young and people together.'

'If they had fun then maybe it was that old people did not live so long, long ago. I could make fun and I could laugh if I was rid of Nappy.' 'And I of Eilis.' 'And I of my blister.' They raised a storm around Brigid. She lifted down the boiling kettle and wet the tea.

'Ah stop it, stop it,' Sorcha protested, 'stop it I tell you and let me ask Brigid something. Why is it, Brigid, that you are so sure that Tom will go on this errand for you? That is one thing I cannot make out. Let Mary say yes, or say no, you say Tom will go.' Brigid nodded. They sat silent, waiting. 'Tom will go, and do you know why?' They shook their heads slowly. 'Then I will give you why in one word, Briany.' 'Briany,' they roared. They were angry now. Sorcha hushed them to silence. 'Do not leave me puzzled, Brigid,' she pleaded, 'put my mind, anyway, at ease on Tom, and I will sleep at night.' Brigid poured the tea. Sorcha passed round the bowls quickly. Brigid seated herself among them. 'You think Briany is little better than a tramp; a foolish man that wears a dickey and does not slave himself in the fields. If you listen to Tom, then every now and again you will hear Briany has more sheep than another. You will only hear serious talk on Briany from Tom. Tom sits with Briany and Tom draws enlightenment from Briany's talk, for that is the kind of mind Briany has, great understanding. Wait till I tell you the comfort Briany was to me. . . .'

They were at a loss what to say when she finished her story of the day Briany came to her to borrow the ladder. But they sipped their tea and listened. 'Talking about hatching hens and fighting cocks,' Nelly said, stuttering a little, 'I see Mary has a pair of red-combed beauties. I wonder why Mary is keeping two cockerels around.' She winked at Susan and Sorcha without bothering to hide her wink from Brigid. Brigid looked from one to the other, puzzled. 'Oh, fine you know,' Susan scoffed, 'fine you know.' Sorcha leaned nearer. 'Are you going to tell us, Brigid, you know nothing of what Mary has in mind feeding those cocks?' Brigid shook her head. The others exchanged uneasy glances, and one elbowed the other to tell and in the end they all put in a word to make known to Brigid how, when a woman in labour passed into a storm of outrageous pain and her life was thought to be in danger, the greatest charm in the world was the death struggle of two live cocks buried in a hole in the ground to take the woman's struggle into the earth itself to be resolved there. All she had to do then was lie there. She could go unconscious if she liked and waken up with her job done. Brigid was on her feet by the time the story was finished. 'There, now, you put the glen itself into scarecrow's rags, to make it like an old hag to frighten me. If I had to give in to the darkness of such talk I would smother. I would smother I tell you.' She slumped on her knees by Peggy's bed. They gathered round her, blaming themselves, and they raised her to her feet. They wiped her face of its tears. 'I should be able to laugh at you. If Eilis and Nappy talked of such things to me I could laugh at them. It would be fun to me. I suppose now I am fun to you, letting myself be upset . . .' They scolded her at that. This was no fun to them. From now on, no such talk would cross their lips. Brigid saw them on their way. They talked together for a long time at the parting of their casans.

Black Donal and Peggy rode back with young Donal's son, small Donal, a sturdy child of four, perched in front of his grandfather. Brigid was on watch and she hurried to meet them. 'You have good news, Peggy,' she whispered, linking her across the street, as Black Donal and small Donal led the horse away. She fussed over Peggy, making her take off her boots, and settle herself on her creepy before telling her story.

'I have a story to tell, Brigid. It was a sore day for me. Young Donal was on watch for us. Grania — that is her name — came outside when she heard the voices. "You are welcome," says she to me, putting me in my place. "Thank you," says I. She had the upper hand of me. I followed her into as shiny and trig a kitchen as there is in the parish; they live in a kitchen belonging to an aunt of hers who went out of it for them. I thought shame. To make it worse she looked tired. She is pale. It is not your shade of paleness Brigid, but a worn paleness, and the sharpness in her features is not nature either. She is not as tall as you.'

'You don't have to measure her against me, Peggy.' 'That is all I had in mind, going over and coming back, would she have some of your nature, thinking of Black Donal. That is all I ask now, Black Donal to be happy. I told her what brought me, and she said young Donal would be glad to get back to the glen. There was no sharpness in her when she said that. It was just that she had young Donal in her mind. That was another sting. If she has any hatred in her for me, because of what I did, I saw no sign of it. The only one of her people that darkened the door was her brother, and he talked like there never was any huff between the two families; they must be fine, upstanding people. But mind you, Brigid, I think Grania and myself took a liking to one another. I think I must be near my end, Brigid, for I came back feeling friendly with the whole world.' Brigid bent over her and hugged her. 'So you are dying again are you?' Peggy beat at her. 'I should know better than to open my mind to you, but now that I am at it let me leave nothing unsaid. For fear Grania would not think of it, I want Mary Manus by my bedside when I am dying. I want her because I know I am sure to be scared.' Brigid sat on a creepy across the fire from her. 'I suppose everybody is scared then,' she said thoughtfully. 'Not Mary Manus. Wait till I tell you, Brigid. Somehow it was in my mind coming back. When the time came for Black Donal's mother to die I stood by her night and day; I can say that for myself. She died on a harvest day. The people were abroad in the fields shearing oats. She asked for a drink and I gave it to her. "Call Mary," says she, and although I was young, and Mary was young and the glen was full of Marys, I knew she had Mary Manus in mind, so I called her and she came. I mind she carried her reaping hook in her hand, for her children were in the field, and she laid the hook on the floor there by the end of the dresser, out of harm's way. She was a young woman then. I mind her wiping the sweat off her forehead with her forearm. I pointed to the bed, and I was standing beside her when the old, creaky voice spoke. "Thank God you came to me, Mary Brian." I opened my mouth to say this was Mary Manus, Mary Brian's daughter, but Mary pressed her foot on my foot. "I am afraid, Mary," says the one in the bed, "I am scared. I am frightened to face God." I mind her eyes. Mary and myself were bent down to catch the words, and Mary laughed. I can hear it like it was now, a real laugh, no let-on, no put-on, only a real laugh. "That is the oldest trick in the devil's bag, Ouida," — Sorcha's Ouida is called after the same grandmother — "the oldest trick in the devil's bag. When all else fails him he tries to frighten you, when you are dying. You can laugh at him." Bear in mind, Brigid, Mary Manus was a young woman then, and the world a burden to her, for Manus was already dead. At that minute Ouida's mind cleared. "You are young Mary," says she, and, if anything, I thought she was glad. "I am young Mary and I am old Mary, and what I say is true. You just put your fear away from you. You had the priest. Let us leave all that is past to God's mercy now, and let you have no fear; no fear at all." Ouida settled down. Mary half turned to me and she pointed to the blessed candle, and I lit it, and Mary put it in Ouida's hand, and she closed the old fingers round it, and I went to the door and I shouted and the neighbours came running and I was crying and they all knelt and they filled the house with the rosary. And then — God Almighty will I ever forget it — Ouida's voice came up, as clear as a lark, in a song she used to sing and Mary leaned closer to her and she put her voice to Ouida's voice, and Mary had a grand voice, and they sang together, and we all knew then, that this was Ouida's last sound ever, and we prayed louder. All at once Ouida's voice broke, and Mary, at the same breath, changed from a song to a prayer. Ouida was dead. Is it any wonder, thinking of that day this day, that I said to myself I want Mary Manus with me, when my hour comes, sinner that I am.'

Brigid rose slowly. 'Do you know something, Peggy. Bear in mind, will you, for fear I would forget it, to leave word with Grania to put no stop at all on us playing ourselves at your wake, for if ever there was a wake that should be noisy it will be your wake.'

'Well,' Peggy gasped, 'well.' She took up the tongs. 'The devil rattle every bone in your body if that is all you have to say to me, and me all but crying, looking at myself, stretched out, dying. I declare to heaven if I had you on my floor, there would be times when Black Donal would have to rope me in a stall in the byre, else I would leave my mark on you.' Brigid picked up the milking pails. Black Donal trudged in. 'That will be the hardest thing on me, Black Donal, when it comes my turn to put my hands in my lap in the corner, having to let a strange woman get between me and my cows, and maybe the cows make no fight at all but give in to her.' 'Get out,' Peggy roared. 'Ho, ho, poor Mary Manus, but I pity her.' She watched Brigid cross the street to the byre. She sighed happily. 'We did a good day's work, Black Donal. I would never have the courage to do it only she will be in and out to us.' Brigid's voice rose, in the byre, in song.

15

Peggy crossed the field, knitting as she walked, small Donal clinging to her skirts. She paused by a potato field in blossom, raised her eyes to the thin wisps of fog by the Loch. She called a child by name and pointed to cows snapping a few hurried mouthfuls of growing oats. 'Lucky for you your father did not come on you,' she scolded, keeping her voice low. She turned to face Bella driving two young animals towards the mountain, but Bella had no wish to come within reach of Peggy just then, so she called her dog to send the cattle on their way, more at the threat of his name called loudly than from any idea to set him on them. The dog was nearer at hand than Bella knew, and he was a young dog, and he read urgency in the loud call. He leaped around barking and ducks lazing on the green started up in fright and made for the Big Hole, and he mistook them for his task. He rushed in among them, and some of them took wing and one he pounced on, and a puff of feathers arose. Peggy joined Bella bellowing at him to lay off, and neighbours raised their heads to see what was to do. They saw Bella take up the duck in her arms, and they heard her cry out in distress that the bird was undone. 'The thing to do,' Peggy advised, 'is to draw its blood.' She shouted for Grania and Grania showed in the door-way and Peggy ordered her to fetch the sharp knife, she would know it for it had a broken bone handle with a piece of rag wrapped round it. Susan was in view now. Peggy told Susan one of her ducks was killed and Nappy heard her too and Nappy wanted to know which of the ducks. 'What odds which duck,' Susan chided.

'Ho, ho, what odds which duck,' Nappy scoffed, 'there is talk for you. What if it is the one duck left out of a whole hatching of ducks, the weasel destroyed, the best duck in the glen. What if that is the duck?' Eilis spoke mildly to Nappy. 'Do not upset yourself and do not begrudge your duck, let it be any duck. The harm of the year go with it. Begrudge nothing that dies.' She joined Nappy and kept pace with her across the green. They could see Peggy stooped now, and they knew what she was doing. Nappy raised her voice in warning. 'Do not be too ready with that knife, Peggy,' she ordered. 'Many a duck I saw that looked dead, after a dog pounced on her, and she came to.' But Peggy was erect again now and she held the duck out from herself, head down while it exhausted its last few spasms. The dog yelped as Bella found him with an angry clod, and he lay on his back, and she beat him with the rod in her hand and she kicked him with her bare feet. 'I never liked him anyway,' she stormed. 'I said to Phil first sight I got of him he would turn out a fool of a dog. He is the living likeness of Briany's dog, an idiot of a dog.'

Peggy took the dog's side. She taunted Bella that fault was not in the dog but in herself. Many a time she saw Bella watching her children making a fool of the dog. How could a dog learn sense that way? He got no teaching, no teaching at all. Even now when Bella called him the dog had no way of knowing what was wanted of him. Bella turned on Peggy. Was Peggy trying to say she destroyed the duck out of badness? She had to turn from Peggy to face Nappy, for this was the duck of all ducks that Nappy hoped it might not be. Nappy would rather it was any two ducks than that it should be this duck. Too bad, too bad that a duck that lived through the torment and the terror of the weasel's night of murder should have to be caught short in this way, in broad daylight, in no mischief. Eilis tried to get her word in, to warn Nappy it was wrong not to say, 'The harm of the year go with it.' Nappy waddled around angrily. She blamed Susan. She said to Susan to send one of the children with the ducks to the Loch, and Susan did not do it.

'Choking to you, Nappy,' Peggy chided, 'go on home and put your duck in the pot. It will not do you a bit of harm. And do not be making out it is a cow you lost. It is only a duck.'

'Only a duck,' Nappy rapped. She turned to Grania. 'Do not you be taken in by this talk,' she advised. 'Let Peggy say to you to drive your ducks to the Loch and let you not do it and then let the like of this happen, and you will get a different tune from Peggy.' Bella spoke up angrily to tell Nappy go down to her place and take her pick among Bella's ducks, to take two ducks if she thought the dead duck was such a wonder, only to shut her mouth. Nappy was taken aback, for her mind had been on Susan. She took the dead duck in her hand and turned for home and Eilis walked with her and Mary joined them. The young women delayed. This was the first time Grania was in their midst at a moment of excitement. Grania chuckled and she kept her voice low when she spoke.

'The thing is, Nappy had the right of it. Peggy was too free with the knife. The duck looked dead enough when Peggy put her between her knees, but at the first nick of the knife the wings beat like mad and then Peggy knew she made a mistake. It is not Bella but us should give Susan a duck.' They glanced at one another. Was this how it was between Grania and Peggy already, Grania ready to pass blame over to Peggy? Grania turned to Kitty. 'You saw the wings flapping, Kitty.'

'If I did I had no mind to say it,' Kitty said. Grania laughed. 'God knows, Grania, you are after my own heart,' Brigid rejoiced. 'Even it was a bigger thing it would be right not to hide it and anyway Peggy will tell Nappy for you will see that Peggy and Nappy and Mary will keep together until the duck is plucked to see is there much of a bruise, and as like as not Mary will maybe open the duck to see was any harm done to her insides.' Brigid was a step back from them, and her glance went from one face to the other. 'Do not be looking for sharpness between Grania and Peggy. Are you not noticing Peggy, how she is over and back on the casans. She never sits. Peggy is making herself an example to the world. She withdrew her hand from the tongs and from the besom and she withdrew her mind from the rule she used to have over such things. Peggy will be what I said she would be, the best old woman ever.' Grania nodded agreement. 'I said to Peggy, this glen has a bad name, and I told her how it was in our glen where we have a name for peace.' They moved closer to her. 'The way it is, old people should be let run around and put their heads together and the one that finds fault will maybe not like to hear somebody else agree with her, and even they all agree it helps them empty out their minds. And it does nobody any harm.' She laughed and it was strange to them that she should produce a snuff box, for none of the younger women carried snuff boxes.

'So this now is how it is to be,' Susan taunted, 'Grania and Peggy will be the wonder from now on. First the island woman makes Mary dance to her tune and now Grania. How does it come we do not know how to make such things happen? Are we thick forby, Grania and Brigid?'

Grania put back the lid on her snuff box. 'It is always said in our glen that this glen knows more about other people's business than any people in the parish, because the men bring back news like they were women.' She waited till the angry blast of talk ended. 'That is all the good you will hear of it, however: if you want news go to Glenmore: if you want sense keep out of it.' They stormed at her again. The sense of light-hearted mischief in her puzzled them. 'Did one of you ever say to Peggy in the past ten years she was making an idiot of herself putting a bar up against me?' 'Be fair to Peggy, Grania,' Brigid intervened, 'it was not because of you — anyway, what odds now why. You will get to like Peggy more and more.'

'We will have to talk of these things,' Sorcha said earnestly. 'I said it to myself, it is making brightness, Peggy walking

around. Wait till I tell you something.' She found herself
a seat and the others sat, or went down on one knee. 'Peggy
headed our way yesterday, one of the children ran in to say
she was coming. Ouida let a grunt out of her. "Give me my
petticoat," says she, angry as you like. I could not believe
my eyes. She slid out of bed and I had to drop her petticoat
down over her head. She was in mortal terror of what Peggy
would say. God knows maybe that is what is wrong, we keep
the old woman too much on a tether. There has to be sense
in things somehow, else we are idiots, out and out. Take
care is Peggy not going to turn out a blessing for the glen.'
She laughed. 'Will I ever forget the morning Brigid set out
for the island.' 'Choking to you,' Susan scolded, and Nelly
protested too. 'It is a story one of us will tell you some day,
Brigid,' Sorcha promised, 'only not now for I have to run.'
They all had to run for it was near the hour for their men's
tea. Susan slowed her step to keep pace with Brigid. It was
a calm, still day now, the men were in the meadow fields,
mowing. They chanced, at that moment, to stand up to
sharpen their scythes, and children herding nearby cried
'Crake, crake' as if mistaking the rasping sounds for that
bird's night call and their rhythm upset the men so that they
threatened fiercely and the children cheered. The sun was
bright on the heathery hillside and Brigid asked Susan to
notice it. 'We make fun of you among ourselves, Brigid,'
Susan scoffed, 'with your talk of the mountain changing its
skirts and the like nonsense. You put me in mind of a story of
a woman in this glen, one time, that used to sit watching the
mountains. She said she wanted her child to be tall; she
was married to a wee bit of a man. And right enough she had
a tall child, but some people wondered was that because she
had a tall neighbour.' With a gay shout she waved Brigid a
farewell. 'Ho, ho, Tom Manus,' she shouted, 'I am warning
you if it is a red-headed child I will take on the rearing of it,
it will be my right.' They saw Garvey's cartman lead his
horse out from the quarry floor on to the rough boreen, making for middle glen. The cartman saw Briany and hailed

him. He had news of a battle between the Boers and the English. There was word in Carrick that, if the English lost another battle, they would send gun-boats round to gather up men for their armies. The reason why they had venom in them to do that was because they found out Kruger was Parnell himself. More power to him. But this news of a gun-boat, was this what was in the prophecy, could it be the gun-boat instead of the train? Sean Mor, rapping the ground sharply, walked among the harvesters and at dusk the men crowded together and discussed this news. Man O man, if it should turn out that Parnell was not dead after all. Next day the cartman reappeared, this time on horseback. Hannah Garvey sent him with word the police were on their way, looking for dog-licences. Ho, ho, dog-licences. This was a sign. This was in the prophecy. This was a trick to get an excuse to destroy the dogs so there would be no warning at night. Let the children go up the mountain and bring the dogs and stay there till dark. God pity the people, wanting the Boers to win and in dread their war would reach into the glen. . . .

The oats ripened early that year, and women took their reaping hooks to work alongside their men, or else they made straps and tied sheaves after the scythes. It was on a busy, light-hearted harvest day that Mary stood on her own street and shouted Tom's name in a way that made everybody look up and told all within hearing that this now was the hour. It seemed indeed as if at that moment they all caught sight of themselves in the setting of their own fields, with the day itself shining over them, and Tom striding across the green, for somehow they all seemed to have a picture of it in their minds when they talked later; even long afterwards. One would say: 'I can see myself like I see you now, standing there, a half-finished sheaf between my feet and everybody in sight standing . . .' But that talk was later. At that moment they had eyes only for Tom. Bella alone raised a voice: 'Ho, ho,' she bugled, 'ho, ho, the big windows again. More airs, more nonsense,' but not a head turned her way. They saw

Tom lead out his horse, already saddled; so Tom knew. Suddenly they were light-hearted. They moved towards the mearns so they could banter each other, making fun of Tom. One of Susan's children raced up to her in the field to say Mary said she was to come to her. 'And will you tell her,' Dan Rua joked, 'that if she gives in, like she should give in, to have a man with clay on his hands lean over her in the bed to give her three shakes, a red-headed man is best, and I am willing.' 'I would as soon I could stay where I am,' Susan worried, 'what will I say to that man when he comes?' She hurried on her way. Wee Conail hopped lightly over the stone fence, and they smoked their pipes together. The children chose to make a game for themselves out of it all. They gathered on a hillock and chanted, 'The doctor is coming, hurrah, hurrah, the doctor is coming, hurrah, hurrah.' Their parents shouted at them and they let on to fly in panic. They drove a donkey ahead of them. They turned aside and rounded up all the donkeys they could find and piled on to their backs, heading towards the mountains. Black Donal had oats ready for building and Wee Conail and Dan Rua went to him and it suited others to stook what they had reaped, and then go across to Black Donal's haggard in a kind of holiday spirit, tending more and more to make a mock of Tom's race for the doctor. They could not believe in it. Some men got soft at such a time and made fools of themselves; some with talk, some in drink. Tom's way was a new way. Sean Mor came, and it pleased them to make him angry by making little of Brigid, a woman that had need of help for such a simple thing. They were having fun when Susan cried out, panic in her voice, to tell Dan Rua he was to ride for the priest. 'Hurry let you,' she shouted, 'hurry let you.' He vaulted the haggard wall, and he ran, letting down his shirt-sleeves as he went, and shouting to one child to put a fistful of oats in a bucket and bring it to him, and to another to bring him his coat. It was while he was coaxing his horse, rustling the oats in the bucket, that the doctor's buggy appeared over the brae with Tom riding behind.

Susan was outside and she waved urgently, and they all waved and shouted to the doctor to hurry himself. Susan ran to meet them. The doctor walked quickly, a gangling, long-legged man, wearing a two-peak cap and riding breeches and a home spun coat. The children gathered to watch him pass, raced ahead and re-formed, and the men moved forward from Black Donal's haggard, halting by a fence. 'Is the whole glen having this child?' the doctor joked. 'Hurry yourself, man,' Susan snapped. She broke into a half-run and he kept pace with her. Dan Rua stood by his horse, uncertain. Only Sean Mor spoke. 'I tell you, you need have no fear for that woman. Above all the women ever I saw, she has the frame for it. Let you have no fear. . . .'

'What in the name of God am I to do?' Dan Rua grumbled. He led his horse closer to the open door. Susan stood in it. She signalled to him, and he slipped the bridle from his horse and set him free. 'Devil such a to-do ever I saw,' Nelly grumbled, 'no such gathering of men did I ever see.' The men, grumbling at themselves, turned back to their work. Women clustered by Nelly's door. 'I hope to heavens he will talk to us,' Sorcha said, 'it would be a great thing, him to talk to us. We had a right to warn Susan to say to him that we wanted him to talk to us.' Susan walked out into the open again. She ran lightly up on the mound at the gable and looked around for Tom. He was over at the quarry walking the two horses. 'Hoigh, Tom Manus,' she shouted, 'you big ugly devil, you have a son, as hairy and as ugly as yourself. Hair for luck,' she shouted into the listening day. Sorcha hailed her and Susan waited for Sorcha to come to her. She promised to ask Mary to say to the doctor they would like him to talk to them. Sorcha hailed Nelly and those with her, and they churned forward to join her on the green. They saw the doctor in the half-light inside the door. He came outside, his pipe in his fingers, and they ran to him. Susan brought him a chair and he sat and they went on their knees on the grass by him. He plucked a knitting needle out of the bun of Sorcha's hair to pick out his pipe.

They wanted to know what caused Mary Manus to take fright. Had she cause for fright? He was patient with them and now and then he laughed loudly and they laughed with him. His eyes went past them to the manure heap and he rose quickly. He found fault with the dung-hill. No dung-hill should occupy such a position. He would like a change in such things. 'For heaven's sake, doctor,' Sorcha pleaded, 'do not start finding fault. If you frighten the men into thinking that every time you come something will have to be changed there will be no hope for us. Cannot you see that we are scared of our lives of you?' He put the needle back in the bun of her hair, and he lit his pipe. They noticed his gaze fasten on something behind them and they turned their heads. Ann the Hill stood against a broom bush. She ran rapidly along the fence and crouched in a gap. She dashed across an open stretch and went out of sight behind Tom's house. 'She is simple,' Sorcha said, glancing at the others uneasily. 'You are afraid of her,' he said quietly. They nodded. 'Brigid is not afraid of her,' Sorcha said quickly; eagerly. He nodded. 'She would not be. I suppose it is no use asking why you are afraid of her?' They all bent their heads. He thumbed out his pipe and picked up his bag. Mary walked with him part of the way to the quarry and they waited for her to come back, and they asked her, too, what it was frightened her and it startled them to see her wipe her eyes. She told them it was God's own pity the glen had to wait until that day to enjoy this man's skill. It frightened them that Mary should cry. They let her go back into the house alone.

16

DAN RUA took his place before his neighbours for a while, following the birth of a son to Tom and Brigid. The glen had no need to make an affair of the christening, so it passed almost without notice, Peggy and Black Donal acting sponsors. At first Dan Rua held his own easily against the scattered traffic of women that came within shout of him in his potato field. He roared out his contempt for the doctor's view on his midden. Rather than put himself about, in such a way, he would cart Susan out and unload her on the doctor's door-step. It looked like the potato crop was going to be plentiful. There was no sign of rot. He roared out light-heartedly.

But Sorcha kept at him. Nelly taunted him too. Nappy put in a word. 'I would see him in hell, before I would be a penny boy at his bidding. Let you not make an idiot of yourself.' Dan Rua's temper gave way. Men and women alike baited him. And soon he was not just helping them play a game, his roars merely part of the performance. Susan became uneasy and she carried her trouble to Tom. He was busy cutting scraws on a stretch of old pasture, and had just laid the spade aside to roll up the ten-foot length of yard-wide skin of grass to place with the other rolls to be laid under the clay on his potato pit later. She began in mockery. 'Some men get more than their share of luck. You got by without any noise over your midden. Everybody has not your luck.' Tom worked rapidly. He rested his foot on the finished roll of scraw and stood up. 'Are you not noticing he is in a bad temper?' Tom nodded. 'Why but you take your shovel and pick, some morning, and walk over to him and say you best begin this work? He is afraid you all will jeer him.' Tom held the lit match cupped in his hand. He nodded. Kitty was nearby, knitting as she walked.

Wee Conail asked leave to cut scraws on Tom's land, not for his pit, but for his byre. He must strip a stretch by the eave and put new scraws over the rafters under the rye thatch. He looked up at Susan. 'Let me tell you, if Dan Rua thinks fit to change his midden that will be the last step I will ever take in any changes from now on.' Susan flashed a quick smile at Tom. 'Tell Dan Rua yourselves.' Next morning Tom carried a pick and shovel over his shoulder when he crossed to Dan Rua's.

Bella alone offered battle. She did not raise her voice against the work itself, but wrought on Sean Mor so that she roused him, and said things to him the glen was welcome to overhear and take to itself. She found fault with Brigid and this roused him in her praise and they both raised their voices. Bella directed her talk at an audience of mid and lower glen people and their laughter was on her side. There was no doubt Brigid gave herself airs; upper glen itself was always given to air; Briany and his dickey was a fair brand for upper glen. Grania, who was of themselves was invited to join in their laughter. She offered battle to Bella instead. 'From the first I had pity for Brigid, because of what I heard and what the world knows about your grudge against any outside women: I am not thinking of my own case. Even now when she is caring for Sean Mor like she is, you sour your minds against her at a word.' They all turned with interest, challenging her to say in what new way Brigid cared for Sean Mor. She half-turned from them. 'I have the story from Peggy but not to tell it.' She faced Bella again. 'For shame on you I will tell it. You are angry because Sean Mor blesses her in your hearing. He has cause. When his eyes went clean out of control with pain she filled them with breast milk, so she did, because Mary was afraid the cold tea would only drive them mad, and she kept at them, so she did, till she quietened them and he can sleep at night. Was that airs? I would not do it nor would I blame any woman for saying no, but Brigid did it. She knows a prayer. Now will you mind your tongue, Bella?' And they all scolded Bella and she gave way to them, and crossed the fields to Tom's, and she sat with Mary and Brigid and they drank tea together and Bella wept a little over her treatment of Sean Mor, pleading however how her stomach would be at her if she had to stand over him and look into the anger in his eyes . . . 'I heard my mother say that it came to pass with her nursing my grandfather, on my father's side, who had cancer, that it was like that with her, her stomach would turn over at sight of his sores and she went to the priest, and he asked her if she ever had any liking for him and she said no, and he said that the cure for her was to see the torn body of Christ every time she looked at my grandfather's body and she did, and she got courage, and she could sleep and eat.' Bella asked Brigid to teach her the prayer and it came easy to her, and other women learned it too. 'It does a body good to know you have power over pain,' Sorcha said.

Susan's time came and the doctor paid his second visit. He was in a gay mood and he accepted Mary's invitation to a cup of tea with herself and Brigid, and he agreed that he would talk to whoever watched him drink, and women of lower glen came, too, under Grania's shelter, and they rejoiced in the doctor's mocking ways, and counted out how many cases were ripening for him in their end of the glen, and when he asked what other sickness was among them they felt they must oblige him without letting him see too deeply into their lives, so they nudged one another and Sorcha told of the strange behaviour of Sean Mor's eyes, and how Brigid brought peace to them. The doctor listened gravely. Women of the roads would be likely people to have a store of knowledge of cures, he said. There could be something in breast milk that was not in other milk; something the text books had not got at yet. He puffed at his pipe. 'There is one thing, I would give a good few pounds to be able to paint a picture of that scene.' They were puzzled now, suspicious a little that he was laughing. 'Do you not give in that the woman that made the cure first of all was none other than the Mother of God herself, and that the strength of the cure is in the prayer?' 'I only know what is in the books or what makes sense.' They glanced at one another and moved closer. 'Many an old cure makes sense. Sometimes a man or woman with no book learning, working in a field with people who have greater book learning, shoots past them all through some gift of understanding. Look at the midwife up the country that took a live child out of a woman's side, and then held the wound while the cobbler stitched it . . .' Nobody took an eye from his face until Mary slumped in a faint against the bed and her snore startled them all . . . She came to herself quickly. 'It was thinking back on something,' she said shyly, 'thinking back . . .' The doctor put a hand on her shoulder. 'If you think back you will be able to put yourself in mind of miracles you wrought, I am sure of that. The thought came to you once?' She nodded. 'I used to look at my hands and wonder if I had the courage would that child be alive . . . But I never knew of the like, except in a story; and that was only a story.' She glanced at Brigid. 'Maybe it was not a story after all, but a thing that happened.'

'Tell us one other thing.' Sorcha spoke hurriedly and the doctor, on his way to the door, halted. Sorcha touched her lips with her tongue. 'Have the books any advice for people, advice to help young people and old people live in peace? There is peace in the house,' she added hurriedly. The doctor rested his two hands on the back of a chair. 'Here is how things are with me . . .' She told the story of herself and Eilis. He nodded encouragement as she spoke and when she finished she felt at her ease with him. 'Maybe there is no cure,' he said. 'My mother lives with me. She thinks my wife is far too free with the wine when other women call. That is one thing they disagree over, the wine, and sometimes it starts a big squall . . .' They laughed, almost cheered now, 'God's truth it is a comfort to hear what you say and we wondering was it some curse was on us that touched nobody else.' 'God bless you, but you are the outspoken man . . .' They watched him ride away.

'Pity such a fine man, believing in nothing but books and learning, a great pity,' Mary sorrowed. 'It is a good job for the world God is free with his mercy.' She picked up her beads.

Brigid, out of doors, saw Briany go by and she beckoned him to her. She asked why he went by the door so much lately without looking in to light his pipe. 'Tom says you are drinking, Briany.' She found herself a seat and he sat too. He tossed his head. 'Ach, Brigid, ach.' He half rose. 'The way it is with me, Brigid, I had it in mind that when Home Rule came I would take to the roads of Ireland with my pack and watch the country build itself up; tell people things I saw done in one place when I went to another. An excuse to get away. Once the country broke Parnell and killed itself what was there to see then along the roads of Ireland? Now I am wondering with the war on will Home Rule rise again? It would be easy now if only Parnell was here. I read in the paper the other day . . .' He rose abruptly. 'That is how it is. I would like to sell a field and fill a pack and take to the roads.'

'God bless us, Briany, God bless us.' Brigid spoke quietly. 'If you want to fill a pack you have no need to sell a field. Why do you not talk to Tom?' He paused in the gap. He came towards her slowly. 'Do you know something, Brigid. I think maybe Mary is right about me. I am a bit touched. I give my mind over to things. Maybe if Tom said there is the money for your field, take to the road with your pack, I would no more take to the road than cut my stick for Boston. People will laugh. . . .'

'Nobody will laugh for nobody will know.' He put his dickey in place and patted it hard. He jerked his shoulders, 'Maybe in God I would see myself on the road yet, with the pack on my back and my stick in my hand.'

The glen trenched its potato pits against sheep and cattle, now that the glen was one great grazing common for the winter months. The gay winter nights were at hand. They had to be ushered in. Carrick Day had to be held. The whole glen — lower glen, mid glen and upper glen — all had to go in a procession of carts, men, women and children, gay and noisy, to lay in a store of things for the winter. Nobody knew what depth of root there was to the habit, but as far back as anybody could mind Carrick Day was a big day. One big day stood out above all its big days, and that was the year the glen fixed its visit to Carrick on the date of Parnell's meeting, after his fall. That was the day. The men of the glen made a ring round Parnell, cleared a path for him out of the village; not without cost to themselves, for one man died within the year of the beating he got, and another had to go to Boston, on his banishment, because of a blow he struck. Ho, ho, that was the day Glenmore men dazzled the world. . . .

The idea was not strange to Brigid. The island had its big day at the end of the herring fishing. The island did not set out in a procession of boats, however. The drive from the glen village to Carrick village would be unlike anything that came her way so far. She rode with Peggy — this was another of Peggy's last days — and Peggy had her mind made up this must be a day to talk of for ever. She shouted at everybody, taunted, mocked, encouraged the youths who skirmished round the carts in continuous conflict through the townlands by the roadside. Brigid knew already from Mary what to expect, but the hostility between the carts and the people by the roadside upset her. The men drove, looking ahead, like Tom that first day with dogs in anger around him, leaving the war to the youths, and the encouraging shouts to their women. Peggy roared, and cheered, punched Brigid in her excitement. 'Do not put a face on you, girl. This day is medicine. You have to scour out every now and then and this is the best scour of the year. Shout let you.'

'Well God knows it is no harm this is your last Carrick Day. Stop it, Peggy. You will do your throat harm. Look at the blackguards . . .' The glen youth raced past in headlong flight from angry men, goaded beyond endurance by their attempt to tumble a stack of oats. The men still drove steadily, looking ahead. The women shouted their challenge and abuse. Brigid drew her shawl out over her head. She raised a furtive hand in greeting to Andy, riding behind. It was a surprise to her to hear from Tom that Andy always took part in Carrick Day, and that always his cart was a shade the reddest wheeled cart of them all. Strange thing about Andy. He always bought ribbons and a packet of safety-pins for Ann. He would never buy with anybody looking on, but always he stole away, and young ones used to sneak after him and watch. When there was a spell of quiet Brigid said to Peggy it was a shame no woman offered to shop for Andy.

'Leave such talk till you get home, girl. Take that shawl down off your head. This day is not something you will tame or beat; not the grey cow, nor the black cow. You will not make your own of this day, so let you go with it. Roar and shout. Ho, ho, my life on you, boy . . .' Glen youths went into battle with rivals in wait for them at a cross-roads. 'God knows I saw many an unruly tide, but never such stream of uproar and confusion as this,' she grumbled. Tom flicked his reins and spoke to his horse.

The carts made a brave show in Carrick village. They were drawn up on both sides of the street. There was stabling, and shelter for the horses in Garvey's yard. Jane Garvey was at hand herself to offer a welcome; untidy, friendly, sharp-eyed, and she was Jane to them all. They mocked her, that they supposed she had marked everything up three prices. 'You have to, Jane,' Wee Conail scolded, 'how else could you keep yourselves in feathers, and gee-gaws, except by stealing from the countryside round you? It is not enough you have our eggs in your bellies for half nothing but you must rook and rob us . . .' The stream of visitors divided. The men went to the bar at the far end of the grocery. The women followed Jane to the drapery shop, the children silenced, expectant, a shade awed, close on their heels, to be fitted with winter boots.

When the drapery purchases were finished there was an interval before buying heavy groceries. Jane led the women to the bar to stand her yearly 'treat'. By now the men were well on their way to their ultimate state of vivid drunkenness which would make loading them on to the carts a job for the united effort of women, children, and Jane Garvey's staff; with Carrick village, superior and entertained, in attendance. Their noisy gaiety at this period drew an audience by the door, but Jane saw to it that none of the villagers sponged on Glenmore on its big day.

Brigid stuck by Peggy, a growing unhappiness separating her from the clamour around her, the thought of driving back over the same hostile road worrying her. She hoped no island boat would reach the village that day, for the island never got drunk in such a turbulent way. Island men grew fonder and fonder of everybody when they got drunk, and indeed that was why the island women always accompanied them on the pay day at the end of the fishing season, to see the sots and drunks of the world did not sponge on them. She kept an eye on Tom. He seemed as far gone in drink as the next. Briany surprised her. He was noisier than anybody, belligerent too. She laughed. Somehow it was good to think of Briany unafraid and aggressive. 'Bully on you,' Peggy whispered, 'bully on you. This day is medicine. Ho, ho, Glenmore for ever. There are the men for you, fists like sledges and the hearts of bulls. Show me the beating of them in the world . . .' Brigid elbowed sharply. 'The devil is in you, Aunt Peggy, do you want a war?' 'Up Kruger,' Peggy shouted, 'up Kruger.'

And that was their slogan on leaving the village, the men loaded into the carts, the women driving, the youths again skirmishing by the wheels, the police massed by Garvey's arch ready to interfere. Brigid rode with Tom this time, to handle the reins, thankful that the horse could be trusted to keep his place without guidance. Tom raised himself on his elbow; he had been one of the most difficult to load. They were now clear of the village. He watched Brigid fumble with the reins and laughed. She turned slowly. He winked. 'Can you see Black Donal, is he stretched out?' She leaned closer to him. 'Tell me, Tom Manus, are you not drunk?' He laughed again and sat up. She was suspicious, reluctant to yield the reins. He convinced her he was sober. She got a new vision of the procession. The men, like Tom, boys making noise. She hugged him and laughed. 'Lie down, like a good boy. Here is Dan Rua dancing on his toes. And will you for God's sake look at Briany with his coat off?' She cheered Briany. 'Ho, ho, my heart in you,' Peggy greeted and Brigid, turning, raised her whip in answer. 'My heart in you, Brigid,' Peggy exulted, 'my heart in you. . . .'

Most of those left behind waited the return of the cavalcade of carts at the old quarry, old people well to the fore. Children spilled out of the carts, grabbed the parcels and were beset by younger members who had been left behind, and battle broke out so that there was an order that all parcels must go back into the carts. Now without errand or mission the children looked around for other diversion and promptly ranged themselves in three armies, upper glen, mid glen, lower glen. They took up stations and flung clods, and one party rushing through whins flushed Ann the Hill, who fled from them screeching her strange screech, racing with her strange sideways skip, and in a flash the whole throng of youths and children gave chase; and even grownups cheered them on. A group of fleet-footed young people burst through a gap to head Ann from the shelter of her own house and they all jeered, and yelped the short yelp of dogs in chase. At sight of this new danger Ann halted. The nearest group of pursuers halted too, and stooped to pick clods to fling, for they had no wish to catch up with her. Ann leaped her stiff-legged leap and screeched her screech that was like a hare in a snare and she staggered, and, with a stoop now, she scurried onwards again and the hunt noises grew louder. The Loch was in her way. She headed straight for it. Brigid's cry of alarm was drowned in the noise. She called Tom's name. 'Jesus, Mary and Joseph, Tom,' she pleaded. He put his fingers to his mouth and whistled, the sharp whistle he used to call off his dog; that all the glen men used to call off their dogs. He whistled again and there was silence. Brigid alone stirred now. She hurried through a slap, calling Ann's name, and Ann turned to her. She was on the flat flag by the water's edge. She stopped, raised her hands sideways and fell; it was as if she folded into herself. Her head stirred for a moment and then it, too, was still. Brigid turned to gesture to the neighbours to withdraw and they withdrew. Andy, staggering as he went, followed Brigid. 'What, in the name of God, madness got into us?' Sorcha asked. 'Shut your mouth,' Susan Dan scolded, 'what was it but fun.'

'Fun,' Sorcha scoffed, 'were you listening to us. I tell you we were mad. Should some of us go to Brigid?' Nobody said go or stay, and Sorcha took her own casan home.

17

IT was maybe an hour later when Mary said to Tom one of them should go on over to Andy's to be home with Brigid, seeing that it was night. He rubbed the back of his head. It was in his own mind to go, only it could be, Ann, in her fright, would be like a child and Brigid would have to stay with her till she fell asleep, and maybe a strange step would upset her. 'It could be Ann is dead,' Mary interrupted sharply. He took the pipe from his mouth and turned quickly. 'I saw Andy carry in two buckets of water,' she explained. 'Then he went outside and into the byre. He did not stagger. He stayed in the byre; like a man would.' Tom thumbed out his pipe with a quick, hard poke and put it away. He paused on the doorstep. 'If you thought that, why but you sent somebody to her? It is not right Brigid should have to lay out a corpse.' Mary smiled at him. 'It will come easy to her. There is great respect in that woman.' She followed him on to the street. 'If Ann is dead raise the lantern up and down at the gable, for somebody will have to go there to free her, so that you can bring her home without leaving Andy alone.'

Tom found Brigid draping the recessed bed in the kitchen. There was such little bulk in Ann's body Brigid had to stand aside to let the light touch her face. He took off his cap and blessed himself. Brigid took up a candle so that he might see how young Ann's face looked in death. She was dressed in a blouse he knew to be Brigid's and she was laid out in finery of safety-pins and a brooch, with the cross of Brigid's beads in her fingers. 'Life was a great misery to her,' Brigid said quietly. 'There was a lump the size of my two fists under her breast.' He became aware of Andy in the shadow by the dresser. 'Too bad, Andy, God knows it was too bad.' He spoke angrily for he was perplexed. 'Like Brigid says, life was a scourge to her, Tom. Death was an ease. Let people not blame themselves.' 'You will have need of things for the wake, Andy. Let me go out to the cross-roads for them.' He picked up the lantern which was an extra light to the one candle and the byre lamp, and he went to the gable and he made a signal to his mother, and he waited until she came and Black Donal with her.

It was well on towards bedtime by the time the neighbours could gain the confidence for any general movement towards the wake house, and even at that they gathered into Dan Rua's first to learn for certain that Andy blamed nobody; Brigid was back home now but the door was shut, so they went by her. Tom was not back from the shop with the tea, sugar, bread, snuff, candles, tobacco. It seemed best to them that they should delay to be in to Andy's with Tom. 'It is not to face Andy I dread,' Sorcha worried, 'but Brigid. Brigid heard us.' They growled at Sorcha. 'It was the day did it; a day for noise. Any other day there would not have been such a hunt. It was a pity, a great pity that the like happened, but it was the day did it.' 'The day will never do the like again for there will never be another Carrick Day,' Wee Conail threatened. 'Like Sorcha says, we went beyond ourselves. The glen is like that lately, for ever going beyond itself.' 'Say what you will,' Susan proclaimed, 'and I will say with you that it was the day, but I will not let on that it is any heartbreak to me, Ann to be dead. I am glad she is dead. A scourge and torment, that is what she was. Who is there among you that would have this day's work undone? I will face Brigid and I will say what I say now. And I will swear to you Andy has no tears. Talk, let you . . .' Briany had a word of warning. If any news of this got out, the police would be into the glen. It would be a fine excuse for them. Away-out-of-here, there would be sure to be trouble over a business like this. Ach, away-out-of-here, and police. Look. No breath of this would go out of the glen; God's truth, Glenmore that was a shelter for men with a hunt on their heels and money on their heads . . . But they were uneasy. What would Brigid's mind be? Sorcha took it on herself to answer for her. A fine how-do-you-do, to wonder would Brigid keep this to herself. After all, every one of them in turn let out the darkest troubles of her mind to Brigid without a word ever hiccoughing back. Was it not to Brigid alone Ann the Hill spoke her secrets? Let people mind their own tongues; no need to fear Brigid. . . .

Youngsters rushed in to say Tom Manus was back. Briany was first man out the door. He helped Tom carry the groceries to Andy's. Tom had a tale to tell. The priest got word about him buying snuff and tobacco and bread and jam, and he knew that could only mean a wake so he came round and took Tom aside and Tom said Ann the Hill was dead; that she just stumbled and fell and was dead. 'And nobody thought fit to come for me,' the priest challenged. 'What got between your minds and me?' So then Tom told the whole story. 'The thing is, Briany, you will have to go out and pacify him. He says we killed her.' Behind Tom and Andy followed a multitude for the wake. All stragglers hurried forward and joined them. 'You will have to make our peace with Brigid, Tom,' Sorcha pleaded. 'I know fine Brigid blames us. She has the door shut. I would rather face Andy; a dozen times rather.'

There was a table by the bed. Briany laid the pipes, and tobacco and snuff on it. He knelt and they all knelt. Briany recited the De Profundis in Latin. At every glen wake Briany recited the De Profundis in Latin. He shook hands with Andy. 'Everybody's heart is sore for you, Andy; everybody's heart is sore.' The neighbours murmured their sympathy and found themselves seats. Briany took out his knife and began to make the pipes ready. Always Briany sat at the head of a wake house table and cut and teased the tobacco and handed round the pipes and the snuff. 'It was too bad,

Andy, Ann to be caught short, but there was no sin on Ann's soul more than the child with the water of baptism still wet on him. No sin surely,' Kitty intoned, 'no sin.' 'Away out of here, death often strikes like that. I mind one winter in Boston . . .' Their hearts warmed to Briany. He was making himself a shelter and a comfort. At any other wake their first talk would be of the dead person; ever and always it had to be like that. Everybody's life story had to be told. If there was anything in it that gave excitement to the glen for an hour, that had to be told and retold, each neighbour giving his memory of it. Clearly that could not be done in Ann's case, for if people went back to the days that were lived in the sun, what about those others covered with shadow? Good on yourself, Briany. Talk Boston, Boston, and let everybody help. Black Donal rubbed his stubble of whisker. He should be able to give Briany a hand. 'Do you know what I am going to take and tell you, Briany, it often puzzles me, all you saw in Boston, unlike me. I have to wonder at myself, listening to you, for I never saw the wonders in Boston you saw. I am going to take and tell you, Briany, I saw more wonders on a summer fair day in Carrick, long ago, than ever I saw in Boston.' They all but cheered Black Donal. He raised his head and looked around at them, puzzled. 'Upon my soul I did.' He spoke to the kitchen full of people at large. 'Now, take the lame ballad singer and his wife. You do not see them any more. She used to make a prop of herself to ease the weight on his bad leg when it was a long song. Then she used to go round whiles selling the ballads and cadging pennies. If there was one note he could not get up to, she would make for it, letting out a screech that shook the fair.' They all remembered the tall, lame ballad singer and his wife. They had memory of his ballads. 'Ho, ho, match Black Donal's story, Briany.'

'So Black Donal saw wonders in Carrick, on a summer fair day long ago, like he never saw in Boston.' They elbowed one another. 'Tell me, Black Donal, did you see many black men in Carrick on a summer fair day?' Black Donal rubbed his forehead hard. He had to give in he saw no black men, nor Chinamen in Carrick. He had to give in, too, he saw no such long streets of houses nor such big houses as he saw in Boston. 'Tell me, Black Donal, there was a big crowd that day in Carrick, was it as big as the crowds on a Saturday night on the streets of Boston?' But Black Donal could join issue now. He saw no crowds in Boston on a Saturday night; for that matter, he saw little any day or night, for this was how it was: he lived with his aunt and he walked to his work with her man. He walked back with him and there were other people from the glen, too, and everybody was in a hurry and if there was any word among them it was about some letter from home. When he got to his aunt's, he washed and he had a bite and he went out with his aunt's man to the Glenmore Saloon; Red Mick Miley's place. They all drank and they talked, and maybe they went to a neighbour's house to play cards or to hear a letter read. Above all, on a Saturday night, he saw nothing outside the street he lived in, for if his aunt's man was not drunk that night — and he likely would be, and if he was he needed watching going home for he had a feud with a man from Mayo, married to his cousin, and if he was left to himself he would be up hammering on the door; the damnedest business. . . .

('Bully on you, Black Donal, bully on you.') 'I saw no wonders in Boston. How could I see wonders in Boston?' The wake house was in a gay mood now and the young people gathering by the door decided this was their hour, and they stormed in and they launched out on the recognized games for the wake of an old person, and those of their elders, too sober to join in with them, withdrew.

But, for all that the first night's wake went by so well, there was still some awkwardness. Brigid did not walk abroad next morning. Susan had reason to believe Brigid knew of her outburst on Ann's death. She wished now she had held her tongue. When a body came to think back, she confessed, you would have to blame yourself. Maybe the fault was in clodding Ann back the first day. She recalled other days, further off, before Ann went queer. Ann was a great one for tricks. She could do things with her face. Sorcha ventured in to Brigid. She found her quiet in herself, willing to talk of Ann. She even laughed telling of Ann's tricks of voice and look. Tom was there at the time and Tom had his own tales of Ann. Tom spoke freely, recalling school-days, although if there was any hint of anger in anybody it was in Tom. 'Ach, man dear, ach, man dear,' he said, pushing back his chair. Sorcha got to her feet at that too. It was her intention, going in, to blame herself and everybody else for what happened to Ann but she came out without saying a word of it. 'Somehow my mind went into a tremble, listening to them. I was as like to cry as speak if I opened my mouth. . . .'

Andy was a comfort. He was at himself, fully sober, in the morning, no stray of any kind in his mind and he had no blame for anybody. His talk of Ann was of her later days; his nights without sleep and her yelps of pain, and her way of crying like a child, not like a grown body that knew why she cried. He had praise for Brigid. When she cried at night time, Ann often called Brigid; like a child might. 'Let there be no sorrow on anybody over what happened to Ann. It was God's doing, to free her from pain. . . .'

Nelly faced Brigid: 'Are you blaming people, or are you not?' she challenged. 'Ann was a hurt poor body, in a fire of pain, and every day she lived would be a day's agony. I blame myself . . .' She did not go beyond that. 'Then go across to the wake house and let you sit with your neigh-bours, and let them see your understanding and your calm-ness. Above all, do not blame Susan. Susan thinks she was the main cause of the hunt; she knows she gave the first blast of anger. Let you listen to Susan.'

'I am not denying what I said, Brigid. I said I am glad Ann is off the casans for good,' Susan proclaimed, standing at her gable for Brigid and Nelly and Kitty on their way to the wake house to come that far. 'If you have it in for me over that, Brigid, I am not going back on it.' 'Ann had the life frightened out of you, Susan, and I had no fear of her. I got to have a great liking for her. If I had your fear of her there would be an excuse for me. I alone wronged her. I should have made a better fight, liking her as I did . . .' 'It was easy for you to like her. You came before her eye a stranger. She had nothing to cast up to you. . . .'

'I tell you, I have more than any of you to cast up at myself.' Brigid's anger startled them. 'You were afraid of her, but I had only fondness for her. With God's broad daylight in my mind I went back on her. I should have walked abroad with her by the hand, not juking or hiding. She should have been in and out on my floor; not creeping in and out of creels, not to be seen. I am the one to blame.' When she wept they all wept and they all blamed themselves.

'God's curse on it for a world,' Susan exploded, 'why has it to be like this, people biting and scratching and then crying. . . .'

'You have no cause to cry, no one of you has any cause,' Andy scolded. 'It is peace for herself and a great lightness.' He walked across to shift the bacan so that his tethered cow might have a change of grass. Nelly, watching him, touched Susan with her elbow. She pressed her foot on Brigid's, winked at Sorcha. 'A great lightness. Will you look at the step of him for God's sake. He will be out "houlting" at the dances before the winter is half through. Ho, ho, the men for you. . . .'

Ann's death passed out of the talk. Andy alive took its place. Ho, ho, now the fun would start. A well-preserved root of a man, the same Andy. No help all those years, but tethered to the house to keep watch on Ann, he looked after his land with so little rambling or distraction his fields were healthy. The kindliest part of the mountain ran down to the Loch and his sheep got good of it. A good warm home for some girl. . . .

And that brought them back to Brigid. She had only to say the word and Andy would put the ring on whatever girl was her choice; not that she had not the like in mind from

the start. That was how the world went; if you were in luck
you did a thing and you benefited by it. Hell to her anyway,
she was rising too fast. If people put their heads together they
might get between her and Andy. The glen broke out in
gay talk and laughter. A man was ready to marry, and he
had his head up looking around him. It would be fun to
best Brigid. . . .

They buried Ann. They could see the priest was in a bad
humour. There was another funeral that day and there were
stragglers from it within hearing. 'I will be in to you on
stations soon,' the priest said grimly. They elbowed one
another. He was not going to let out their story; a grand
man. He would be no fun at the station. Many a scolding
he gave them, only up until now it was poteen, or suspicion
that the glen men were out with the moonlighters. The one
day he got them angry was when he spoke against Parnell.
That was the day. Ho, ho, Sean Mor let a roar out of him
that day, and so did Black Donal and Peggy. That was the
one time ever that Mary Manus showed anger. It was in
face of her anger the priest shut his mouth. There was
sprinkle of drink among them on the way home; and boast-
fulness. 'We have to build Andy a house,' Tom announced.
'They say once the sickness takes a grip on a house that the
thing to do is leave it.' So, that was how it was. Brigid was
that far ahead of them all. She had Tom out telling people
what to do for her. Their minds hardened and their faces
and their voices. Black Donal said with Tom. Let there be
a new house. Andy must step out of his loneliness. Yon was
no place for a house. He would give Andy a place on Ardan
Rua. Let him marry, let him rust, only let him be within
shout of his neighbours. . . .

Peggy delayed for a meal with Brigid. 'Now you will see
fun,' she laughed. 'Andy will not go far now but there will
be ears cocked. Let him come in on this floor and I will swear
Kitty will be on his heels, or Susan, or for that matter Nelly.
Let him go to a house with a girl of a ripe age, and the
women will raise such a laugh that grown men will be blow-

ing bottles round the house. Take care will you be let have your way.' Brigid warned Peggy to cease. Kitty tripped in; no matter how cautiously Kitty approached she always entered a house with an air of hurry. 'I had to run into you with the news. Andy took a glass after the funeral, and Andy's tongue always breaks loose when he has a glass in him; which all his life was seldom. The last time he had drink in him was after his mother's funeral and he bragged the world to fight him. You mind the day, Mary, and you, Peggy . . .' They nodded. 'Well this time what comes out do you think? Not anger, nor blame, but a whisper. I have to laugh. He has Hanna Rua in mind. All the time and he saddled with Ann had he not Hanna Rua in mind.' She turned to Brigid. 'From the lower end of mid glen, I might say from lower glen, aunt to Dan Rua; a young aunt . . .' Peggy felt for Brigid's foot with her foot but Kitty was watching.

'Dan Rua will be well fixed if Andy marries Hanna Rua,' Peggy said with easy friendliness. 'He will have three farms waiting for his children, for I suppose it is to one of Dan's children Briany's farm will go too. Still I suppose he will let the sod settle on Ann first.' 'Ach, Ann; it is not as if Ann was a person. What was Ann but a shadow.' Kitty accepted Mary's snuff box. 'Some say Andy would be for looking further afield, only he was told a stranger would want a new house.'

Peggy held up her knitting to count stitches. 'Indeed then Hanna Rua would have no reason to be afraid to make her bed in Andy's: at her age there would be nothing for her to fear; I would think; a fine hearty neighbourly woman.' 'A good-hearted neighbour,' Mary endorsed. She saw Kitty off the street. She raised her two hands and beat them together and laughed, standing by her bed. 'Hanna Rua for Andy. In their minds Andy is another Ann. Nappy's greed is at her. The greed is in Dan Rua himself.' She seated herself on her creepy. 'It would be wrong, Brigid, to let Dan Rua outgrow his neighbours. He could become a rough, coarse man if his greed got rein; a country-side of land, Brigid, would be bad for him. His father — God be good to him — tried to wrench a field from me. Take Andy under your care, Brigid.'

'How could Andy listen to Brigid when she would want him to burn down his house and build a new one? . . .'

'I will be content if he just makes byres of the old house.' Brigid chuckled quietly. 'I am not letting Andy with them to waste his life on him, what is left of it.'

'Bully on you,' Mary rejoiced, 'bully on you. There is life enough left in Andy.' Peggy rested her hands in her lap. 'So you have a woman in mind for him?' Brigid nodded. 'Then let me tell you, you best stir yourself. If you are going to be stubborn about a new house, rouse Tom and let Tom raise his voice and say to build it. Black Donal will give place for a house on Ardan Rua.' She took up her knitting. 'I talked to him. He will make a fair swap with Andy, no fairer.' She rid her throat angrily. 'What kind of a clip are you bringing in among us? Would it kill you to talk; to be civil? Will she have a hat on her?' Brigid's mood puzzled Peggy. She got to her feet and raised her fist. 'You are not taking a hand at people are you, saying a thing only to raise contention and talk? You have somebody in mind?'

'I have somebody in mind,' Brigid assured her, but there was still a mockery in her that still angered Peggy. Mary followed Peggy out. 'What do you make of her, Mary? We are not at the bottom of that woman's mind. There be times when I could brain her. All night I will be going over what she is up to. I know she would not let us make idiots of our-selves. One thing, Mary: make her go to Black Donal herself and ask him will he swap Ardan Rua with that sour patch of Andy's back of our garden; and say to her to go to Andy. Others will not be backward. The one thing for her now is, Andy not to go to the forge with anybody that would boost him up with drink and settle him in with Hanna Rua.' She sighed heavily. 'The like happened before. The glen is on its tiptoe. . . .'

And right enough, at the first word that the swap was made more voices came into the contention, and argument and laughter than hitherto, for mid glen had to deal with Sorcha, and Andy's own people in lower glen took kindly to it also. It was almost like some fault could be found in them that upper glen should brand Ann as a kind of witch. Now upper glen confessed itself in the wrong; at least that rumour was abroad. There was discord in the voices, a kind of muttering against Brigid within the gaiety. It would be all right building a house for Andy, only was there not another finger in the business. Who was to come stepping in when the house was up?

Andy was keeping to himself, without letting on not to see people like before. He seemed busier than ever. He called his dog oftener. He was wearing his Sunday trousers and coat. He took his place at night in the card school. So far as could be seen no whisper passed between him and anybody. Always there was somebody; should it have to be a child. For all that somehow the way Andy walked, and the ease in him when he talked, all hinted at a mind made up in a pleasing way. It was known Andy and Black Donal had agreed to the swap, but there was more meaning in Andy's gait of going than that. Peggy clucked and scolded. She did not give a curse who Andy married only now that the world knew Brigid was in the tussle for him there would be a great laugh if he went past her choice. 'Tell me, Brigid . . .' Mary and Peggy and Brigid were together by the fireside, tea bowls in their hands. 'I will tell you who I have in mind, Peggy, only one or other of you is not as much as to breathe it: Winnie.' 'Winnie!' Peggy's voice shot past her. She clapped her palm flat across her mouth. She gave Mary a push with the other hand. She signalled to Brigid to shut the door. 'You will have to let me laugh. God O God, when this gets out; the glen with its hand over its eyes watching the brae expecting an island woman, while all the time . . .' Mary shushed and gestured Peggy to quietness. Mary was pleased too. She saw that Brigid was happy and had no need of a woman of her own people. Peggy wiped her eyes. 'There is a mountain of nature in you, Brigid. Does Andy know?' Brigid nodded. 'Now how under God did you get word to Andy? Winnie knows too?' 'Winnie knows; Tom's doing.' 'Ho, ho, so Tom knows. Listen to me, Brigid, let me tell Black Donal. He will shake the buttons off his clothes laughing. This will make one laugh of the whole glen, one nature and one laugh. And not a word nor a whisper.'

But that was where Peggy erred. God knows how it happened. Maybe Winnie put a ribbon in her hair, or laughed in a way that drew an eye on her, but all of a sudden the word was out. In its first flash it had the edge of its laugh against Brigid, but without a word from her or anybody else the truth dawned on people. That evening the biggest gathering ever crowded into Tom's. Let the house be put up. The day was fixed then and there for the ceremony of the marking of the site.

Brigid had no knowledge of the ritual laid down for the building of a new house. She agreed light-heartedly that whatever was laid down should be done. She joined in the bustle of people from the houses around and was as gay as the next waiting at Ardan Rua for the ceremony to begin. The site was already pegged out and while they waited people argued whether the house should face one way or the other, so as to enjoy a good draught in the chimney, and much of the argument was mischievous. The gathering was even a bit uproarious when shush was called and passage for Sean Mor. For this was his hour. He stood before his people. A man of authority sanctioned from afar. Brigid noticed how he had made himself ready. There was a button on his coat. A loose patch on his knee was newly sewn. There was a whang in one shoe. 'If I had only known,' she whispered to Mary. 'Why did not somebody tell me?' Sean Mor was apart from them all now, in the centre of the marked site, a small-bladed, short-handled spade in his hand. He jerked his hand up and down and there was silence. The eyes of his world were on him now.

His own gaze passed along the faces of his neighbours. It passed over their heads to the mountains, thick thighed, grey shouldered, attentive, and his voice when he spoke was pitched for distance. 'Be it made known then, by the turning of this sod, that Andy Melly has in mind to raise the walls and roof a house in this ground so be that the ground is free.' He turned over a small sod, already hacked clean on three sides, while still entangled in grasses on the fourth. He straightened his back slowly. 'If the ground be not free but in use and if it be that whosoever is using the ground will not take to a new road, then let the same be made known in the manner laid down. Let it be made known in the manner laid down . . . in the manner laid down.' He faced north, south, east, west, in turn. He trudged along the stretched cord, rested his eyes on his neighbours again, raised them to the world beyond, and levered up the second sod and spoke again. A third time and a fourth time he said his words, and there was a stagger in his feet as he took up position again in the centre of the marked ground. 'And for seven days and seven nights these sods are live things that nobody dare lay hand or foot on but at their peril.' He took the spade in his two hands. 'And I have to do what is laid down for me to do, for my day is past, and my hour is at hand. Come here to me, Tom Manus.' And Tom Manus went to him and he placed the spade in Tom's hands. He gestured the people to be on their way and they knew there were words Sean Mor must give to Tom to carry into other days along with the spade of history.

Mary put a hand on Brigid's elbow and hurried her home. They were silent on the way home. 'I would wish Sean Mor had to make some other choice than Tom.' She gestured Brigid to her creepy. 'Tom will put the spade up back of the roof tree. There will be cobwebs. Tom himself will have to gather them and put them into a dry bottle, with a grass cork; a loose grass cork of bleached grass. You will not make little of this, Brigid?' 'I will say nothing at all,' Brigid promised; 'nothing at all.'

But that evening the talk was of the ceremony on Ardan Rua. Briany had no mind to make little of anything that came down from the old people, but it was his belief this business made a different kind of sense. The Sapper had such an idea and the Sapper was a man of great understanding of things; a man going round making maps hears things. He said a Sapper's spade was not unlike this spade above. It was his belief these sods were no more than marks men made when they put their eye on a place for a house and did not know would they be welcome to build there, and had no knowledge which way to turn to ask. You made your marks and you maybe went on your way and took work and then you came back and you saw if the ground was free, or not. . . .

What was strange to Brigid, was that if people had to seek a blessing in any way it was not from the priest they sought it. No, no, the priest is not to be brought in ahead of his time. His turn will come when the house is up. He always gives out the station in a new house. Once it is up, let the priest bless it. There was a man one time . . . It was a great evening of stories of men who built themselves houses without by-your-leave to the fairies, and how they lived to be sorry. Brigid had no story to go with their story. The only sign from the world without that the island gave in to was lights. It was a bad thing above all to see a light running along the skin of the water, especially if there was a sound with it, like water plunging in boots. She contributed her tale.

After the rosary she blessed herself quickly. 'Tell me this, was ever a sod turned back in the glen? If the like happened what would become of Andy?' Mary kissed the cross of her beads and sat up. 'Well, not a hand, nor hand kind, would be laid on pick or shovel, and if a hand was put out to put a stone in place it would be withered before the year was out; for all the world like you cut down a gentle bush.' 'But if somebody out of badness turned back a sod?' Brigid pressed. 'God almighty, Brigid, such a thing could never be. Such a thought, Brigid.' Even Tom was startled. 'It would be a wrong thing to say, Brigid.' He picked up a coal and put it to his pipe. 'There is never any notice taken of marking a site; I mind Sean Mor marking the ground for our stable. It was in the early morning. I was herding and I saw him. He was alone. The glen was in swarm this day because people are glad about Andy and Winnie.' He was pleased himself, puffing contentedly, the toes moving on his bare feet in front of the fire. 'This glen is in a hurry now to help Andy catch up on all it maybe denied him so far . . .' Mary's mind drifted away on its own thoughts.

'God knows I have to laugh,' Brigid chuckled. Tom took his pipe from his mouth and waited, but she turned back on her knees to add a word to her night prayers.

18

THE women of the glen were in a cluster by the chapel gate and they closed in round Brigid, and they knew it must put her in mind of that other Sunday; it was, maybe, their wish to redeem themselves on just that spot. They made a procession of themselves up the gravel avenue and down the aisle. They packed themselves into the seats by the baptismal font, with nobody behind them, and when their men tramped in, a solid clump within the general tide of men, they whispered together and laughed so the police sergeant's wife turned round and glared at them, and others turned too, and frowned. A woman, pushing past the sergeant's wife, knocked her hat awry and more than Glenmore laughed. The priest came out on the altar, and with a deep sigh of happiness Glenmore buried itself in its prayers. The sermon was on devotion to the souls in purgatory. It was not until people were on their way home again, after visiting their graves, that their gaiety was restored.

'Do you hear us, Brigid?' Sorcha shouted, 'this wedding will be the biggest night ever in Glenmore; whenever anybody alive now talks of a big night, when we are through with this night ahead of us they will remember this as the crown of all.' Now that Brigid could speak her mind freely she scolded them. She all but gave way at the knees at the chapel gate, listening to their nonsense. What did they wish to make of her. . . .

'It is not what we wish to make of you, but what you make of us. You had no call to befriend Winnie, but we had, for we all knew, and we were ready to tramp over her.' 'Get a bit of sense,' Brigid scolded. 'Only that Andy was the age he is when he got an open fireside he would need nobody's help; any more than Tom. To marry young you must court young.'

'Court young and head for Boston,' Bella mocked. 'Let me see two young people in hoults and I will name two for Boston. Andy was maybe lucky I tripped up Winnie when she had a mind to fly. By the time a man of the glen has freedom to marry, what fun is left in him for courting? He goes after a woman like he might sit under a cow to milk her.'

They cheered Bella, mocked men within hearing, bantered Winnie, shouted at Andy, and the youths raised their voices and shocked everybody.

'God damn it, I never heard this kind of talk given out in this glen,' Wee Conail protested. 'People should bear in mind there are children around. And there is another thing; all this talk of a big night. How will it be if the glen loses hold of itself and is carried to such lengths in its carry-on it makes a mock of Andy and Winnie? If ever a wedding had to have a sense of right behaviour it is that wedding. . . .'

And as if to give edge to Wee Conail's words, the youths of the glen, on Sunday night, misbehaved themselves on a grand scale. Girls masqueraded as boys, boys as girls, they beat on doors, shouted at windows, loosed cattle out of byres, entered Andy's house — he spent the evening at Black Donal's — killed, plucked, and cooked three hens, ended up with a bonfire of gorse over by the old quarry, and such roaring and shouting as was never heard. 'There is no great harm where there is great noise,' Mary commented. 'That was what Big Father Dan said when the sergeant's wife went to him to complain about the fighting on a Patrick's night dance. Let them play themselves on the doorstep to Boston. They will have something to laugh over together later on. Best open some barn to them for the dances. . . .'

In the shelter of the noise made by their elders, children sallied forth at night, now that there was a moon and a breath of frost. Boys in lower glen took the casans as a band based on two tin-whistles, with oddments of drum effects. Upper glen boasted a flute. Mid glen contented itself with changing sides as the fortunes swayed from one gang to the other. Schoolgirls added their voices. The whins on the slope of Ardan Rua became a favourite battle ground. Parental authority, sure of itself, rested by the firesides. Word went round that Andy and Winnie would marry before Lent. Time enough to have their house up and warmed by then. . . .

The glen surely was in good heart towards itself. And yet in that hour its world shook. . . .

The sods marking the site on Ardan Rua went back into the earth. It would not be easy to say who first noticed that the four black blobs so easily within view from half a dozen door-ways were gone. By the time Andy walked out from his own door to give a day's threshing to Black Donal there were people in every door, at every gable; except Black Donal's, for Peggy had not the heart to cry warning, nor yet to be a witness to what he must see once he came round her gable. She heard his step, and she heard its rhythm break. She heard his step go away from the door. She went inside and by then the morning was full of people and shouts. She watched the rush of people to Ardan Rua. She called Tom and he came to her. 'Beats all,' he said, standing puzzled on the floor, his palm moving against the bowl of his pipe.

'What did she say, Tom?'

'She asked who did it.'

Mary scudded in. 'You best go on home, Tom. I never saw a woman so upset.' He put the dead pipe in his mouth. Took it in his hand. The stem snapped in his fingers.

'Do you think somebody did it?' He asked without anger, a challenge. Mary shook her head. Peggy raised her two hands and let them fall heavily. 'The like has to be in it, else what sense in what comes down from the old people? Poor Andy, he is back again in the cloud we thought was past him.

'There is no good in saying this or that, nobody would put a hand to pick or shovel now.' He looked back from the doorstep. 'If this was somebody's hand, it will come out.'

That evening, Wee Conail's eldest daughter — Eilis for her grandmother — saw a light on Ardan Rua. She was shutting in the ducks at the time and came screeching in the door. It took a little while to get her story. She saw one light, then she saw more lights than there were stars, all small lights, and they were going round and round, round and round. Wee Conail himself put her to bed. He was worried. He never saw such fright in a child. Her whole body was in a tremble; like a fledgling might be in your palm. Next day there were other rumours. One of Bella's children, in the dusk searching for the donkey to put her in because of the threat of snow, heard shouting over on Ardan Rua; angry shouting. It was an idle day, for snow fell during the night.

There was a movement of people between the houses. Lower glen women came into upper glen. One brought a story of the like happening in lower glen, long ago. The people went to the priest. He said to them to try again and to light a fire in the middle of the marked ground and keep it alight all seven nights and they did it and the sods were shrivelled and dead at the end of the seven nights and there never was a family thrived like that family. She wandered into Peggy. From Peggy she crossed to Mary Manus. Sorcha was in with Susan at the time and she persuaded Susan to come with her and make Brigid see sense. 'Talk about Andy shutting himself into a cloud back of the Loch, if this goes on Brigid will be more of a stranger than when she was barely a name to us.'

Mary, who made the lower glen woman welcome, kept the talk away from Ardan Rua for a while. She had to ask her visitor about the state of her health and the health of her people, and how they were off for fodder, facing what she judged would be a severe winter. The visitor drew Brigid into the talk and Brigid added her word when manners

called for it. Sorcha and Susan came in and they shook
hands with the stranger and seated themselves, and Mary,
as if she must break in on this purely courtesy visit, turned to
the woman from lower glen. 'I suppose you heard about the
great upset and sorrow that is on us all because of the setback
Andy got?' Sorcha and Susan had their eyes on Brigid, but
Brigid sat on her creepy and darned, and was silent until she
heard how the priest advised a fire. She laughed at that.
'The priest was like me, he knew it was somebody's doing,
and whoever the somebody was would be baffled by the
light and somebody watching.' She put down the wool, for
the kettle was boiling. 'Please God, come Sunday I will go
to the priest. I am putting no tooth on it, this was somebody's doing.' She stood with the tea-pot in her hand. 'If I
had to give in to the like of this, I would smother. It will be,
God help whoever did this, and whoever knows and says
nothing. . . .'

It was threshing time now and groups of men gathered at
barns, some to work, some to watch. There was more bad-
tempered talk than anybody remembered; up and down the
length of the glen there was argument and confusion. Some
said it was a job for lower glen families sib to Andy to en-
courage him to ask leave to build a second time, some argued
it was up to his neighbours, again there were those who
pooh-poohed the idea of a new house and said Andy should
marry and stay in his old home. But nobody went to him.
He kept his door shut and his head stooped.

And all the time children in upper glen were a worry.
Their fear of ghosts went so far that no one would take a
drink to a calf in the byre without having a second by the
hand, and even then they both wanted somebody to stand
in the door. Wee Conail stormed against the endless talk
about Ardan Rua. Unless an end was put to it children
would lose their reason. There was that girl of his, Eilis, a
frail child, much given to listening to stories, a gentle
child. . . .

It was uncanny, really. It was as if the glen was overheard whispering to itself by everybody in it at the same moment. Mary walked into Brigid. 'So you had the truth of it.' She took to her creepy and peeked out her head shawl. Briany was on Mary's heels. He glanced from her to Brigid. 'The children, I suppose?' Brigid said. Mary raised her head at that. 'That is the one comfort. The children did it out of no harm, but in play; wrong play. God help the people. . . .'

'What ails the people,' Brigid challenged, 'now that they know. Let them rouse themselves now and get to work . . .' Mary pushed back her shawl. 'Eilis wakened up out of her sleep crying; that is how it came out. They all pledged themselves not to tell. Dan Rua's children were in it, and Bella's, and two big lumps of boys from mid glen. The like never was known. There was no telling. The only thing like it was once seven drunk men uprooted a gentle bush. Next thing, one of them had his right side paralysed. . . .'

Dawn was still an hour away when Wee Conail came rapping on Mary's window. She was out of bed at the first call of her name, and she dropped her petticoat over her head as she hurried to the door. Tom was little behind. He stood in the room door, one leg in his trousers, one fumbling and kicking as Wee Conail entered. He staggered in, and Mary murmuring a prayer, called Tom. She guided Wee Conail to a chair. 'It is not Nelly?' He shook his head. He buried his head in his hands and great sobs shook his body. 'Stop it I tell you,' Mary ordered, 'stop it and tell me.' Brigid dressed quickly in the bedroom door. Mary pulled the rakings together. Tom lit the lamp. 'It is wee Eilis,' he said. 'It is she is to pay.' Mary had her feet in a pair of Tom's boots now. Brigid helped her into a coat of Tom's. 'Here, out with us, Wee Conail.' He put his hands to his face. 'I cannot bear to look at her, Mary. It is like hands are at her throat choking her to death. She is likely dead by now.' Mary put a hand on his shoulder. 'Let you stay here, Wee Conail. One thing let you say. Welcome be the will of God. Then if it is His will your child will not be held in her agony.' His voice was steady enough now. 'I bow myself to the will of God.' He said solemnly. 'Go with her, Tom,' Brigid urged. Brigid went on her knees by Wee Conail's chair. 'Tell me, Wee Conail.'

'Something woke me, Brigid. There was a roar of wind in the chimney and a crackle of hail on the window. I knew it was not that. I edged out of the bed, then I heard the choking and I knew it was Eilis. I shouted. I did a terrible thing, for I roared out, "Not Eilis. Let who will be struck down but not Eilis." I was expecting the like and I had a fear for Eilis. I knew someone of the children that took part, me or Nelly, or Dan Rua, or Susan, or . . . someone.' The door was thrust in roughly. Dan Rua strode in, Susan on his heels, and after Susan, Nappy. Tom returned. He put his back to the door and looked at the ground. 'Is she calling for me, Tom?' 'Say you give her,' Nappy ordered. 'Do not withhold her, for fear of worse. This is a punishment. It is like the lightning, it strikes where it likes, and there is no withstanding it.' Wee Conail, pale, but composed now, turned to Dan Rua and Susan. 'I wish no harm to anybody.'

'Listen to me, Wee Conail,' Brigid stammered. She turned to Tom. 'It is a sickness; tell them it is a sickness.' 'I would be said by her Wee Conail.' Brigid put a hand on Wee Conail's arm. 'Say to Tom to go for the doctor, Wee Conail. Let him bring the priest too.'

'Let you not,' Nappy snapped, 'not doctor, not priest. This is beyond doctor and priest; like the lightning. It is a punishment.'

'I saw her,' Susan spoke hurriedly. 'It is like nothing ever was Brigid; yon choking. Nelly will not give in to let her go, so this choking goes on and goes on. . . .'

'I tell you it is a sickness.' Brigid was roused now. 'Say to Tom to bring the doctor.' 'Let you not, Wee Conail,' Nappy warned. 'Let you whist,' Brigid stormed.

Sorcha and Bella rushed in. 'Mary is yonder, a hard face on her and it sharp as a hatchet. She has wee Eilis on pillows on the hearth, so she can kick. But Mary is not calling for

Doon Well water, or Saint Brigid's cross. Once she shouted at Nelly to give over crying and resign herself, and at that minute an ease came to wee Eilis and she looked at her mother, and her mother broke out again in a great gush of crying, and behold you . . .' She paused. 'You tell it, Bella.' 'I saw fingers. I saw the flesh pushed in and I saw the track of fingers. . . .'

'Let you speak, Wee Conail,' Tom broke in. 'In God's name, then, Tom Manus.' 'Let you not,' Nappy shouted, lurching towards the door, but Tom thrust her aside and went out, and there was silence.

'Will he come for a child?' Sorcha asked. 'And the priest, is it right? The old people always said . . .' 'Let you pray,' Brigid pleaded, 'let you pray that Tom gets the doctor in time.' She plucked a shawl off the line. 'It is not right to leave Mary alone.' She went out alone.

'You had no right to do such a thing, Wee Conail, it is not right anybody interfering.'

'A fine thing, if she was to call me and look around for me and no sign of me. . . .'

'Go after him, Dan Rua; he will do something. . . .'

'God knows people are to be pitied,' Sorcha said, not knowing what to say with and what to deny. 'Let us do like Brigid said, pray. . . .'

Tom's kitchen filled with neighbours, and women shuttled over and back with news. They never saw Mary like she was, the sweat in beads on her forehead and when she spoke her voice quiet and every word bare as a knuckle. Any minute now, in a new burst of distress, the child must die. . . .

And then Tom's dog barked and they knew he was at hand. They rushed out into the frost and the glistening snow and the stillness, and heard voices and they shouted at somebody in Wee Conail's open door that the doctor was at hand, and then for fear he would be shut out they raced for Wee Conail's themselves, and knelt and crouched and waited, scarcely breathing, in hope he would let them stay.

He paused on the doorstep, his great coat about his ears. His glance went past them Mary, standing by the kitchen table wee Eilis in blankets on it. He pulled off his gloves. Tom, at his shoulder, handed him his bag. 'God knows this glen is all one person.' They wondered that he could chuckle. He stood by the table. They got to their feet with as little noise as possible, and pressed closer. 'So far as I know there have been no other such cases. There is no case like this in the glen,' Mary said grimly. He glanced sharply at her. 'You never saw the like of this?' She shook her head. 'A frightening thing to look at.' He lifted away the potato poultice, opened his bag and laid a piece of gauze on the child's face. He let chloroform drip on it. 'This will end the spasm.' His glance rested on Brigid. Her looks puzzled him. He looked from her to Mary and back. 'Of course we will cure this child,' he said quietly. 'I can promise you all that.' Now what the hell — for suddenly the kitchen full of people rocked with deep-drawn sobs. He busied himself with his patient. 'There was a great theatre sister lost in you, Mary Manus,' he said, laying his hand on her shoulder; 'or maybe she was not lost. And now maybe you will tell me what this is all about, or why does one child's sickness shake the heart of you all: I would have thought the one plentiful thing would be children.'

'I will tell you,' Nappy said. 'Save this child and some other child dies.' The doctor waited, puzzled. 'This is no sickness. This is a punishment.' 'Do not talk nonsense,' the doctor rapped. 'This is a plain case of croupus laryngitis; a simple case, fortunately. Did this child get a fright?' He saw the quick sideways glances. He went to the bed-side at a signal from Mary. He seemed pleased. Mary was pleased too. 'It is but right you should know what has us frightened.' She was in the midst of her story when the priest walked in. She let the priest have the part of her story he missed. He listened attentively. So did the doctor. 'I suppose indeed you will laugh at us . . .' Both shook their heads. 'Fitter for me to cry,' the priest said quietly. 'It would ill become me too, if I made light of your story,' the doctor sighed. 'Talk to us, let both of you, let you tell us,' Sorcha pleaded. The priest left it to the doctor to explain how this highly imaginative child, listening and fearing, brought this sickness on herself. 'As a rule children escape the blast of pishrogue,' he went on. 'It is big people suffer.' They sought the priest's guidance. He nodded. They rustled with interest and pressed closer. 'You dig up something in your garden; a lump of butter.' They were startled. He pulled at his pipe until it drew freely. 'You could become very scared. You could get so frightened that some weakness in you would become so aggravated you could die; of the fright not of magic in the pishrogue. This child was lucky. Croupus laryngitis, in this form, is frightening to look at but it is not so terrible. The child will need some medicine, and soon she will be racing around. And you will be the better for this night.' He smiled at the priest. 'It was I brought them past the fairies; my medicine and I. You will have to be patient. They were scared. Fear is the beginning of wisdom.'

'Fear without faith is the end of wisdom.'

'Are you both agreed on this, there is no fear another child will be stricken?' Dan Rua asked.

'I would not think there is any danger,' the doctor said lightly, 'unless some old body starts some fool scare.' He glanced at Nappy.

'There will be no more fool scares,' Dan Rua thundered, 'none ever.' 'Out with us and let the world breathe. We have work to do.' 'Croupus laryngitis.' 'We have to build a house.' 'Croupus laryngitis.'

It was broad daylight now. A shaft of sunlight directed on to the Loch through a break in the clouds touched Andy's gable. He halted by his door, interested in the movement of people around Wee Conail's. Dan Rua signalled to him. He picked up Wee Conail's spade. He handed Tom a pick. 'Go get your tools. The glen is going past the gander. Croupus laryngitis,' he roared. 'Croupus laryngitis,' they all bellowed, following on his heels.

Briany stayed back with the doctor and the priest. Brigid and Mary walked off together. Mary staggered and Brigid put an arm round her. A roar of laughter came from Ardan Rua. 'Bear in mind, Father, it was I led them past the fairies,' the doctor joked. 'The island woman had a good hand in it,' the priest said, 'so had the glen woman.' 'That is all you know,' Briany said quickly, 'when you do not put Tom's name on top. It is I know the full story.' There was a new burst of merriment back on Ardan Rua. 'Whatever the glen is doing to itself at this hour it is doing gaily,' the doctor said. Briany carried the doctor's bag and led the way to the horses.

19

And there maybe the story should end only then you would not understand how it ever came to be told. Brigid and the glen had little more to do to one another for Tom was killed, in the footiest way you could think of, that very day, and for her the glen died with him. The head flew off Dan Rua's sledge and hit him on the forehead. It was a heavy blow and it stretched him out, but he came to quickly, and made light of it; although he let himself be persuaded to go to bed early. He was up at his usual hour next day, to work on the site. He was lacing his boots when he slumped forward and fell dead at Brigid's feet; the priest said there was life in his body still, when he reached him.

The glen waked Tom Manus and buried him and withdrew back into itself in a silence and sorrow never known before. On the day following the funeral Brigid went into the house to Dan Rua and Susan and she asked Dan Rua to call the others to him and go over to Ardan Rua and build Andy his house. Dan Rua listened to her and he said he would do what she asked.

And Wee Conail went to Ardan Rua, and Black Donal, and Bella's brother, and men from lower glen, keeping watch for a signal, joined them. And, day after day, they gathered and worked and they put up the house. They put down a floor of blue clay, and the children were sent in to toughen it with their tramping and that was the first laughter that arose in the glen from Tom's death. Andy and Winnie married and it was the quietest wedding ever, and they went to live in the new house.

Brigid and Mary lived in peace together and Peggy was in

and out daily and Peggy made no secret of a great uneasiness in herself. The two women were altogether too calm. It was true Mary cried easily when you talked of Tom, whereas Brigid maintained the terrible quiet that was in her all through the wake, and again at the graveside. 'It is like you have to wait for the thaw, and not know what, under God, is in her mind to come out then.'

They watched her; they all watched Brigid and Mary, eager to rejoice in every sign that life was returning to Brigid. Mary was back in her old ways, busy around her byres and haggard, and at the first breath of spring, attentive to her fields. She stripped the clay off a pit of potatoes and Brigid sat with her, turning over the potatoes, flinging out such as the rot had touched, separating out the best size for seed. Dan Rua came on them at it, and ordered them away. He was angry. 'God damn it, woman,' he stormed at Mary, 'you know you have but to raise a finger. . . .'

But that was not Mary's way. She found a break in a fence and she mended it, found a choked drain and she freed it. 'She is setting Brigid an example,' one said. 'She is maybe driving her,' another said. Sorcha asked Peggy to speak to Brigid, how was it between herself and Mary, in case somebody should talk to Mary. 'If it has come to pass that she needs our shelter now, we should be a comfort to her.' 'Let you do as I am doing,' Peggy sighed, 'let you pray.'

Peggy was by herself on a Sunday afternoon, Grania was on a visit to her people in lower glen, Black Donal wandering around outside, when Brigid came into the doorway and again a hen was trapped, only this time Brigid stepped back to let her flutter out. 'Well, God knows, I was going over in my mind in bed last night that you did not darken that door since a week last Thursday. It is good for a body to walk abroad.' Brigid picked a creepy from under the kitchen table. Peggy took the corner across from her. 'I see you are letting out the field back of the haggard in meadow.' Brigid smiled. 'Mary thinks that is best.'

'Black Donal, too, says it is best.'

'When land is in weak hands the grass is easiest; that is what Mary says.'

'Whose land is in weak hands?' Peggy challenged, 'not yours. The hands of the men of the glen are over your land. I hear them talking.'

'For this year, and next year ; maybe the year after.'

'More of Mary's talk?' Brigid shook her head. 'Let nobody ever say a wintry word to Mary. I am sorry for myself. I am in agony for Mary.' And then very gently she cried and Peggy wept with her.

Brigid dried her eyes quickly and got to her feet. 'I will not wait for tea, Peggy; I only ran over for a minute.' She looked out the window. 'I got to like the mountains in the end, mind you. I mind asking Tom once how far up the mountains he thought he could drive his fields, with the power of two strong arms. He said the mountain was bad as the ram, always showing its face in the fields that you won from it. Such land has to be in strong hands.'

'I told you, there is no land in stronger hands than yours. What, under God, is going on in your mind, Brigid?' Brigid turned slowly. 'Fine you know how it must be, Peggy. Fine Mary knows.'

'I tell you, Brigid, the men have their minds on you. I hear them talking. More grass, more cattle, more sheep. Your fields have no cause to complain,' she urged. 'Mary is not at you, saying to you "do this," "do that" . . .' Brigid sighed. 'I am telling you, Peggy, Mary is the pity, like her land is to be pitied. Mary is,' she paused, 'once you said she was holy. That is the wisest thing ever you said, Peggy.' She embraced Peggy quickly, kissed her and hurried to the door. Black Donal trudged round the corner. 'I thought there would be tea, that you would sit.' 'I only ran over,' Brigid explained. She took a step past him. 'I always liked the view from this door.' The three of them stood close together. Mary came outside to feed her hens. Her voice carried to them clearly. 'There is a great calmness in everything,' Brigid said, 'like in the sea, often.' She walked away slowly. Peggy caught Black Donal's hand.

Next morning at dawn she left the glen, taking her child with her. Briany drove her to the mail car in the grey of the dawn, and she spent her waiting time in the graveyard. The news spread abroad quickly. The people talked of her and talked of her and they set down all things that touched on her days among them, in such a way that when a man with an ear for the like, who was forby sib to Brigid herself, spent a while in the glen all he had to do was to write down the story. It would not be fair to say who of them all was alive then, or what became of her, beyond that she never entered the glen again; Tom's unmarried brother in Boston returned and married a girl of the glen. Brigid was on her way to becoming folk-lore by the time the story was set down, and because of her Peggy will be talked of and Mary, and Briany, and Sean Mor, and Black Donal for many a day, even though the glen itself losing strength — of that she was maybe a messenger herself — may smother her story with its casans under the creeping heather.